THE
EMPEROR
OF
ANY PLACE

THE
EMPEROR
OF
ANY PLACE

TIM WYNNE-JONES

CANDLEWICK PRESS

The author acknowledges the support of the Canada Council for the Arts,
which last year invested $157 million to bring the arts
to Canadians throughout the country.

L'auteur remercie le Conseil des arts du Canada de son soutien.
L'an dernier, le Conseil a investi 157 millions de dollars pour mettre de l'art
dans la vie des Canadiennes et des Canadiens de tout le pays.

Canada Council   Conseil des arts
for the Arts   du Canada

Calligraphy by Sawako Shirota

Extract from "A Process in the Weather of the Heart" by Dylan Thomas,
from *The Poems of Dylan Thomas,* copyright 1939 by New Directions
Publishing Corp. Reprinted by permission of New Directions Publishing
Corp. in U.S.A. and Canada and by permission of David Higham Associates
Limited in rest of English-language territories throughout the world.

First edition 2015

Library of Congress Catalog Card Number 2014953457
ISBN 978-0-7636-6973-7

15 16 17 18 19 20 BVG 10 9 8 7 6 5 4 3 2 1

Printed in Berryville, VA, U.S.A.

This book was typeset in Granjon and Weiss.

Candlewick Press
99 Dover Street
Somerville, Massachusetts 02144

visit us at www.candlewick.com

This book is dedicated to my father,
Lieutenant-Colonel S. T. Wynne-Jones,
Royal Engineers,
1912–1981

A process in the weather of the world,

Turns ghost to ghost; each mothered child

Sits in their double shade.

A process blows the moon into the sun,

Pulls down the shabby curtains of the skin;

And the heart gives up its dead.

—Dylan Thomas

CHAPTER ONE

Evan stands at the door to his father's study. There is a sign at eye level: THE DOCKYARD. It was a present he gave to his father last Christmas, made of cork so that if the house sank, at least the sign would still float. Their little joke.

He raises his hand to knock—a habit he can begin to unlearn. So much of grief is unlearning. He opens the door, steps inside, and takes a shallow breath, afraid of what might be lingering on the air. But there are only the old familiar smells: Royal Lime aftershave, glue, sawdust.

This is where he found him.

He thought his father had fallen asleep. The only sign that anything was wrong was the new model ship lying on its side on the carpet. His father had finished it the evening before—fourteen days ago. Evan had picked up the ship; it wasn't damaged. He found a space for it on the shelf with the other ships, a couple dozen of them. He placed it there to join his father's bottled armada. "Not so grand as an armada," his father had once said. "More like a flotilla."

Clifford E. Griffin III, a modest man.

It was strange doing that, picking up the boat and placing it carefully on the shelf, pretending his father was asleep behind him. Only asleep. There was no blood, no sign of a struggle, just the boat in its bottle on its side on the floor. And his father pitched over his desk, his face strained, his eyelids and jaw tense, rigor mortis setting in. He even died modestly.

Hypertrophic cardiomyopathy. The muscle of his heart had been thickening. Evan had watched his father rub his chest a fair bit, the look on his face more annoyance than pain. And he would get short of breath when he was gardening. That was about it.

And then that was it.

Fourteen days ago. No—fifteen.

Now Evan moves into the room, heads over to the desk, the chair pushed back so hard against the wall by the paramedics that it left a dent in the plaster just under the window. The chair is still there up against the wall. The plants on the sill are dead. One more thing Evan has forgotten to do. There are dried leaves on the floor.

The ambulance arrived thirteen minutes after he called 911. The fire truck got there three minutes faster. Evan stood shivering at the open front door in his boxers and T-shirt, watching the cartoon-red ladder truck pull into the driveway, wondering whether he'd somehow called the wrong number. Huge men, dressed for putting out fires, piled out of the vehicle,

2

sniffed the air, looked up into the early morning haze for smoke or flames—the kind of stuff they were good at. Then two of them set off at a run around the perimeter of the house—one this way, one that—while three of them entered, so large, they seemed to fill up the place and suck out all the air. Evan thought maybe he was suffocating.

One of them checked out the Dockyard. Another one found a blanket somewhere and wrapped Evan up in it, made him sit in the living room, trembling even though it was July. The third fireman brought him water in a glass from the kitchen.

"Is there someone we should call?"

Evan shook his head. His dad was retired now, so he wasn't going to be late for work. Oh! The fireman meant family: another parent or auntie, an older sibling—that kind of someone. But there really wasn't anyone. Not one he could think of right then, that is—right at that precise moment. Just him and Dad.

The book lies on the desk, precisely where his father's head had landed. He remembers that now, looking down at the desktop: his father's sallow cheek against the brighter yellow of the binding. He touches the book tentatively, turns it to face him with the tip of his index finger, like it's booby-trapped—something that might go off in his face.

Kokoro-Jima, the Heart-Shaped Island.

The title is embossed in gold on leather that is pebbly, like sun-smacked sand. The man who phoned this morning had described it that way: sand colored.

Evan wishes he hadn't taken the call.

He should have let it go to his father's cheery message, a message Evan can't erase or change because he doesn't know the drill, because the house phone was his father's territory—and, anyway, what would he change the message to: "Sorry, we're not in. Actually, Evan might be in, but if you're Evan's friend, you'd call him on his cell phone. Clifford is dead, so don't leave a message."

Fifteen days and counting . . .

Most of the time he lets the calls go to voice mail. But sometimes he can't stand the ringing — the jangling of it. "Just fucking go away!" he shouts to the empty house. But then sometimes he answers, just for something to do. And sometimes he doesn't tell the caller the news, just pretends his father is out. Not that it is comforting to delude himself, but because it is so uncomfortable to tell the truth. Embarrassing, as if you have somehow fallen down in your responsibilities. "What? You didn't know the walls of his heart were hardening? What kind of a son are you?"

Anyway. Anyway.

When he told the truth, it felt as if he were playing this cruel game on the caller — the kind of smart-ass retort you save for telemarketers. "Sorry, the owner of the house is dead. Have a nice day."

But this morning he had just said, "He's not in. Can I take a message?"

"Do you know when he'll be back?"

"Sorry, I wish I could tell you."

"Is your mother around?"

"No. She's not."

"But she —"

"Left."

"Oh."

"Yeah. Like when I was three. So . . ."

"Oh . . ."

There was the pause where the guy tried to think of something appropriate to say. Evan waited, sharing the discomfort, almost enjoying it. If you're going to shove a knife into an unsuspecting stranger's gut, the least you can do is hang around and watch him writhe a bit.

"So you're Clifford's son?"

"Yeah, Evan."

"Evan. Hi. My name's Leo . . . Leo Kraft?" He waited in case the name rang a bell. "I've been leaving messages. I don't mean to be impatient, but I really just wanted to know whether the book arrived?"

"The book?"

"Yeah. It's called *Kokoro-Jima*. Have you seen it? It's yellow, hand-bound — kind of sand colored."

And immediately Evan saw it in his mind's eye. "Yeah," he said. "It's here."

"Oh, good. Great." He could hear the relief in Kraft's voice. "Thanks. Listen, could you ask your father to get back to me when he gets a chance?"

"I'll —" Evan stopped. There was only so long you could carry on the charade. "I'll do what I can," he said. An odd thing to say, come to think of it.

And now here he is in the Dockyard, staring at the book, his father's last resting place, this hard pillow. He half expects to see an impression on the cover, a stain of drool. The thought makes him woozy. He leans hard against the edge of the desk. Gets his breath back. He picks up the book, feels the warmth of it from the sun streaming through the window, through the dry spines of the dead plants. He opens it, and there's a letter. He sinks into his father's chair, unfolds the letter, and reads.

5

Leonardo Kraft
4586 Santa Cruz Road
Menlo Park, California 94025
June 21, 2014

Dear Clifford:

Thanks so much for getting back to me. Here's the book. As you will see, my father lavished attention on it. I believe it was one of the most exciting projects he ever undertook in a lifetime of many accomplishments. I only wish he had lived long enough to complete the goal he refers to in the prologue. And I wish he'd lived long enough to dispel the shadow that hangs over the story's ambiguous and disturbing conclusion. As I might have mentioned, he held off bringing the book out, hoping for answers, but when your father proved to be so obstinate, he went ahead. Leaving us with a mystery.

What happened to Isamu Ōshiro?

I think, when you've read the book, you'll see why this is a delicate matter. As I mentioned, Griff has not replied to any of our inquiries. You said he was "difficult." What more can we do? We cannot proceed without his approval; our legal counsel has made that point abundantly clear.

If you could prevail upon him to talk to us, we would be so grateful. If going to see him would help, we will of course reimburse you for any expenses.

Please let me know that you received the book. Thanking you again for your help, I am, most sincerely,

Yours,

Leo Kraft

Evan leans back in his father's swivel chair, lets the letter fall to his lap.

Griff has not replied to any of our inquiries.

That would be the infamous Griff, all right: his father's father.

We cannot proceed without his approval.

Evan wonders who "we" is—a we that includes lawyers. Proceed to do what? A creepy feeling comes over him. He leans forward. Thinks hard. As if he has some inkling of what this is about. Something his father said. Something was on his father's mind that last day. What was it?

Evan gets sidetracked. Happens a lot, lately. It's that word "last." He thinks how weird it is that you can suddenly pin that adjective to something. At the time, it didn't feel like the last day—the last anything. It was just Thursday, July third. No big deal. A sunny early summer's day that drifted into a soft evening, a warm night. Evan wasn't going to be starting his job at Hardboiled Inc. until July fifteenth. It was going to be very cool: printing T-shirts, which was a change from flipping hamburgers as far as summer jobs go. But for the time being, it was pure holiday time. He'd been at Rollo's with the guys all that afternoon.

Just Thursday. The evening before the morning when . . .

There were no big plans for the summer except for the job and, before it started, a little road trip with his dad. Now it wouldn't happen. It would never happen. There were these things to unlearn; a whole lot of Never to get used to.

He goes limp. The letter slips from his lap and flutters to the floor. He stares at it. Then his eyes drift back to the book, lying in his shadow. If he leans away, the cover blinds him with sun glare.

There is a bookmark lying on the desktop. Another

Christmas present from Big Spender Evan. It's a slip of glossy cardboard with a 3-D pair of feet in socks and Top-Siders hanging off the bottom end, so that when the marker is in a book, it looks as if there were a person in there who has been squashed. Except the bookmark is on the desk. *What does that mean, Sherlock?*

Well, Watson, it suggests Clifford had finished the book. Finished it and then died. Evan thinks back to that Thursday, two weeks ago. His father had been obsessing. Obsessing about *his* father. Evan leans back in the chair, which squawks in protest.

He understands grandfathers only as a concept. He's never met Griff, but he is going to very shortly and the irony is kind of astounding. If his father had not been so preoccupied with Griff the day before he died, Evan isn't even sure he would have remembered whether the old man was still alive. So when concerned friends began to say he should contact his grandfather, he did it, obediently, in a kind of a trance. That was another part of grief: the kind of stupor he found himself in a whole lot. Days of daze. Good to have a relative around to pick up the slack, even if it's one you've never met and your father hated. Hmm. There was a gap in the logic there, somewhere, but . . . well, logic had not been trending in his life lately.

And so Griff is coming. And now Evan can't help wondering if he has made some very big-ass mistake.

CHAPTER TWO

Fifteen days earlier

Evan walked along Plateau Crescent pulling a Radio Flyer Big Red Classic. It was dusk. The wheels on the Flyer went round and round, the only sound on the block but for the hiss of the lawn sprinklers, the odd bark of a dog, and the sound of *Jeopardy!* on someone's TV set. A neighbor bearing an uncanny resemblance to Mr. Rogers chatted over his fence to a neighbor also bearing an uncanny resemblance to Mr. Rogers. Neighbots.

Behind them the traffic hummed in C-flat major on the Don Valley Expressway. Don Mills, an island of calm, the most ordinary place in the world.

There was a Fender Mini guitar amp loaded on the wagon, a guitar case strapped to Evan's back. With Scott leaving for the summer, they had figured it was time to put the band in cold storage.

"Cold Storage would be a better name for us," Scott said.

"Except that people might confuse us with Coldplay," said Rollo. Ha-ha. It was often like this at practice. They came up with way more names for the band than actual songs: Resin, Omar Kayak, Boys without Handlebars, The Frenzied Gnomes, Cold Storage.

He stopped outside 123 Any Place, waved at Lexie Jane Reidinger mowing the lawn next door. The Reidingers on the right, the Guptas on the left, and the Griffins in the middle. Three pretty-well-identical houses with three different-colored doors. Lexie waves back. Everybody in Any Place waves back. The lights were on in his house although it was only dusk. Dad was framed in the dining-room window sitting at the table, looking as if he was ready to launch a new ship. Evan walked up the driveway, peered in the window—a Peeping Evan. His father didn't look up.

Sometimes his dad brought all his model-making stuff out of the Dockyard and worked while he ate his dinner. A change of scenery. The bare bulbs of the candelabrum above the table shone down on his balding head. The camera of Evan's eye zoomed in, slowly. There should have been some seafaring music as background to this nautical scene. "Yo, Heave-Ho, Dad."

It struck him how odd it was that you could live with someone, day in, day out, and then suddenly see them like this, so clearly. Dad was wearing his ancient *Axis: Bold as Love* T-shirt: Jimi Hendrix and the boys in Day-Glo orange, blue, and pink printed over gold foil. The tee was stretched taut, the logo cracked and faded over his expanded belly. Not much gold left. It was hard to think of Clifford as lean, sporting John Lennon

10

glasses, paisley bell-bottoms, a strip of linen wrapped around his forehead with a peace sign on it. It was hard to think of him with hair.

Evan parked the Radio Flyer by the crumbling back step in the carport and hefted the amp through the screen door and into the kitchen.

"That you, Ev?"

"Got it in one, Dad."

His father was not only wearing *Axis* — he was listening to it. "Little Wing" was playing. *My dad,* he thought, *hopelessly trapped in the sixties.* Evan left the amp by the door with the flip-flops and his father's mud-stained gardening clogs. He stripped the guitar from his back and leaned it against the amp. There was stir-fry on the stove: chicken, broccoli, mushrooms — all shining and glutinous. He scooped a bowlful and threw it in the microwave.

"There's stir-fry," said Dad.

Evan smiled. Clifford E. Griffin III, always just that one beat behind.

"What's this one?" asked Evan. He stood, bowl in hand, across the dining-room table looking at the tiny boat his father has inserted into the neck of a dimpled scotch bottle.

"A frigate," said Dad.

"Frigate," said Evan. He said it again a couple of times.

"Sounds like you've got a frog in your throat," said Dad, without looking up.

Evan took a seat, examined the miniature ship. "Looks a lot like the last one," he said.

"It won't," said Dad, bending in close to do some tricky maneuvering with tweezers. "They all look pretty much the same until you get the masts up and the sails unfurled."

"Is that a valuable life lesson, Dad?"

"It is. Glad you noticed."

"You're very dependable that way, Dad."

"I am. When do I ever miss an opportunity to impart the wisdom of the ages to my impressionable son?"

Evan worried the meat off a piece of gristle, then spit it out onto the table. Dad frowned but he didn't protest. *It's just us boys,* thought Evan—and, anyway, the table was covered with newspaper, littered with tiny tools, a tube of glue, saucers of paint. And an unfinished bowl of stir-fry left to harden.

"The *Cutty Sark* was a clipper. This is going to be the USS *Constitution.*"

"Frigate," said Evan.

"Correct," said Dad.

"You Got Me Floatin'" ended and "Castles Made of Sand" came on, psychedelic guitar warped and weaving through a phase shifter. Evan watched as his father pulled a thread and the masts rose steadily inside the bottle, like some kind of strange butterfly unfurling its wings. A tiny contained ship that wasn't going anywhere. *Just like my dad,* thought Evan fondly.

His father stopped what he was doing, looked up. "I learned something interesting today," he said.

"Something even more interesting than a frigate?"

"Way more," said his father. "It's about Griff."

It took Evan a moment. "Your father?"

"The infamous Griff."

"Right," says Evan. "The infamous Griff. He was a general or something, right?"

"A sergeant major. And you do not make mistakes like that around Griff."

Evan stopped eating. "You mean he's coming here?"

"Hell, no!" His father looked up as if Evan had just announced an alien invasion. "What made you say that?"

"You sounded like you were warning me, like I should be prepared."

"If he were coming, I'd be sandbagging the place and planting land mines."

"Cool," said Evan. "Fort Any Place." He picked through the stir-fry for chicken. He'd eaten all the good bits. He put the bowl down. "But it's kind of too bad. I thought maybe he'd phoned and said he was homeless and we were going to have to put him up."

"I'd take poison first."

His father tied off the lines. The sails were raised.

"So?" said Evan.

"Huh?"

"Your father. You learned something?"

"Oh, right. Well, not much to my surprise, it turns out the man is a murderer."

Evan nodded. "Uh-huh," he said. "What else?"

"Murder isn't enough?"

Evan had heard all this before, and anyway his mind was wandering. "It would be kind of cool if he showed up, wouldn't it. Like the premise for a really bad sitcom."

His father laughed, but it was not the kind of laugh you got from a studio audience. "You obviously weren't listening closely to what I said."

"He's a murderer. Boring."

"It's true."

"I *know,* Dad. He was in the army, right?"

"No, the marines. A leatherneck."

"Yeah, so killing people sort of comes with the territory."

His father's eyes gleamed. "In a war, yes. But when the war is over? What kind of a guy goes on killing when the fight is officially over?"

Evan rolled his eyes. "Keep on trucking, Dad, like it's nineteen sixty-seven."

His father acknowledged the reproach with a grin. "Okay, I hear you. I'm ranting. But this is different. This is actually murder." The smile on his father's face was a little maniacal.

"This is what you learned today?"

"This is what I learned today."

"Like, it was on CNN, or something?"

"Not yet. But that's not a bad idea."

"Dad, stop being mysterious."

His father chuckled. He shook his head, returned his attention to the brand-new ship in a bottle. The deranged smile turned into a grimace — indigestion, judging from the stir-fry. He rubbed his chest. Some of the decrepit Day-Glo rubbed off on the heel of his hand. Jimi was fading away to nothing.

"So are you going to tell me or what?" said Evan.

His father frowned for a moment, shook his head. "Sometime, maybe." Then the frown lifted and he smiled radiantly at Evan as if he'd only just seen him and the boy was a miracle. He looked down, gazing, kind of sadly, at the ship in the bottle. He seemed flushed.

"Dad, are you okay?"

Clifford shook his head.

"What is it? What's wrong?"

Clifford shook his head a second time. "It's this murder thing. I mean, on one hand, why would I be surprised, right? But, on the other . . . it's as if, for some reason, I don't believe it. There's something wrong with the picture."

Evan watched and waited. What picture? But with one last

shake of the head, his father seemed to dismiss whatever it was he was thinking about.

"So," he said, finding a stash of smiles somewhere and trying one on. But the "so" didn't lead anywhere. The room was silent. There was just Evan, Clifford, *Axis: Bold as Love,* and the newly reconstituted USS *Constitution.*

CHAPTER THREE

Later that night, fifteen days ago

Evan came up from the rec room. He was in his sweats and a sopping T-shirt. He'd been working out on the rowing machine, listening to "Angry Workout Mix," not getting anywhere. That was the thing about rowing machines.

His father sat in the living room listening to jazz. His favorite chair in the sweet spot between two tall electrostatic speakers. He took his listening seriously.

"Very mellow," said Evan.

His dad looked up and smiled. "Miles Davis," he said. *"Kind of Blue."* He was drinking a scotch. He sat up a bit straighter, paused the sound. "Sorry for getting all bent out of shape earlier."

"No prob, Dad. I love it when you get sentimental about the good ole days."

"Like I said, sorry." He swayed a bit as if the music were still playing. "It's just that I've been thinking about Griff a lot lately." There was something in his voice that made Evan pull up an ottoman.

"What's up?"

"Ah, it doesn't matter. I'll tell you about it sometime. I'm kind of glad you put me in my place earlier."

"Dad, I—"

"No, no. It's ridiculous—*I'm* ridiculous. I know it." His face got pinched. "The man still gets to me, even now. Like I'm haunted." Then he pushed the pause button again, let the music out of its box. It floated up into the room, and the stand-up bass seemed to Evan like a boy with a kite—and the kite was Miles Davis on his muted horn out of sight in the air up there.

"Maybe you *should* get in touch with him."

Clifford seemed for just a moment to consider the idea, but then gently shook his head—or was he just noting the slow rhythm of the song? The window was open. A night breeze stole into the room and was doing a slow dance under the jazz. Evan could feel it on the back of his neck, the sweat on him cooling. He shivered.

"Dad?" His father looked at Evan. "What's going on?"

"Memories," he said. He leaned forward and patted Evan's knee, then sank back into his seat. "Just memories."

CHAPTER FOUR

Now

Evan looks out the window at the garden in the rain. He's standing over the kitchen sink eating a casserole that Mrs. Cope from up the street brought over. Rachel Cope is . . . was . . .

Start again, Ev.

Rachel Cope *was* his father's gardening buddy. Dad called her his pusher lady, dropping by with bulbs and cuttings and things in plain brown bags. Evan wondered once whether there was something between them.

"Nah," said his dad. "Just bulbs."

She'd offered to help Evan out with the flower beds. Was he supposed to phone her about that or would she just come? Looking out the window now, at the drenched greenery, Evan isn't sure which are flowers and which are weeds. He's not sure what he's supposed to do about annuals and perennials, except that with perennials, you probably have to do it more often. He isn't sure what to do about the lawn. Mow it probably. Or get a goat.

He isn't sure about this casserole, either. Eating it cold right out of the dish probably isn't helping. It's got hamburger in it and a tomato base. That much he can identify. But there are other textures, other flavors — some alien vegetable, strange spices. He stops, stares at it.

Other people's food is weird.

He's got a freezer full of other people's food: casseroles, soups, and stews. He's grateful, but one of these days, he's just going to have to make himself something he recognizes.

His father had been building a fishpond in the back. He can see it from the window. There's just the hole and a pile of topsoil sitting on a black tarp. There's a rubber liner, folded and waiting, the rain beading on its matte-black surface. A delivery of paving stones arrived only yesterday, all paid for. What do you say to the deliverymen? Nothing. You sign the sheet where the guy says, and you've got yourself forty square feet of polished granite.

He wonders if he should finish the fishpond. The hole and the pile of dirt have been his excuse for not mowing the lawn. How long can he put it off? He doesn't have anything else to do. Then he wonders if he should just shovel all the earth back into the hole. There's a pool of muddy water at the bottom of it, like an empty grave.

Maybe he could put his father's ashes there.

Right now they're sitting in The Box.

The Box is sitting on the kitchen counter, where he left it when he came back from the funeral parlor. The Box is a plain brown sturdy plastic container, too fat for a cereal box, too short to be laundry detergent—a box that should *in no way* be sitting on the kitchen counter.

Dave, a friend of his father's, helped organize the cremation, the funeral. Evan shared a checking account with his father that they used for household expenses, groceries, random bills, and whatnot. This was clearly the "whatnot" he could never have seen coming. Anyway, there was money, for now. As for the big picture, well, that remained to be seen.

He was pretty sure everything was his: the house, the car, the savings. He didn't think his father had some secret lover who would suddenly come out of the woodwork and cause trouble. There wouldn't be a charity he'd signed all his money over to: the Ship-in-a-Bottle Foundation. At least he didn't expect so. His mother was long gone. He thought of all those stories of people sitting in a lawyer's office and learning the horrible truth that they've been cut out of the will. He really didn't expect anything like that. Dad wasn't one for mysteries. If there was one thing he knew it was that his father loved him more than anyone or anything else. That was pretty amazing.

And it wasn't making any of this easier.

So there was money, apparently; how to get at it was another thing. He needed help. He was over sixteen, an adult. Whoa! That came as a surprise. Driving the car was one thing; settling an estate was something else.

"If you were from my homeland, you'd be a ward of the state." This nugget of information came from Olivia Schlaepfer; Olivia who walked her Siamese cat on a leash. Any Place's resident steampunker.

"Where are you from?" Evan asked. "A Dickens novel?"

"No," she said, as if his question had been serious. "Switzerland." It was at the brunch after the memorial service. When he first saw her arrive at the chapel, he almost cried at the thoughtfulness of her showing up, even if she was in a studded black leather jerkin, white crinoline, and black aviator boots. She had an ancient black aviator cap on her head, too. She looked like an Oreo. Then she came over to talk to him, and soon enough he really was on the verge of crying — or screaming. "You're not an adult until you turn eighteen in Switzerland," she said.

"Well, good for them," he said. "I'm an adult here. Children's Aid won't take me." He threw out his hands like *What's a guy supposed to do? Move to Switzerland?*

"So, you're an orphan," she said, with a gleam in her eye that suggested the idea seemed attractive, if only in a steampunk kind of way.

He could correct her on the orphan thing: technically there was a mother somewhere, in England, last he'd heard. But, no, he had no proof of that. "I guess so."

She nodded and smiled as if they were sharing a very special secret.

He did what people advised him to do: the bank manager, Dad's friend Dave, and nice Mr. Gupta next door. "Family, Evan," said Mr. Gupta. "In the end, always family. Surely, you must have someone?"

Mr. Gupta didn't lack for relatives. How do you explain having no one? *Actually, Mr. Gupta, sir, I was born in a test tube.*

A relative.

Well, there was one at least. So he looked in his father's address book and was a little surprised to find a series of addresses, all scratched off but for the last: "Hope Manor." Whatever his father might have said, he always knew where the infamous Griff was. North Carolina, it turned out. Where his father was born and lived until he was Evan's age, when he turned into Wily Draft Dodger Man and made his way to the True North Strong and Free.

And so when Evan got up the courage, he phoned.

The irony of it rushes over him again. Double-digit irony. Irony to the power of ten. The reason Griff was even on Evan's radar was because of his father going on about him like that. Griff the murderer.

But that was just Dad being Dad, wasn't it? Just Hyperbole. (Yet another of the many band names he and the boys had rejected.)

My father is dead and so I have asked a murderer to come and help out around the house.

Evan puts down the dish, half eaten. He feels the rumbling in his stomach. Whatever it was Mrs. Cope made for him, he was going to get to taste it again, very, very soon.

KOKORO-JIMA
THE HEART-SHAPED ISLAND

being an account
of Lance Corporal Isamu Ōshiro
Imperial Japanese Army, Fiftieth Division,
Marooned in the Northern Marianas,
July 1944 to September 1945

With a prologue, epilogue, footnotes,
and additional chapters by
Flight Lieutenant Derwood Kraft
Second Combat Cargo Group, Fifth Air Force,
U.S. Army

COPY NUMBER *12* OF TWENTY

CHAPTER FIVE

Evan closes the book. Stares at nothing. Then, with an effort, he opens it to the title page again. Twenty copies. That's all? So this is what: for family and friends only? He closes it. But wait . . . He opens it, confused. How do lawyers get involved with something when there are only twenty copies of it in existence? He shakes his head, flips the page, reads the dedication, flips to the next page.

A prologue. He hates prologues.

Why would you say something *before* you said the something you wanted to say? He closes the book again.

"Are you going to read it, Evan?"

He looks up, shields his eyes from the sun. He's in the backyard on a lawn chair, sitting up to his butt in dandelions. Mr.

Gupta is on the flat roof of his carport. Who knows why? He is wearing work gloves.

"Hi," says Evan. "What did you say?"

"The book. You have opened it many times now."

Evan stares at the yellow-bound volume, closed again, just lying there. It reminds him of a cat—a very rectangular cat—that jumped up when he was napping and has fallen asleep on his lap. He looks back at his neighbor, shrugs.

"If you would like something very entertaining, I have just finished a work of science fiction by Mr. Robert J. Sawyer, *The Terminal Experiment*. Do you know this book?"

All Evan knows is that he should have stayed indoors. "Uh, no, sir."

"Ah," says Mr. Gupta. "Well, it is a shocker, let me tell you: a murder mystery but also a very interesting treatise on ethical philosophy. Most intriguing." As Evan watches in horror, his neighbor takes off his work gloves and heads toward the ladder.

No, no, no! No more help. No more nice people!

"Uh, thanks, Mr. Gupta. But actually this is something I have to read."

That stops him. *Thank you, God, if that's your real name.* Mr. Gupta climbs back up the two rungs he had descended and steps back onto the roof. He puts his work gloves on again. "I thought school was out?"

"It is, but you know . . ." He can't think of anything to say. "Thanks, anyway, for the offer."

"You are very welcome, Evan. *The Terminal Experiment*. Remember that."

"I will. Yeah."

"Anytime, my friend."

Evan opens the book again.

Prologue

What you are holding in your hands is a rare and extraordinary document, not just in its content but in its very existence, the fact that it has survived the journey it has taken. To that end, I owe a debt of gratitude to Sergeant Major Clifford E. "Griff" Griffin II, who rescued the original manuscript and was kind enough to forward it to me, knowing, or should I say, hypothesizing my relationship to Corporal Ōshiro. That this account, written in the dying year of the War of the Pacific, is only now coming to light is another aspect of the miracle. When Griff discovered the manuscript in 1945, he intended to send it to me, forthwith. That was what he said in the cover letter that accompanied the material when it appeared, so surprisingly, on my doorstep, more than half a century later. He apologized for taking so long, but no apology was required. I know how war and its aftermath tend to push aside the best of intentions. The cessation of conflict only lets us see the chaos that war has left behind, and small personal matters are forgotten, as a soldier attempts to find his way back to something like "ordinary" life. That certainly was my own experience. The manuscript had been shoved away somewhere and miraculously *not* been lost or left behind in any of a number of moves. Picking up stakes is the fate of a lifer in the armed forces, like Griff. So it was only when he was preparing to move into a retirement home, at the end of a distinguished career, that he rediscovered the document.

I did not know the sergeant major well or for very long. We were, as they say, ships passing in the night. And so it is all the more extraordinary that he remembered me and went to the trouble of tracking me down. For that I am eternally grateful.

There is a mystery here, however. Griff could not have known the content of these writings. *Isamu's memoir was written in Japanese.* This point is important, as you will see when you come to the end of the story.

Before you read it, however, let me say a little something about myself. I do so not out of any vanity but only to try to place in context material that will undoubtedly strike the reader as far-fetched, the maundering of a mind set adrift. That might very well be the case! War does funny things to men.

I have spent my life as a man of science. After demobilization, I became a student at the Massachusetts Institute of Technology. I ended up doing a PhD and then followed my mentor, John McCarthy, when he left the Institute to go west in the early fifties. "Uncle John" was a cognitive scientist and among the earliest of a new breed of computer men. He was the one, in fact, who invented the term "artificial intelligence." I didn't have to think twice about accepting the invitation to join his staff at Stanford, where the university had created the first technologically focused industrial park to be found anywhere in the world. I am still affiliated with the university as a professor emeritus and a longtime denizen of that industrial park—that hive of activity—known now around the world as Silicon Valley.

So I think I am safe in declaring myself *compos mentis.* And therefore you may ask yourself, "Do I believe everything that is written herein?" I can only answer in the affirmative. Monsters, ghostly children, eaters of the dead . . . It cannot be so, you say, and yet it is what it is. I concur with everything Isamu describes, and his description, as you will soon see, is vivid and detailed. Oh, there is a passage in the opening chapter that is clearly fanciful—hallucinatory. Isamu seems to acknowledge it as such, the effect of shell-shock, as we used to call it. But from the moment he arrives on the desert island he named Kokoro-Jima, his refuge and later my own, I can vouch for everything that he saw and experienced there. Indeed, I have added my own recollections, interspersed with his, where I felt further explication might be warranted, fantastical though it might seem. I cannot explain any of it rationally, even now, so many years later. So it is worth repeating: War does funny things to men. Reading Isamu's account revived in me those long-ago memories. A fear I have never known. A friendship like no other.

I wish I could proclaim here in this prologue that I had been able to track down Isamu's beloved Hisako, to whom this memoir was dedicated. Nor have I been able to track down any relatives. How I would have loved to present this book to her, to them. I have tried, with the help of my son, Leonardo, to locate survivors of the family. The war effort in Saipan resulted in massive casualties to the population of the island, not just the combatants. Isamu was an immigrant to Saipan from Okinawa. That island was also devastated in the last great offensive of World War II. We keep searching, Leo and I. Who knows? In this age of global communication, the technology to which I have contributed in my own small way, we might still find heirs. And it is important that we try. This document, when you strip away all that is strange, all that might be a product of fright and horror, is more than anything else a remarkable love story. And I am still able to wish, despite the hard truths of this worrisome world, that every love story should have a satisfactory conclusion. I owe it to my friend Isamu Ōshiro to finish what he began.

Professor Derwood Kraft
Palo Alto, California

Evan looks up. Hears a lawn mower. Not exactly a startling sound in Any Place. In fact, he's not sure of this, but he has a feeling you are given a lawn mower when you sign a lease to live here. There's probably a law saying you have to use it, too. Like the law about no clotheslines.

Then Evan sits up straight. There *is* something strange about the sound, after all. He gets up, leaves the book on the lawn chair, and makes his way through the carport to the front. Lexie Jane Reidinger is mowing Evan's lawn. She's wearing her favorite snake T-shirt, the one that looks like you've got a boa around your neck—a boa constrictor, that is—draped around your shoulders with its tongue licking your belly button. She's got earphones on, and she's mouthing along with whatever song she's listening to.

A twelve-year-old is mowing my lawn for me, thinks Evan. *I am now certifiably pathetic.*

He waves. Moves down the driveway a bit, stones poking his bare feet, just in case his guilt isn't painful enough. He waves again to get her attention. She sees him finally, stops the lawn mower, pauses her iPod, and takes off her earphones.

"Thanks, Lexie," he says. "You didn't have to do this."

"My dad said I did," she says with a frown.

Great, thinks Evan. *Alienate the neighbors.* Maybe he should get some chickens, a hound dog, and a rusty car or two. "I'm really sorry," he says. "I had been meaning to get to it . . ."

"It's okay," she says. "You don't have to pay me."

"Oh. Right. Uh, thanks."

"But . . ." She stretches the word out.

"Here it comes," he says. "What is it? My LEGO collection?"

She rolls her eyes; proof positive that she's almost a teenager. But then her expression changes to unadulterated excitement; proof positive that she's not.

"I was wondering if I could see how the frigate turned out."

For a moment, Evan is lost.

"The boat?" She's got a "duh" look on her face. "The one your dad was . . . you know . . ." Now her expression changes. She looks a bit worried, as if this was one of those things you weren't supposed to say to the bereaved.

"Oh, right!" says Evan. "The frigate." He thinks a bit. "The USS *Constitution*."

"Yeah."

"I'd forgotten. You were his . . . What'd he call you?"

"His navvy slave," she says with enthusiasm.

He has to laugh. "You're in luck, slave girl—he finished it." Then he gets an idea. "Wait here," he says. He holds up his index finger. "One sec." She nods excitedly, pushes the hair out of her eyes. And he heads into the house, takes the stairs up to the Dockyard, two at a time.

The newest boat is there on the shelf where he placed it. Sixteen days ago, now, that morning when he found it on the floor. He picks it up in two hands. *This is such a good idea,* he thinks. Then he sees the dust on the shoulders of the bottle, the clean space on the shelf where the bottle sat, outlined in dust. Everything covered in dust. And dust . . . he knows what dust is.

Give it to her. Go on. Let it go. You can do it.

But he can't.

Slowly he places the bottle back on the shelf.

He leaves the room, closes the door behind him, and stands at the top of the stairs. Then he turns one-eighty and heads to his room. He lies down on his bed and closes his eyes. He thinks of Lexie Jane standing out there on the lawn waiting. Waiting for one sec. He's not sure how long it is before he hears the lawn mower fire up again.

CHAPTER SIX

Evan sits in his bed, the book open in his lap propped against his raised knees. It is late, raining again. There is distant thunder, sheet lightning. His window is open and a sheen of raindrops paints the windowsill. A breeze stirs the curtains and wanders around the room checking out his stuff, riffling paper on his desk, the feathers on a dream catcher, the right bottom corner of a poster of the Three Stooges. A breeze cool enough to make him glad of a summer-weight duvet.

He hadn't noticed at first, but there is a title embossed on the back of the book as well. The gold letters in kanji must be the Japanese for the title on the front. And if he opens the book that way up, sure enough there is a title page in Japanese, and then the body of the book in reverse order to the English translation. Which is how Japanese is read, he guesses, right to left.

He pages through the reproduced photographs of the original manuscript, tiny kanji characters, written in pencil and pen—the "monograph," as it's identified in the acknowledgments. Then he flips to the English translation. Two translators are acknowledged in the book's front matter, a professor and a graduate student, as if this thing were an archaeological specimen. Something dug up and dusted off and handled with white gloves and a magnifying glass.

For some reason he is full of trepidation.

Why me, he thinks. Why does he suddenly have a grandfather with a mysterious past? What was it Leo had written in the letter: something about the "ambiguous and disturbing conclusion." There was something in the prologue, too. He flips back, finds the paragraph . . . yeah, here it is: "Griff could not have known the content of these writings."

What was that supposed to mean?

And then he recalls that look on his father's face, the last night, as if he was trying to recall something, a lost memory.

There's something wrong with the picture.

Evan leans back and closes his eyes for a moment. The memory of his father's words has spooked him. The whole thing spooks him. How does a book like this float up onto the shore of 123 Any Place, a perfectly ordinary island in the perfectly ordinary sea of Don Mills?

KOKORO-JIMA

— I —

I Escape from Tinian

My name is Isamu Ōshiro. I was born in Okinawa but left for Saipan in 1938, when I was just sixteen. There was work there harvesting sugarcane, and no father to slap me for reading too much and for being a dreamer. I wanted to be a mechanic and soon found work fixing cars and trucks. But you know all that, Hisako. I only mention it in case this book falls into the hands of a stranger. Your name and address are plainly displayed on the book's cover, for it is into your hands that I wish it to be delivered, into your arms that I wish myself to be delivered. How I wish to share with you my most intimate thoughts. Trust that I hold many sweet memories of you in my heart.

I think too much, I talk too much—have you not told me many times? But there is precious little paper for my yammering. Ah, the miracle of these pages! You will have to wait to find out how the paper came to me along with the implement to write down my adventure. Patience.

You know everything about me until the day I boarded the troop carrier for Tinian, and after that, nothing. There was no time for letters. Everything happened so fast. So I will pick up the story of my life at the moment when it looked as if it was most likely to come to an end. It was the day after the invasion of Tinian.[1]

I remember little of the fighting. At one point it was all around me, the loudest thing in the world. And I was part of the noise, but my rifle did all the talking for me! Then there was a very loud whooshing sound, a wall of heat, and everything went dark. Time passed with no help from me to count the minutes or the hours.

The next thing I remember was pain. How strange it was to not be able to really see or hear or think at all but only feel this searing pain all over. I rolled onto my back, breathing heavily from the effort and gritting my teeth. I opened my eyes and lay there several minutes sucking in air, greedily, while the dizzy sky swirled above me. Then I raised myself onto my elbow and, dreading what I would see, I looked down at my body. Yellow pus oozed from my left flank, discoloring my torn uniform, which was already brown with dried blood. I had been scorched. I shuddered and shook. My heart was racing. Septicemia was setting in. I wiped the sweat off my face, knuckled it out of my eyes, looked up, looked around. My rifle lay a few feet away, as scorched as I was, broken. The chrysanthemum etched into the stock was filled with dirt. Everywhere was quiet. Dead quiet.

Rolling onto my front, I dragged myself painfully forward on my elbows toward a stand of new bamboo. I parted the culms with my hand. I blinked. Blinked again, for what I saw could not be. What insanity was this?

---

[1] The Battle of Tinian began on July 24, 1944, and was over in not much more than a week. Over 30,000 American marines landed on an island defended by fewer than 9,000 Japanese soldiers. The Japanese lost more than 8,000 soldiers. Only 313 were taken as prisoners. The Americans lost fewer than 400 soldiers.

Amidst the smoke, a terrible battle was being fought in utter silence.

By puppets!

Bunraku puppets shot at one another with bright-blue rifles or slashed with yellow swords. This one held a red dagger in his polished wooden fist, which came down repeatedly on the inflated torso of another puppet, who twisted and turned this way and that, throwing up its hands, its clever glass eyes rolling in its wooden head. Over there, another puppet twirled around and around, shooting a green handgun, out of the barrel of which rained a silvery cascade of confetti.

Parts of soldiers flew off, this way and that.

The puppets were elaborately dressed: on one side, brave samurai warriors in orange-colored armor with ferocious grins; and on the other side, grotesque ogres, pale with white noses as long as daikon radishes.

For every puppet there were three puppeteers, one to operate the feet and legs, the other to operate the left hand, and one—the master puppeteer—to operate the right hand and the head. The puppeteers were all but invisible. I squinted to see them at all, for they were dressed in black from head to toe, with black hoods over their heads as if they were death's own helpers. What Dancers they were—blind Dancers under the blazing sun. War Dancers holding aloft warriors with child-bright weapons, and hungry mouths open to reveal the whitest of chompers and the pinkest of tongues.

Now this one's head flew off and rolled toward me, so that when it stopped I could see the worn handhold in the hollowed-out neck. This was a puppet that had fought in many battles. Had he lost his head every time?

There was something terribly wrong with the performance, but I was so delirious it took me a while to realize what it was.

Ah, yes! There was no chanter to tell the story. There were no musicians: no one to pluck the *shamisen*, to drum on the *taiko*, or to blow on the *shakuhachi*.

There was no noise at all, and what is a battle without noise?

My grandfather had taken me to see *Bunraku* when I was a child. Did I ever tell you that, Hisako? No, I mostly complained about my father, didn't I. Ah, but my grandfather—how I miss him. I remembered him explaining how the chanter always held up the text before the play and bowed to it, promising the audience that he would follow the author's story, faithfully. So this was a performance without sound, and without an author or a story. And how could such a story be true? How could such a story ever end?

Now, from the midst of the swirling mayhem, stepped the most impressive of samurai with a mighty ax, which he swung at the loftiest of the ogres. The ogre ducked but not fast enough, for the top of his head was sheared clear off! As you can imagine, I gasped in astonishment. Then as if all this were not strange enough, out of the white ogre's skull appeared the head of another miniature ogre. A hatchling that rose on tiny white wings and floated into the air above his fallen father, higher and higher, until he hovered above the battle. All the brave samurai stopped their fighting to look up in awe. The hatchling held a rose-colored orb with a fuse that flashed and sparked.

A bomb!

If there were black-gloved hands holding that flying ogre-child aloft, I swear I could not see them. The mightiest of the samurai, stunned by what had happened, regained his composure, raised his ax, and swung at the tiny winged warrior, back and forth, leaping and twirling and lashing out. How comical he was—deadly comical. But with great alacrity the ogre's offspring averted every blow, rising to just the right height above the battle scene.

The fuse grew shorter and shorter.

And then the bomb went off.

A hot wind made the bamboo culms click together. I did not open my eyes this time, afraid of what I might see. I was thinking about something I had been told, something that had been drummed into me, when I became a soldier. "There can be no surrender. A great man should die as a shattered jewel."

A great man, yes. But I, Lance Corporal Isamu Ōshiro, knew I was not a great man. I was a burned man, a broken man. A puppet deserted and left to die by my manipulators. I was nineteen, married not four months, before I was called to serve my country and my Emperor. Which I had done and failed. Failed not once but twice, for I was too weak now to throw myself on my own sword. To be fair, I had no sword. But I was too weak to throw myself on the sword of the conqueror.

There was even greater shame inside me. In my heart of hearts, I knew that, given the chance, I *would* be a tile under the invaders' feet—would suffer the infamy of becoming a prisoner of war—if it meant eventually I could be with you again, Hisako. If you have survived on your island, then I would live on this one, with any amount of shame, just to be with you there again. I did not then know that there was a third island, a third choice. Ah, but I get ahead of myself.

There I lay. Tears sprang from my eyes, I will tell you, and mingled with the sand, which coated my cheek. The burning in my side throbbed and throbbed. My breath came in sobs.

I dreamed of you, your face so somber and strong. "Live," you said to me. "I will live, if you will, too. Live and come back to me."

* * *

I woke a third time to the thumping of a bittern. I could hear again! I listened to the wind stir the leaves of the trees. Is there a more glorious sound in the world? Then I heard human sounds, voices. Not the cries of war, but of men talking. I lay perfectly still. A burst of tired laughter split the air. One voice louder than the others sounded on the verge of hysteria. I knew that kind of laugh only too well, but I could not understand what the voices might be saying. From the pitch and the lazy timbre I could tell they were *gaijin*.

It was dawn. A day and a night had passed. Or maybe several days and several nights—how would I know? I raised my head, scraped at the sand coating my cheek. Dug the sand out of my ear. The voices were still there. They were not a dream, although it had been a night of uncommonly strange dreams!

I cleared the sleep out of my eyes. Then carefully, I rose on my knees and peered again through the bamboo. This is what I saw: American soldiers walking amongst the dead and dying, eyes peeled, rifles fitted with bayonets. A wounded Japanese soldier was helped to his feet. He was frisked and led away, without a struggle. The two Americans and their prisoner crossed a slight rise and disappeared from view, and I waited for the single shot of execution. None came.

Another warrior writhed in pain. A marine called out, and two men appeared with a stretcher, and the three of them loaded the man onto it. A farmer, by the look of him, for many of the citizens of the island had joined us in the last-ditch effort against the invaders.[2] I had heard, Hisako, as have you, what

---

[2] On July 31, the Japanese launched a suicide attack, which included many residents of the island, including farmers, women, and children. This raises the question of just how long Ōshiro lay wounded. He spoke earlier of it being the day after the invasion, whereas the suicide attack was seven days later. The suicide attack signaled the end of the invasion, for all intents and purposes.

the Americans do to the wounded—the torture, the humiliation they inflict. And yet that was not what I was seeing here. The stretcher-bearers carried the warrior to a place where there were many stretchers and where the wounded were being treated, Americans, Japanese, soldiers and commoners alike.

Then a baby started to cry.

A baby? Now you will think I am hallucinating again. Believe me I thought so, too. I punched my head with the heel of my hand as if my untrustworthy ears had deceived me. But no, across the battlefield a marine leaned his rifle against a tree and gently released a child from the dead arms of its mother. Awkwardly he cradled it.

"Will you look at this," he called out. No, I cannot understand English, as you well know, but that is what he must have said, for another soldier approached him. "Well, what do you know," he said, or words of that kind. I wanted to turn away, for fear of what would happen next. *They would kill it. They would throw it to the ground and tread on it. They would snap its neck like a market chicken.* This was what we had been told. I had to do something!

My rifle was ruined, but I still had my handgun. I rolled onto my side, almost screaming with pain, but biting down on my tongue to keep from giving myself away. I reached for my Nambu, struggling to pull it from its holster. But by the time all of this had transpired and I had rolled back onto my stomach to fire—nauseous from the exertion—there were three soldiers gathered around the child. It was howling now, and the first soldier held the baby at arm's length and wrinkled his nose. The others laughed.

I took aim, or tried to; my hand shook too violently.

The newest of the trio had pushed his helmet off the back of his head and taken the baby, placing it across his shoulder. He patted its back tenderly. I lowered my gun. The soldier's face was black. Black, I thought, from the smoke of war. But no, so were his arms and hands: black because he was black.

The black man cooed at the baby.

What was I to do? I lay my head down in the sand, too weak to hold it up, confused and ashamed. Surely war is madness. Meanwhile, the baby, quiet now, was carried away, back through the dead and dying, back to the living and recovering. And I faded off again, exhausted by the attempt to care.

I awoke another time and it was evening. Another day was coming to an end, although how many had passed I have no idea. The birds told one another the news of the battle in excited chatter and shrieks. I sat up and with my good hand tugged at the string around my neck. The little red-and-gold sack came free of my shirt, my *omamori*: the amulet you gave me on the day we wed, meant to keep me safe.

Gingerly, I opened the top of the sack and with two fingers slipped out the photo of you, my bride, Hisako.

I will live, if you will, too.

It was time, I thought. Your face gave me courage. I tenderly placed the picture back in my *omamori* and tucked the little sack back into my filthy shirt.

And so . . .

I was prepared for anything now. I gathered up my strength and climbed to my feet. I wobbled like a drunken man, then stepped through the vale of bamboo and stood unsteadily at attention, staring straight ahead across the clearing. There were still soldiers there; the cleanup from the massacre would go on long into the night, whichever night it was.

But no one saw me.

Their eyes were cast down at the carnage. I would have called out but found I had no voice. I would have gone to them — given myself up, but you, Hisako, you snapped at me!

"Iie!" you said. "No!" Such a shock. I could have sworn I heard you.

So I stood there a moment longer, the longest moment of my life. Then I turned and shambled off the other way. I held myself as tall as a limping burned man can, and I waited for the shout, the gunfire, the end, but it didn't come.

I am leaving this war, I thought. *It is no defeat to live.* Isn't that what you meant when your voice snapped at me from the amulet lying next to my heart?

It is funny. We have been married so little time that I have never heard you raise your voice except to sing! But I am glad you shouted at me like that, even if it was most impolite of you.

I came to the brink of the sea. I looked down at the beach below. The tide was in, lapping at the wreckage of the American amphibious landing vehicles. There were landing ramps,[3] constructed by the Americans, to scale the bank. The tide was high, a spring tide. One of the ramps floated, the wooden platform torn free from its base.

A raft waited for me in the floating world.

I washed up on a shore at low tide. It was early evening. My raft was deposited on a wide strand of beach, littered with all manner of flotsam, the debris of battle: what was left when the war was over but not over. From the fringe of the beach, where the grasses waved in the onshore breeze, I could just make out hungry ghosts watching and waiting, impatiently. I thought to

---

[3] These ramps were called "doodlebugs" by the Seabees who constructed them: the United States Navy Construction Battalion (CB).

myself, *Isamu, beware! When you are good and dead, they will feast on you.* But then, before my eyes, children appeared, unraveling from the air, first one, then another, and so on, until there were a number of them — too many to count in my half-dead state. The nearest came to my side, a ghost boy, who might have been nine or ten to look at, if years count for anything in the in-between world. He rested his vaporous hand on my shoulder. And although I could feel nothing, I closed my eyes again with a feeling of peace coming over me. *These ghost children will protect me from the other ghosts,* I thought. It was not a very rational kind of thought, but it was my last in what had been an endlessly long day.

CHAPTER SEVEN

Evan looks up, stunned, not sure what has roused his attention. The phone. The house phone is ringing. He's not sure how many times it has rung. He was a long way off. He waits, perfectly still, until the ringing stops, until there is just the rain again, splattering against the window and the wind gusting in the trees like the tide on a distant beach. The water on the sill dribbles down the wall. There is a wet spot on the carpet — a semicircle of darker beige. There is the shimmer of summer lightning, then thunder rumbling, low. He remembers to breathe, looks at his cell phone. It's just after ten thirty. His friends only know his cell number. It's too late for robocalls. He leans back against his pillow. Closing his eyes, he sees a raft at sea, a body half dead, an island shrouded in mist heaving into view. And then the phone rings again.

Leo Kraft?

Evan remembers the address on the letter. California. It would only be seven thirty there.

He pushes the covers off, praying that the ringing doesn't stop. He runs silently to his father's bedroom at the end of the hall, to the cordless on the bedside table.

"Hello?"

There is a hollowness at the other end of the line and then the echoey sound of a loudspeaker announcement. Evan can't make out the words, but he can guess the location.

"Evan?" The voice is deep. Not Leo Kraft.

"Hi."

"It's your grandfather." There is a pause while he waits for Evan to say something. Evan says nothing. "I'm at the airport."

With effort, Evan lines up enough neurons to kick-start his vocal cords. "Which airport?"

"Is there more than one?"

"Here, you mean? Pearson International?"

"That's it. It's late. Thought I'd give you a heads-up."

"But you were coming—"

"Next Saturday. I know. That was the soonest I could imagine getting away. Turned out there was nothing stopping me from coming a week early." He pauses. "The earlier the better, I figured."

Evan doesn't know what to say.

"I guess I should have called."

It's a prompt, Evan, your turn—say something.

"Is this inconvenient, son?"

"No, sir. I was just . . . Sorry. I was asleep." It's almost true; the story he left in the other room seems dreamlike to him.

"I can make my way there," says Griff. He recites the address and Evan nods, then remembers to say yes. "No need to pick me up. Perhaps, if you're tired, you could leave a key under the mat."

"It's not locked. The door. We don't . . ."

"Right, then."

"I'll be up," says Evan.

"There's no need, soldier. Get some shut-eye. We'll talk in the morning." Then he hangs up before Evan can say another word.

"Shut-eye," says Evan to the darkened bedroom. "Soldier."

Back in his room, Evan slips an old Blue Jays ticket stub into the book to mark his place. He sets it on his bedside table, then some instinct makes him pick it up again, hold it in both hands for one indecisive moment, before slipping it under the bed, out of sight. He clambers into the clothes he's worn the last three days and makes his way downstairs.

The house is a split-level: at the entry level, there is a living room, dining room, and kitchen, then up a short flight of stairs to the bedrooms, or down a short flight to the rec room and basement. He's going to put Griff in the rec room. The couch folds out into a bed. He finds sheets and pillowcases. He and his father have always shared the housekeeping duties. He even remembers clean towels. "You are going to make some woman a fine wife," his father used to say. He stops at the door as he's leaving and looks back to see if everything looks right. The rowing machine has been folded up and leans against the wall, out of the way. The free weights are on the dumbbell rack. Exercise is just another thing that's gone by the wayside.

There's a lava lamp sitting on the bar in the corner. He walks over and turns it on. He smiles to himself, trying to imagine whether the leatherneck with the gravelly voice will appreciate it.

He's looking out the side window of the front door when

the taxi pulls up. The rain has slackened some, but not the wind; it punches holes in the willow on the lawn, grabs at the wings of Griff's raincoat, as he gathers his briefcase and suitcase from the trunk. The cabbie doesn't help, doesn't even crack his door. Then he pulls away in a hurry, spraying the curb, the moment the trunk is closed. What was that about?

Griff walks up the drive, head lowered against the wind. A fierce gust grabs him, and in the wavering light from the streetlamp, he looks like something Tim Burton might have invented, constructed out of cables and dark matter.

Now he stops.

He looks up the driveway toward the carport. Evan wonders what he's looking at. Standing there, like that, on his own long thin shadow, Griff reminds Evan of that poster for *The Exorcist*.

"Oh, shit," he murmurs to himself.

The old man shakes his head slowly, turns, and heads up the pathway toward the front porch. His face is disgruntled, stern, and creased like old stone, eroded. Evan wants to lock the door against him. Run around the house and lock all the doors and windows. Pull down the shades. Instead he just steps back three long paces and then two more and waits for the door to open.

If Griff is surprised to see him standing there, he doesn't act it. Evan hears his father whispering in his ear. "He has stormed a thousand beaches. He's used to hostile welcoming parties."

"Ah, you're up," he says.

"Hi," says Evan, nodding. He watches Griff size him up — sees himself through the old soldier's eyes: lanky, under-weight, with a loaf of dirty-blond hair, the sides buzzed, and a vertical tat on his skinny neck that reads: ".44 caliber love letter." He's dressed in sprayed-on black jeans, a studded belt, and a wrinkled and torn red T-shirt. It's the one with the "March of Evolution" on it: an ape following a less hairy ape walking on

46

his hind legs, following a guy with a club in his hands, following one with a spear on his shoulder. Modern man leads the parade, but this one is turned to face the posse and he looks pissed. "Stop following me!" say the words in the balloon.

Evan is barefoot. And where was it he left his club?

In the same instant he sizes up his grandfather: under the dripping black raincoat, a yellow golf shirt and tan chinos with pleats so sharp you could cut your finger on them. There's no bunching at the knees to suggest the man was sitting on a plane or riding in a taxi. Maybe he stood at attention the whole way from Raleigh-Durham. There's a scar above his right eye, a little white zigzag, where the gray eyebrow hair doesn't grow.

Evan takes the man's raincoat and hangs it up, separating it from what's already hanging there, his father's coats and jackets. He watches Griff open the front zippered pocket of his luggage and pull out a clear plastic bag with a drawstring. He takes out a pair of brown cordovans. With tassels. Griff steps out of his shiny black shoes, beaded with raindrops, and into the cordovans. The skin of his arms and face is almost as brown as his shoes and several degrees darker than healthy. His hair is nothing but gray bristle. "Not a buzz cut," his father's voice whispers to him. "It's called a 'high and tight.'" Evan smiles to himself, remembering his father rubbing his own balding scalp. "The first battleground between the old man and me was the top of my head."

Griff holds Evan's eye as if uncertain where the smile lingering there might have come from. He manages something like a smile, a slight rearrangement of the deep crevices in his face. His eyes are the Griffin-clan blue, except that Griff's are darker, clouded by how much they've seen. The two of them shake hands stiffly. There's nothing old about the man's grip; Evan holds on for dear life.

47

He clears his throat. "Was it an okay flight?"

"No, since you asked. Our ETD was pushed back three times, the coffee was rancid, and there was a mother with a newborn beside me who cried the whole way."

"The mother or the baby?"

Griff does not favor him with a reply. *Note to self: Joking doesn't seem to have any good effect.* The look in Griff's eye reminds Evan of a word he's only ever heard in war movies: insubordination. Whoever is accused of it usually ends up in the brig.

There's this awkward moment. *I should be doing something,* Evan thinks. *Something other than running away, screaming.*

"We can talk in the morning," says Griff, taking charge of the situation. "Where do you want to put me?"

"Uh, the family room," says Evan. "There's a bathroom down there, flat-screen TV, a mini-fridge in the bar, and it's a lot cooler in the summer."

"I'm not buying the place," says Griff.

"Right. Uh . . . Yeah . . . It's this way." Evan holds out his hand, indicating the stairwell, like he's some goofball bellhop at the Hilton.

Griff picks up his bag and briefcase in one huge, knotted hand, and with his other hand clamped to the railing, he one-steps his way, old man style, down the stairs.

"Did I leave the light on in the car?" says Evan.

The man stops and slowly turns. "What's that?"

"You stopped in the driveway and you were staring at the carport. You looked as if you were frowning."

"The Ford Escort," says Griff, shaking his head. He looks peeved, as if there's something he cannot comprehend. "It just seemed remarkable to me that your daddy and I would end up driving the same damn automobile."

Then he turns to go but stops and looks back up at Evan, his face now half in shadows. "Keen observation, soldier," he says.

Keen, says Evan to himself.

Griff stops again at the bottom. "So, shall we say oh-eight-hundred hours for debriefing? Or are you a late sleeper?" Evan would never have guessed that the words "late sleeper" could sound so much like "Satan's spawn."

He shrugs. "Whatever," he says. "I'm not like on a . . . you know, schedule."

"Schedule," says the old man, turning the *ch* into a *k.* From what Evan can make of his expression, the word has a whole different meaning to Griff.

He turns away. The wall-to-wall carpet says *shhh* as he opens the downstairs door and *shhh* as he closes it.

— II —

I Explore My New Home

There was a magic pond. That is what I decided it was. I was so parched, you see—so desperate for water—that until I drank from the pond, it was as if I were not truly alive. I wandered up some path made by animals, crawling part of the way, scarcely able to move at all, hoping that such a well-worn path must lead to water. I parted the rushes with my hands, and there it was, a deep, green pool.

The air was laced with fine blue dragonflies; the sun glanced off their translucent wings. I sank to the soft earth and, leaning forward, placed my hands in the pond. I lifted the water to my face, gasped at the cool of it, opened my cracked and salt-stained lips to receive its blessing. My hands were smoke-blackened, my knuckles scraped raw, and the water felt like a salve. And my throat . . . Ah, my throat opened to the water like a flower to rain.

I leaned back on my ankles, my wet hands resting on my thighs. *"Tasukatta,"* I said to the dragonflies. "What a relief." Then I raised my hands and, placing them together, bowed reverently to the green pond.

When I opened my eyes again, my ghostly family of children was there, scattered around the fringe of the pond, their transparent bodies visible behind the reeds, each watching me reverently with the steady gaze of a newborn child upon its mother. I bowed to them all.

Leaning on my fists, I stared into the shimmering surface of the water. Might it be poisonous? I dismissed the idea. After all, how many times could you die in one day?

In a glossy-leaved bush nearby, a white-throated ground dove whistled at me and chirped. "Hello, *hato-chan*," I said. "Thank you for welcoming me to your island." The dove paid me not the slightest attention, fluttered to the ground, and dipped its beak into the water.

I watched the bird, its plumage so much finer than my own. Ha! I was down to nothing but a loincloth. The bird sipped the water, not six feet from me but undisturbed by my alien presence. And, Hisako, you will forgive me if I admit to you that I had the strangest thought: *This bird has lived forever. The dove is fearless because nothing can kill it.* "So maybe this sweet water is an elixir," I said out loud. "Maybe I will live forever, too."

In the dappled coolness of this clearing, I dipped my hands back into the pond, but this time I dug down deep into the cold, thick mud. At once I felt the healing in it. I scooped up the rich brown sludge, let it drip and slither down my arms. Tentatively I applied the mud to the raw and suppurated flesh of my torso. There were virulent red patches, hideous abscesses, all along my side. Gently I applied the muck to my afflicted body as though it were an expensive ointment. I breathed through my nose, my lips pressed tightly together to suppress the urge to scream with the pain of touching my skin. Then I sat, cross-legged, closed my eyes, and let the mud do its work. I was alive.

But you are worried, perhaps, about the other ghosts I saw when first I landed, the ones standing a ways off watching me with red

51

and ready eyes. You are thinking, *Isamu, you must have been feverish and confused.* But no, it was not so. When first I reopened my eyes, just as I felt the raft begin to move again on the incoming tide, I was startled to see one of the ghoulish creatures only a few feet away. It backed off, its head cast down as if it had been looking for something. I was not fooled. I knew what this fellow was, a *jikininki.* Slim as an eel it was and slimy, a decomposing cadaver, but with those glowing eyes and the sharp claws needed to tear apart a corpse.

"I'm not dead yet, *jikininki,*" I shouted at the creature. It wasn't much of a shout. My throat was parched. But the ghost stepped back a few paces more, and I could see how sad it was that I was not going to be its dinner. I dug my fingers into the wet sand and with a mighty effort hurled a fistful of it at the ghost. "Go! Scat!" I said. And, slope-shouldered, the thing limped off up the beach. My gentle ghost children watched all this with interest but no alarm. They are a peaceful lot. I climbed to my feet, exhausted from the ordeal, and immediately they crowded close to me. I did not like it, despite their angelic faces. But I decided they were only curious and not a threat.

But back, now, to the deep, green pond. Time passed. The dove flew off. The shadows moved. I stood, a little groggily, on my feet, a mud man. How you would have laughed to see me. I was mud from head to toe. I contemplated bathing in the pond. If the waters were indeed magical, surely they would heal me. But then I thought of how my body might contaminate it, the only source of potable water I had found so far. No, I would leave it be. I would bathe in the ocean eventually. But for now, I had to eat.

I headed back toward the beach, through the glinting light filtered down through the palm trees, banana trees, papaya trees. There was food there, all right, but I was in no shape to climb a tree. Not yet. I made my way back down the sloping path, a path made by animals, as I had supposed, for there was one now, a deer, a sambar hind with her fawn. I stopped in my tracks. So did the deer.

"*Konnichiwa, shika-san,*" I said, bowing to the animal. She did not move. The young stag did not move, either. "You are going to the magical pond," I said, very gently, calmly. Then I stepped aside into the dense underbrush and gestured with my hand for the deer to pass. A long minute passed and I stood perfectly still, as still as any tree. And finally she budged, her eyes alert for movement. There was a curious blemish on her neck: a hairless bloodred spot on the underside of her throat, oozing a white liquid. I stared at it as she hurried past, so close I could have patted her yellowy-brown hide. The fawn skittered after her, frisking at one point, kicking out his back hooves. I laughed and watched them proceed up through the tall grass until they were out of sight. I couldn't say why but I felt strangely blessed.

Such wonders I have seen, Hisako-chan.

The sun had passed over the island and was low in the western sky, though it would be hours before it set. I ventured out onto the sand. *Atsu!* Still hot, but bearable, and it was time to see what there might be amongst the wreckage on the beach. I passed by where I had taken off my uniform, what was left of it, and had hung it on the low branches of a tree. I had fashioned my loincloth out of a torn piece of cotton I found, caught in the branches of that very same tree. *These branches shall be my clothing closet,* I thought, *my chest of drawers!* The cloth of my loincloth was dead-leaf yellow, the color of bravery. Ha!

As I had made my way from my makeshift raft up the beach, staggering and crawling and half dead of thirst, I had seen this strip of cloth fluttering, caught by a gust of wind, a tattered flag. And when I reached it—reached the coconut palms and shelter

53

from the scorching sun — I had stripped out of my army uniform, peeling it away from my damaged skin, glad to be free of the stench of it.

I stopped now, beside the uniform, dry and warm to the touch. It was so strange, Hisako, for it was as if I were touching the shoulder of a dead comrade. My hand strayed to my chest, to my *omamori*, your gift to me. There were beads of water on it. I brushed them away.

"I am alive, Hisako," I murmured. "I have no idea whether I am in this world or some other, but I am alive."

Then I turned to scan the beach, my hand raised to my brow, squinting in the brightness after the shadowy coolness of the jungle. My ghostly cavalcade turned with me to look.

There were torn and broken things everywhere.

Crates and broken boards of wood, tangles of rope, all manner of debris. All manner of treasures! It was like a market — a bazaar. I remembered in a sudden flash the busy prefecture where you lived and worked in your father's noodle shop.

"Ah, for a bowl of *miso nikomi*," I said out loud, patting my stomach. But no, there was nothing so comforting there. After a while I did find food, or something like it, half buried in the sand, like pirate treasure. On my knees, digging like a dog for a bone, I cleared away the splintered, sun-bleached wood. I peered into the crate, shoved my arm inside it, and pulled out something wrapped in cellophane. I pulled out tin cans with indecipherable words on them. What else: matches — good!

And what was this? I picked up a slim packet, as long as my hand, flat and wrapped in paper and foil. I opened it to reveal a hard flat brown stick. I smelled it, scraped at the dark surface with my ragged fingernail, sniffed it again. Sweet. Then I tasted it. Ah, *such* sweetness. I dared to bite into it. *Pock!* A piece snapped off in my mouth. I let it sit there. It was not like anything I have ever tasted. I closed my eyes and savored the substance now melting on my tongue.[1]

There were other things, white tablets. I licked one of them.[2]

"*Mazui!*"

I spit and spit to get the taste out of my mouth. Luckily, there was also dried fruit, which I gobbled down greedily. But the dark brown substance, Hisako. How I hope one day you will taste it.

Before nightfall I had explored the eastern side of the island and found no signs of human habitation, other than the detritus on the beach. The jungle was dense enough that there might well be people at the heart of it. But I did not see the smoke of fires nor, as it darkened, the lights of any settlement or camp. I would explore the island in time, for there was nothing else for me to do. And I would have to make myself some kind of a shelter. How long would I be here? I could not say. But by the end of that first day, I was in no hurry to go anywhere. Somehow, I knew, I would have to try to find my way back to Saipan, back to you, Hisako, and to our tiny set of rooms, if indeed there is anything of it left. But I wanted to be whole again, first. I wanted to heal. There was so much healing to do.

At sunset I climbed a grassy hill at the northern end of the island, a hill high enough that I could see the whole island with its white beaches and green heart. And from there I perceived that it was, yes, heart-shaped. Gazing down at the place where the western and eastern shores curved up and around and then

---

[1] Isamu would seem to have tasted chocolate for the very first time. He had stumbled on a box of K rations, the "assault lunch," by the sound of it, which also included caramels and chewing gum.

[2] Probably water purification tablets!

back down until they met in a deep cleft, I suddenly remembered a favorite book of my grandfather's, *Kokoro* by Sōseki Natsume. I love reading, as well you know, and it was only because of *Ojiisan*. I have told you about him, how we talked—or *Ojiisan* talked and I sat at the old man's feet, listening. At least when I was younger I listened, when I still knew how to sit still and be obedient. Before I reached the age where I was in such a hurry to do things my own way.

I sat now on my heart-shaped island, cross-legged, and thought of him.

"A book called *Heart*?"

"Ah," said my grandfather, "there are shades of meaning. It could refer to 'the heart of things' or 'feelings.'" I remember how he patted my chest gently, where my heart was. "It can mean 'Heart and mind'—many things."

I remember frowning, shaking my head at this. What was the use of a word that meant many things? When you said "carburetor," it meant carburetor. When you said "piston," that's what you were talking about. Even as a small boy, I was wild about automobiles and motorbikes—anything that roared and belched smoke. I remembered *Ojiisan* smiling at me kindly. "If only life worked as simply as an automobile. In books things can mean more than one thing, and that makes you *work* at the meaning."

I stood and looked out at my new home. In honor of my *ojiisan*, and in honor of things not being as simple as automobiles, I called the island "Kokoro-Jima."

It was in the cleft at the top of the heart that I discovered the lagoon. A wide barrier reef crossed the northern reach and turned the voluptuously curving V-shaped bay into a warm, sandy-bottomed shallow salt lake. I bathed there that night, tired from my trek along the island's eastern flank. The moon was frozen in its fullness, heavy with light, and I lay on my back in the water staring up at the stars. I imagined you, Hisako, in my arms, the two of us naked in this paradise.

— III —

I Become an Undertaker

I found other rations in the wreckage along the eastern beach of the heart-shaped island. The flat, brown-colored stick was a marvel, but some of the other food items made me wonder if the rumors were true about the Americans being monsters, for there were cans of vile, gelatinous meat, or so I supposed it to be, though the sight and smell of it made me retch.[1] There were also *bisuketto* I could barely crack with my teeth.[2] It was hardly food at all!

But, as I had known from the start, there was food growing on the island. And as I combed the beach, sifting through the debris of the war that I had slipped away from — drifted away from on a piece of broken ramp — I found a good sharp knife to cut down papaya and even a sword to open coconuts. I made a spade to dig up taro. The island provided.

Unfortunately, the island also provided food for the restless *jikininki*. These are not like the friendly children ghosts. No. I knew the *jikininki* for what they were, from the minute I laid

---

[1] I can only assume Isamu is talking about Spam, which was included in certain rations.

[2] Probably hardtack.

eyes on them. Human-eaters. They were harmless to me as long as I stayed healthy, but they were repulsive and a reminder that death was here in this otherwise beautiful place.

"Here!" I shouted, hurling a can of the horrible meat at one of them that ventured too close. The ghoul recoiled and shuffled a few yards off, sniffing the air like a dog, although how it could smell anything with what was left of its decrepit nose was a mystery to me. The *jikininki* stepped from foot to foot as if the sand were too hot for its misshapen, cadaverous feet. "Eat up!" I yelled, pointing to the opened can at the ghost's feet. The creature sniffed again, hissed, then turned and loped awkwardly away. I laughed and slapped my leg. This thing that ate putrid flesh — even it wouldn't touch the canned meat.

It was the *jikininki* that led me to the first corpse.

I came down from the hill one fresh morning and saw several of the ghouls congregating on the beach. As I got closer, I could see that one of them was kneeling on the ground with his hand under the head of a dead man, its shoulder protecting the carcass from its hideous kinsmen, claiming the body as its own, while it lashed out at any of these revolting creatures who dared to come too close.

"Shoo! Off with you!" I shouted, racing across the hard sand toward the gathering, splashing into the low tide, my sword raised in two hands like a samurai. Ah yes, I can hear you say, what a dashing figure I must have cut, Hisako! Oh, how the *jikininki* hissed at me, stumbling out of my way, to the left and right, but not prepared to leave. They spit and slobbered. Then they turned their backs on me, bent over, and farted horribly. You laugh, Hisako, but it was true! Bravely, I covered my nose and waded into their midst, swinging my sword back and forth. You cannot kill what is already dead, but the *jikininki* are tender-skinned nonetheless, I soon found out. They are half rotted and, in any case, afraid of the living. They hate the living; too much of a reminder of what they've lost, I guess.

"Leave him!" I shouted, slashing at the one who had claimed the body. The thing pulled back. Then it opened its horrible maw, from which gobbets of blood and flesh spilled. It tried to growl at me, but its mouth was too full. Sick with revulsion, I pierced the creature through the chest. It squealed hideously, loud as a siren, and clambered to its feet, scuttling away, but not without taking a great hank of flesh in the talons of its left paw. While I stood guard over the corpse, the other *jikininki* circled the one with the food, slavering and screeching, like so many seagulls wanting their share of the bounty.

The flesh-eaters had hideously disfigured the dead man's face, but his tattered uniform proclaimed him to be an American sailor. I wasn't sure what Americans did with their dead; I seemed to think they buried them, but since I was not sure, all I could think to do was to cremate him, as is our custom.

There would be no need to moisten the lips of the soldier with the "water of the last moment." He was lying in the wet sand of low tide, waterlogged. I wondered how long the sailor had been trying to land, washed up and washed back out again by the tide.

It is not hard to die; I had learned that all too well. But I found myself thinking how hard it is to settle, to find a place of rest. With the flesh-eaters around, there would be no rest for this soldier's spirit. So I dragged the man up the sand to dry off. I stayed nearby, for I could sometimes see the ghouls not so far off, watching, waiting for their chance. Then the wind changed and they wandered off. When I felt I could leave him for a moment, I gathered what I needed and built a pyre of driftwood and a bamboo platform for the sailor to lie upon, his body facing north. I talked to him. I wished him luck.

"I have no coins to give you to ford the River of Three Crossings," I said. "I'm sorry. But perhaps your gods do not require payment." Then I lit the fire with one of my precious matches and watched the flames consume the man. I fed the hungry fire to keep it as hot as possible. The *jikininki* returned with the fickle breeze, drew as near as they dared, and howled at their loss, their hands raised to their cadaverous cheeks, but did not dare come too close. Fire, it seemed, was their enemy.

And so I set myself up as the island's undertaker. It was something that needed doing, and I went about it as best I could, sending dead souls to wherever it was dead souls went. Did *gaijin* go to the same place our own people go? I had no idea; I had never given such things much thought. But here I had only to keep myself alive and to get well, and so the days stretched before me with more time to think than I would have thought possible. By the time you next see me, Hisako, I will be a wise man, a philosopher! Meanwhile, the dead floated in on the tide, and I was the only one around to send them on their way to heaven or hell or wherever it was they were going. The destination of the dead was not my business: the vehicle was.

"Am I not an auto mechanic? Is it not my job to make sure people get to where they are going as smoothly as possible?"

I made a spear out of bamboo. Using my trusty raft, I ventured out onto the reef, where I proved an able fisherman. It seems, Hisako, that for all my unkind comments about him, my father did at least teach me something. There were sea urchins, crabs, oysters, octopuses—real food! The gelatinous canned meat did have one great value. It made good bait.

There was some American food I grew to like, especially the beans in a red sauce and a vegetable stew of which there was an abundant supply. But fish became my staple diet. Besides, fishing gave me something to occupy my time.

Once, when I was fishing in deeper waters with a line and improvised hook, taking advantage of a clear, calm day, I looked down and saw the ghostly form of a sunken ship. It might have been the source of my bounty, spilled onto the tides to wash up on the shores of Kokoro-Jima. I knelt on my raft and stared down into the waters at the wreck. I said a blessing to the gods for the bounty and a prayer for the dead I knew must be trapped down there in the green darkness. I had found three other corpses by then. But if the wreck gave up further members of its crew, I would give them a proper send-off. I could do this much.

Days passed into weeks. I had clothes to wear now, and shoes. I had stripped the clothes off more than one dead sailor by then. As I had suspected, other sailors from the wreck washed ashore, and I sent them on their way, getting to them whenever possible before the *jikininki*. I would regularly go on death patrol, which, as awful as it may seem, was better than when I was a soldier and went looking for people to kill!

"Come home in death." It was a line from a song we had learned when I joined up. There were many such songs extolling the proud deaths we soldiers would earn on the battlefield. Curiously, there were not a lot of songs about what to do if you happened to survive.

Sometimes I would wake and find the ghouls hovering near me, longing for me to die, drawn to the stench of the corpses that lingered about me, I suspect. A smell that remained no matter how many times I bathed in the lagoon. But I would not die. I would not give them the satisfaction.

I will return to you, Hisako, when the aroma of the dead is gone from me.

I have not mentioned the other pleasant ghosts for quite a while. I suppose that is because I have become quite used to them, these "children" of mine, for I cannot seem to shake them. I no longer try to frighten them away. I do not waste my breath yelling at them. Though their faces are hardly formed and they cannot speak, they seem to express human emotions. They smile and frown and look angry sometimes, though it is hard for me to know what motivates their feelings. The expression I see most when I gaze at one or another of them is hopefulness. There is one, a boy child, Hisako, who comes closer to me than the others. In some strange way, he reminds me of you. But perhaps that is just my longing for you that makes me look for your features everywhere—even in the clouds.

I have come to taking the clothing from dead men and hanging them over bushes to dry, leaving them until the sun has bleached every last drop of death out of the material. One of the corpses I found was not so big, and his boots fit me quite well. I go barefoot most of the time, in any case, but these boots are good for when the sand is hot or for my sorties into the jungle, where there are snakes and thorns but where there are also luscious fruits for the picking.

Ah, but I have not yet told you of my biggest project! Up on the promontory above the lagoon, I built a shelter, which I work on all the time. It is made out of wooden packing cases, stout bamboo posts and beams, and with a roof of palm leaves. I have notched into one of the posts the number of days I have been here and in that way kept track of the passing of the summer. Of my time on the raft reaching this island, I can only guess. One night, two nights, thirty-one?

I made a hammock of fish netting I found washed up in a terrible snarl on the beach. Ah, the beach. It is like a postbox!

The nights are warm, but I found canvas to hang from the bamboo beams of the shelter for when the breezes pick up, walls that flap and snap in the wind. After every rainfall I add more palm leaves to the roof, once it dries out, so that now my shelter is dry even in a hard downpour. I hope it will be sturdy enough for the monsoon season, but by then, who knows, I might be back with you and we will read this together. Of this, I fondly dream.

Farther along the headland from my dwelling, a stone's throw, at the very highest point on the island, I found a stout coral tree, over eighty feet high, with wide embracing branches. I knew these trees from my youth in Okinawa. There were a few bright crimson flowers on it when I first discovered it, but I knew in the spring it would put on a brilliant show if I were around to see it. There were black tiger's claw spines all over the tree, but I cut and smoothed myself a route up through the prickles and built a platform, a watchtower, where I could see for miles and not be seen from below.

From this high spot at night, I could see the lights of another island. At first I thought it to be a ship far out at sea, but it was there all the time in the same place, never moving. So I had not traveled so far, really! You can't imagine how this renewed my hope of a return to civilization. As I grew stronger, I wrestled with the idea that I should go, for surely the island across the sound must be Tinian, unless it was Saipan—even better![3] If it was Saipan, then that is where you are, Hisako, and there was every reason to want to return. I knew, of course, that Saipan

---

[3] Saipan and Tinian are sister islands in the Northern Marianas, the latter only a little over five miles from the southern shore of Saipan.

was invaded before Tinian, and I knew something of the result of the invasion, the terrible loss of life there. But I also knew this: reports are not always accurate. More important, I knew that *you were alive!* I knew this as well as I knew that I was alive. You, Hisako, were the one shining thing that made my own survival an imperative. And in my braver moments, I imagined making a sail for my raft, the quicker to get to you. There was all manner of machinery on the island, albeit in mangled bits and pieces, some of it. I might even have made myself a motor, rigged up a propeller—*sped* to my beloved!

But the thing that held me back was that the islands, both of them, were now in the hands of the enemy, as far as I knew. And who could say what would happen to me when I landed there, or if I would even make it to land before they opened fire? The image of the American soldiers tending the injured, the black one caring for the baby, haunted me as I tossed and turned some restless nights. I had been led to believe that the *gaijin* would as likely tear a child to pieces with their bare teeth as look at it. My own eyes told me differently. And I dared to believe that you, as a civilian, would be spared any suffering. But what I couldn't know was how they would treat an enemy soldier. Prison camp? I wouldn't mind that. My job now was to stay alive. But why not stay alive here on the heart-shaped island? In time, the war must end. The Empire would rally or fall. I realized that it was wicked to suggest that the Empire might ever be defeated, and if this account was to fall into the wrong hands, I might be had up on a court-martial. So let me quickly add for anyone to see that the Emperor is in my prayers every night, and it is my fervent desire that we will prevail! But in any case, it was just a matter of time. War could not go on and on in a perpetual state forever, could it? Oh, on my bad nights, when the fighting was in me, the killing, the horror, the bone-jarring noises coursing through my memories and bloodstream, I shivered and thought that, yes, war *could* go on forever if one were in the earth prison of purgatory. But then I would wake up, push back my canvas walls, and look out at this beautiful place and my hope was renewed.

I will wait. I will make myself strong. I will cremate the dead to keep them from the hunger of the undead. I will purify myself in this peaceful place. The nightmares will stop, and then the war will be over, yes? There will again be something like civilization to which I might return.

— IV —

The Gooney Bird[1]

I found a pair of binoculars. Sadly, they were wrapped around the neck of a drowned sailor, but apart from a dent or two, they were serviceable. No water had seeped into the lenses. I smacked the side of them, and when I looked, there was my jungle. There was sand in the adjusting wheel, but I was able to fiddle with the binoculars enough to suit my eyes and bring the distance into sharper focus, as if dragging the jungle toward me. I could not wait to take them to my watchtower, but first I had work to do: cremating the dead solider.

One of the *jikininki* dared to approach me just as I was lighting the fire.

"Wait," it said.

I must tell you, Hisako-chan, I jumped with surprise. I had not known they could talk. I had assumed their mouths were only good for squealing and devouring dead flesh. "We could share this one, yes?" the ghoul asked, although it had to say it

---

[1] In the transcript, Isamu scratched out the original title of this section, so that it is unreadable. I doubt he would have heard the name "Gooney Bird" at this point in time, for he learned it from me.

more than once, for its words came out mangled. The creature's tongue was bloated.

I will not repeat what I said to it. I used language only soldiers use and never in the company of a lady. But the creature pleaded with me.

"You have it all wrong," it said, looking at the body at my feet. "It is not really the flesh we crave."

"Ha!" I said to it. "You expect me to believe that?"

Its head swayed as if the smell of the corpse was making it delirious. "Believe me!" the thing insisted. "It is the *memories* we desire."

I had never heard of such a thing, and it brought me up short. "Their memories?"

All the time, the *jikininki* waggled its wretched clawed hands close to its mouth as if it was wafting the odor of the dead man toward its shattered nose, already transporting the rotting flesh to its lipless oral cavity.

"You do not understand," it said. "You *cannot* understand. We are not the ghosts of the dead, as you think."

"Then, what are you?"

"The ghosts of those who were never born."

What a thing to say! But looking at this vile and helpless monster, I could not think that it was trying to trick me.

"That is not what I have heard," I said.

The fiend threw its arms into the air. "You know *nothing* of us. You know fables and cautionary tales told to children." It dared to come a step closer, holding up its arms defensively. "We have no memories, you see. Had we lived, we would have memories of our own. But we never lived and so we must depend on the memories of those who have lived."

You can imagine how startled I was at this odd confession, Hisako.

"So now that you see," said the *jikininki*, "you will sympathize and share . . . share with us?" Then it crouched and reached out toward the leg of the dead sailor.

I answered by taking a burning stick from the pyre and hurling it at the creature. It hobbled off, hissing and farting and threatening revenge. "You will see," it cried, its voice like a cattle beast being dragged to slaughter. "You will learn." It stood twenty yards away in the blowing grass, rubbing its red eyes, moving whenever the smoke blew its way. Then it circled and dared to come toward me once again, upwind. "You wait," the thing said to me. "I shall eat up your memories when you are gone. All your precious memories shall be mine!"

I lay in my hammock that night thinking of the creature's threat. The thought of such a thing eating me seemed almost worse than dying. But I was fascinated by what it had said. It was such a strange thought that I had to wonder if there was some morsel of truth to it. Could there be such a thing as the ghosts of those who never had the chance to live? And if so, who were these other ghosts, the ones who hovered near and only wished my company, not to eat me whole for my memories!

I remember I sat up that night in my hammock and stared out into the yard of my encampment. In the dark there was not much to see of the ghost family. The moon picked out the contours of them, two or three, anyway, like patient guards. You will not be surprised to hear me say that this is the strangest of places, Hisako.

The binoculars were a great advantage. I was astonished when I first looked through them at how the world of distance flooded into focus. This was especially true of the island across the water. It was Tinian, I was quite sure, although it was much transformed.

My attention was especially drawn to the north end. The Americans were not wasting any time turning it to their purposes now that they had control. They were busy day and night. Sometimes, when it was very still, I almost thought I could hear the sounds of lorries and graders, the ringing of hammers, the buzzing of industrial machinery. But this is foolish. I could only imagine the sound, a sound I know so well. But the ships that arrived were not concocted by my imagination. Ships came on a regular basis with earthmoving equipment and building materials—more, always more. Many thousands of slaves had been set to the task. This at least was true of what we have heard: slavery in America still exists, and now I could see that it was so with my own eyes through these wonderful glasses.

One night, long after the moon had set, when darkness held me in the deepest reaches of sleep, where there was still a war raging in my bones and in my liver and in my weary brain, another survivor floated onto Kokoro-Jima—this one from the air. I can only say this from hindsight. If I heard the roar of the plane's engines, the stuttering, and then the whine of too fast a descent, I must have assumed it to be part of the nightmare that I was still in the slow process of escaping. When I try to think about it now, I *must* have heard something. There would have been so much noise: the noise of the jungle screaming its resistance, the earth shaking. There must have been a flash of fire—all part of a great disharmony of noises. But here is the point: the sound of things exploding had become as much a part of me by then as the sound of my own pulse. Did I hear the plane crash? I cannot say for sure, though when I think back, I feel sure that I must have.

This is what I can honestly say that I recall: awaking the next morning to a heavy rainfall and sniffing smoke in the air. Smoke?

70

I sat up enough to see that my cooking station in the compound was thoroughly doused. Indeed, the rain had made a puddle of the fire pit. I sniffed again. Unmistakably smoke.

I stepped outside my hut, hugging myself against the downpour, and scanned the hilltop. Nothing could burn in such conditions. I remember deciding that I would go to my lookout in the coral tree once the rain stopped.

It was mid-September by then, as far as I could reckon, and I had come to think of Kokoro-Jima as my very own island and therefore my responsibility. Perhaps there had been lightning in the night. Dimly I thought I could remember the rumble of thunder. Of course, now I know better, but that morning I recalled thunder. Thunder and lightning made sense. I shuddered and stepped back into my hut. Later I would check.

But the rain persisted and I suppose the smell of smoke must have been washed from the sky. The next day a strong wind wrung the last of it out. So it was several days before I even so much as thought of it again. And it was only the *jikininki* who reminded me.

The rains had passed, but it was overcast. I had gone to the Pond of Sweet Water to fill up an inner tube with potable water, a system I found easier than trying to fill a steel drum and roll it to my hilltop compound. Yes, there were steel drums, some empty and some still filled with oil. Anyway, I could sling the partially filled inner tube over a shoulder, or fill it quite full and roll it along. You see how clever I have become?

I was whistling to myself, walking up the path, when I saw the sambar deer and her youngster grazing not far from the pond. The whistling had gotten their attention. I stopped and waited, and eventually the youth forgot I was there, for he had certainly seen a lot of me. The hind, though, still looked perturbed. Silently, I watched the young one stand on his hind legs to get at some berries growing in a tree. How strong the young deer had grown. I knew it must be the same pair, because when they saw me they did not run. The little one even ventured toward me, while his mother looked on warily.

"I must eat," I told her in my softest voice, "but I will not eat you." Then after a moment of deliberation, I added very quietly, "If I can help it."

The hind suddenly reared her head and her eyes grew wild, as if she had understood my murmured words. She ran off, her young one leaping after her. Which is when I saw *jikininki*—three of them—walking in the shadow of the trees. I was used to seeing them by now, but somehow their pasty forms looked even more ghastly against the vivid green. I turned and saw others heading in the same direction into the deeper jungle. That was odd. And it was then that it came back to me: the smoke and the sounds of thunder that might not have been thunder.

I dropped my empty inner tube by the pond, and, having filled only my canteen, I followed the flesh-eaters into the jungle.

I do not like the jungle. Do not like the insects, the incessant buzzing and shrill birdcalls, the dripping closeness. It was like descending into a green ocean; I found it hard to breathe. With my sword I slashed through the underbrush, keeping the *jikininki* in sight. Were they fully ghosts, they might have been able to glide to their destination over the tops of the undergrowth, but they were stuck in this limbo of limbs, and although they made no rustling sound, they were visibly slowed by the thickness of it, whereas I at least had the benefit of a sharp tool to cut my way through. They yowled at me when they saw what I was doing.

"Go back!" they cried in their awful garbled voices. Some even ventured close enough to try to scare me, swiping at me with their claws from ten yards away, but they dared not get too close, let alone touch me. They were helpless to stop me from following them and not clever enough to try to lead me astray.

My own ghostly family, I noticed, always hovered closer when the *jikininki* got too near. I suppose they sought my protection, though I could not see what they had to fear. By then, I was as used to them as a man who has a pet monkey — used to it sitting on his hip or clambering up to his shoulder. In any case, they stayed very near as we made our way down into the dark lowlands of the island.

However decrepit the *jikininki* were, they had stamina! And whatever was enticing them deeper and deeper into the forest was strong.

After a good solid hour, I found my way to an animal path and reached a clearing looking down upon a deeply forested gully. Below me there was a windfall, a place of broken trees. A cyclone might have touched down creating a pathway, a wide swath. But a tingling in my blood suggested otherwise. I examined this scar on the shadowy jungle floor, a couple hundred feet below. The sun peeped out from behind a cloud and glinted off something metallic. That is when I knew for sure.

The *jikininki* started howling as they plunged down the steep hillside, like bandits descending on a village. I scampered down after them into the valley until at last I stood, sweaty and scratched, in the shattered place. A wound in the earth, a runway — but no, the opposite: for at its end, I saw the wreckage of a cargo plane.

"Get away from there!" I screamed at the flesh-eaters who were pawing at the sides of the plane, smacking the steel with their scabrous palms. There were seven or eight of the creatures already there, but others were coming down from the hills on every side, maybe another twenty or more, and, oh, they set up such a chanting and howling. I rushed at them, but whatever they smelled coming from the plane was powerful enough to make them bold. They snarled and hissed at me. I had to beat them back with my sword, leaving hideous weeping wounds in their wretched bodies. But even then they would try to sidle around me, tripping and falling and crawling to try to get at the fuselage and to what must be inside it. They were hungry and enraged.

What could I do to hold them off?

Aha! I had an idea.

I struggled out of my jacket and hung it over the end of my sword. Then I placed the sword between my knees, fumbled for the matchbox in my pocket, lit a match, and then held it to my jacket until it caught fire.

It only smoked at first, and I had to light it again and again, but the reaction was immediate. The flesh-eaters stumbled away. They backed off, whining and rubbing their faces, shouting curses at me. The smoke stung their viscous glowing eyes. They made horrible heaving noises.

"Ours!" they cried. "Ours!" they insisted. "Ours!"

One of them, braver than the others, strode toward me, despite the smoke. It must have been the one who had talked to me weeks earlier.

"All we want is their stories," it said pleadingly. Its eyes were leaking as if with tears, but that was only the effect of the smoke. I waved the now-flaming coat at the creature and it stumbled away, throwing up its arms in frustration.

Then gradually they stopped bellowing and cursing and simply gave up. They started to leave, one by one, heading back up the gully, as if they had forgotten why they were there in the first place. It was the smoke, I supposed. It not only hurt their eyes; it seemed to obliterate the scent that had brought them here, the scent of death. By the time the jacket was a charred and smoking rag, the last of them was gone. I draped the smoldering remains of the jacket over a dead bush to ward them off. The last wisps of smoke drifted like incense up into the heavy air. They would come back eventually, I knew, but for now I had the wreckage to myself.

The great silver beast lay on its belly, its wheels buried in the forest floor or snapped off—I couldn't tell. The stench of fire clung to the metal carcass. Surely this was what I smelled on the morning air, when was it—a week ago? The smoke and then the heaviness of the rain must have held down the scent of what was inside, keeping it from the flesh-eaters for a while. Now it was my job to make sure they never got at the corpses. There had to be corpses.

The windows of the cockpit were smashed, but the snub nose had bucked up as it came to a stop, so I could not look inside. One wing had been severed at the elbow, the other snapped completely off.

I shuddered, though it was not cold. I felt the steel side of the plane, moist with dew. It was over sixty feet long.

I heard something. Were they back already? I peered into the jungle, scanning the undergrowth, crouching. I listened under the birdsong for some deeper sound. Then I heard a scrabbling sound from much nearer by. It was coming from the cockpit! Could someone possibly be alive?

My hand clutched the hilt of my sword; the *jikininki* were drawn to the dead. But as I knew so well myself, they were also drawn to the *almost* dead. I slid along the downed plane to look for the hatchway. My eyes were so busy scanning the forest that I tripped, crashing headlong to the ground. I cried out as I fell, and suddenly the air was filled with screaming and flapping, so that I threw my arms over my head, fearing for my life. From the broken cockpit windows, a black flock burst into the steaming jungle air, flying to the nearest branches, cawing like mad, angry to have been disturbed.

Jungle crows, thick-billed carrion birds, their feathers ruffled; they roosted in judgment, five or six of them. One of them had a long strand of something hanging from his beak, brown and stringy.

"You are not eating for the memories, are you, crows!" I said, on my feet again and a little embarrassed at having drawn such an ugly crowd.

I rested my back against the fuselage. The explosion of birds had frightened me. I will not say otherwise. I breathed deeply, swatted at the mosquitoes drawn to my sweat. Oh, I do not like the jungle.

I looked down at what I had stumbled over. It was a yellow metal box with wide straps attached to it, a backpack of some kind by the look of it, with rounded corners and two sides curving in, giving the thing a thick waist. I crouched to peer at it more closely. There were dials, two of them like eyes; or one was like an eye and the other a closed eye, a keyhole. And where the mouth should have been on this strange yellow face, there was a larger semicircular dial, as if the machine were frowning.

What was it doing *outside* the plane?

One of the crows cawed and fluttered up from its branch, anxious to get back to work in the cockpit and eyeing me with contempt. *Jikininki* were not the only marauders I was going to have to deal with. I had to get inside.

I found the hatch right behind where the wing had once been. I tried the handle; the door clicked open. This surprised me, exhilarated me, but also troubled me. I am not much used to planes, but surely, I thought, it should not be easy to open one from the outside like this. Through the slimmest of cracks,

I peered into the gloom. The cargo bay was fully loaded. Crates filled the fuselage right to the curved steel ribs of the ceiling. They were all in disarray from the crash. I hoisted myself up and into the plane, silently pulling the door closed behind me and turning left toward the cockpit. The air inside was hot and close, hotter even than the trapped air of the ravine. A fetid odor made me wrinkle my nose. I clambered over the clutter toward the cockpit, making as little sound as possible, although I did not really expect there to be any adversary, really. The crows were not likely to have been dining on anything living. The crates shifted under my weight. I cut myself on a jagged splinter of wood, my attention fixed on the cockpit.

I passed by six portholes and then ducked through the low doorway that led to the cockpit.

The men at the controls were already more jungle than human. The cockpit was stifling hot. The men looked well cooked, their skin leathery. And the crows had been hard at work. An eye dangled against the stripped bone of the pilot's cheek. Through a gaping hole ripped in the underbelly of the fuselage, creeping plants had already begun to climb into the small, enclosed space. The crew, still in their flight jackets, were strapped in.

There was a book lying on the cabin floor, stained with crow droppings. I knelt to pick it up, despite the mess, so pleased was I to see it. I rubbed the ordure off on the copilot's leather sleeve. I muttered a word of apology and bowed to him. He made no reply. I could not read the writing inside, *gaijin* writing, but I could read the numeric figures there: dates, I suspected, and the coordinates of destinations, the codes of airfields. It was the pilot's logbook, an almost new one with only a couple of pages filled in. Flipping through the many blank pages, how I grinned, Hisako. I had wished to keep some kind of a journal of my experience so that when we were reunited I could share every detail of it with you. Here was that journal!

All I needed was a writing implement, and I could see the top of what I supposed to be one in the pilot's breast pocket.

Gingerly I squeezed between the two dead men. My elbow caught the copilot's cheekbone and his head fell sideways, held to his neck and collarbone by leathery strands of cartilage. Wincing at the ravaged face, I groaned.

"Ā, sumimasen," I apologized, bowing nervously to the copilot. How grievously I was treating him!

What was I doing here! *Get out*, I told myself. *I have become too used to traveling amongst the dead.*

But was it such a desecration to steal a man's pen? With shaking fingers, I reached for it. Outside the ragged eyes of the splintered windscreen, there was a fluttering of wings. One of the crows had returned. It squawked at me, spreading its wings in a gesture of defiance.

"Scat!" I shouted, and with a squawk of annoyance, the bird took off. Again, I turned to the corpse. I reached for the pen and only at the last moment snapped my fingers back.

What if the body was booby-trapped? As I pulled the pen from the pocket, would the whole plane explode?

Don't be foolish, I told myself. Surely that would be impossible unless someone had survived the crash. Which is when my mind registered what my eyes had already seen but not fully taken in.

The third seat.

I had walked right past it: the navigator's station. The seat was empty.

There was someone out there! I dropped to a crouch and squatted on the floor of the cockpit, with my hands over my head. I felt like a frightened child hiding from his father. I felt incapable of everything. Oh, I had trouble even breathing at that awful moment. I had to think clearly. You see I had forgotten over the last little while what it was like to be at war, to always be thinking of the enemy because, as it had been drilled into me, the enemy was always thinking of me.

Think, Isamu.

After a while of listening to the jungle sounds sifting in through the empty window, hearing nothing unexpected, I was able to concentrate on the problem at hand. I came up with two possible solutions: One, the navigator parachuted, either at sea, in which case he was undoubtedly dead, or over land, in which case he might be anywhere on this island. But if he was, I had never seen him nor any trace of him. And if he had seen me and successfully hidden from me, would he, this survivor, not then have taken advantage of the element of surprise and taken my life? As gruesome as this idea was, it made sense.

Alternately, he might be dead elsewhere on the plane. He might have been attending to something in the tail end of the vessel. Was there a lavatory on the plane? Maybe he had been trapped there and been unable to make it back to his seat. A vile place to die! But then there were not many good ones when you were at war.

Obviously, I had to investigate. But first the pen. I had heard of booby-trapped bodies, but as far as I knew that was only on the battlefield or in an area where there was likely to be enemy action. What would be the point of rigging up such a thing on a desert island? And why blow up a plane filled with supplies, whatever they were? Food, I dared to hope. More sweet brown sticks—boxes and boxes of them! Still, I was cautious. And then I thought about the crows. They had been at work for some time. If there was a bomb, the crows would have set it off. So I gathered up my courage and plucked the object from the pocket.

It was not something I had ever seen before. Perhaps it was not a pen at all. I tried to pull it open. It would not. Then I pushed the knob at the top and a point appeared at the bottom, although it was not a very sharp point—not anything like a nib. I touched it gingerly. It was round. I rolled it along my finger and blue ink appeared. It was a pen, after all! What a story this would be to write in my journal and the object with which I wrote it would be the subject of the story!

I did not find the third crew member in the plane, but what I did find made my blood run cold. At the back of the cargo bay, I found a blanket lying on a pallet and a pillow made up of a folded jacket wrapped in some kind of gunnysack. A case lay on its side, acting as a low table, upon which sat a medical kit, opened. There were bandages and bottles and tubes and ampoules, squeezed dry and empty, lying higgledy-piggledy on the floor. There was also blood—a lot of blood. It stained the floor, the blanket; there were smears of it on the sides of the crates. In one corner there was a ragged pile of bandages and gauze soaked with gore. Brown. Dried. Whoever had turned this place into a hospital ward had left here on his own two feet.

I sat cross-legged, waiting in the cargo plane. Sitting had not been my first thought. My first thought had been to get out of there and run as fast as my legs would carry me out of the ravine, back to my little home up on the highland overlooking the pretty lagoon, where the air was fresh and the winds kept the mosquitoes at bay. But everything was changed now that I knew there might be someone out there—*was* someone out there. Had I merely been lucky to avoid being seen, or had the navigator been watching me all along, awaiting the right opportunity to dispatch me?

No. The crash was recent. And clearly the man was injured.

Badly. He'd taken cover. Maybe he had even died from his wounds.

Not entirely reassured by this thought, I waited for half an hour or more, and my imagination, on any number of occasions, picked out the sound of someone approaching the plane. But as the time lengthened, I felt my nervousness harden into critical doubt. What a fool I was being. I could almost hear my father snap at me. *Why are you cowering there, boy?*

I looked around at the crates surrounding me. Many of them were cracked and broken, though they were stacked so densely, I had not seen anything of what they contained. Curious, I got to my feet. Ow! Pins and needles. I hobbled around a moment, shaking out the pain. Then I pushed back the wooden top, careful of the nails that had held it shut until the crash.

Rifles.

The cargo plane was loaded with rifles. I pried open another box with my knife: ammunition. I lifted a rifle from the case. They were American firearms, but not so different from my own Arisaka. No chrysanthemum embossed into the steel. I remembered rubbing the cold steel flower with my thumb when I received my first: the chrysanthemum, symbol of perfection. I aimed down the sights of this other rifle and was swallowed by a memory.

Remember when I signed up for the Young Men's Corps early in '39? Ah, no, of course not, for we hadn't met yet. How strange. It feels as if I have known you forever, my Hisako-chan. Anyway, it was a chance to learn a little close drill, how to fire a rifle and use a lance. I learned how to man an observation post and did so proudly, scanning the skies for enemy planes. As an Okinawan, I had grown up under the scarcely concealed intolerance of the Japanese toward my people, especially the soldiers. Then things

81

changed, as you know. With the war in China, Japan had to conveniently expand its view of what a person of Japanese origin might be in order to swell the ranks of the infantry. They extended citizenship as far as the Ryukyu Islands, my homeland.

In the Y.M.C. I discovered a camaraderie that I enjoyed. And when the time came, when in any case conscription seemed likely due to the threat of an American invasion, I went ahead and signed up to become a real soldier. You did not want me to. You never said so, but I know. If all young men, everywhere, listened to their sweethearts, would there be any war?

I lowered the rifle, ashamed. I had never become a real soldier, never a very good one, in any case. But now, it seemed, the war was *not* over? Maybe now I would get my chance.

Outside the light had changed. Through the nearest porthole, I could see that dusk was dipping her long fingers into this steep valley, fingers stained like a smoker's with nicotine. I knew I must get back to my shelter. I most certainly must *not* get myself trapped in this place of death at nightfall. It came on so quickly. Night, I mean. Well, death as well! I loaded my new rifle and stuffed my pockets with ammo, so that my shorts, already baggy, sagged even more. I tightened the rope belt I had made around my skinny waist.

I was about to leave when I remembered the crew. What was I to do about them? Nothing! Not right now, at least. Ahhh. How could I bear to leave them to the carrion crows? I stamped my foot. *This is foolish, Isamu,* I told myself. *There is little enough left of them to ship off to the next world. Get a grip!* But I couldn't do it — couldn't just leave them. I swore and punched one of the crates. Ow! But then an idea occurred to me. The tops of the crates. Yes! With the help of a bayonet, I opened another crate and carried the two tops to the cabin. I managed to block the cracks in the windows. It was not a very effective job, but at least it would keep away the crows. For now. Later? Well, I could not account for later. There were a lot of things to think about, and "later" was not at the top of my list of concerns.

I opened the hatch just a hair and peered cautiously out into the noisy heat. I waited another moment, then, wiping the sweat off my forehead, stepped down onto the jungle floor. Crouching, moving quickly, and running in a zigzag line, I made it to the thick trunk of a flame tree at the edge of the scar. Catching my breath, I waited. No shots rang out. No one had been waiting out there for me. I was a fool to have wasted time sitting there in that steam bath of a plane. Whoever had occupied the blood-stained compartment had hurried away from there as fast as he could or had stumbled out of there to die. Unless, of course, he was playing a cruel game with me — cat and mouse. Well, if that was the case, I had a weapon now, two weapons: a rifle and the best weapon of all, *intelligence! If the navigator had survived . . . well, Isamu will be ready for him. Isamu will be the cat!*

CHAPTER EIGHT

Evan wakes to someone walking by his bedroom door. It is a comforting sound, his father going to the bathroom and returning for a little sleep-in. *A good idea,* thinks Evan.

Where was he?

Running. Running with Isamu, waiting for the gunshot that will bring him down. A desert island — hunter or hunted?

Then he wakes again to reality.

Kokoro-Jima lies beside him on the bedclothes, open, wings spread out like some grounded yellow bird. The story is bleeding into his life. Hurriedly, he closes it and shoves it under his bed. He rubs his eyes, checks his bedroom door. Closed. Would Griff have opened it? He looks at his phone: 10:33, two hours and thirty-three minutes late for debriefing. So, he is now officially the Devil's spawn.

He should get up, but he lies there thinking about this stranger in his house. This man who must be a hundred, or at least — he figures it out on his fingers — at least in his late eighties. And yet he walks tall as if on parade, as if every muscle in his body knows its job, a well-oiled squadron of muscles waiting for deployment.

He thinks of Griff's voice, how disarming it is. How he seems hardly to acknowledge the *g*'s and *r*'s and *t*'s at the ends of words, so that everything *sounds* softened out, like a box of pastel-colored M&M's. Except there's no sweetness, really. It's as if someone melted chocolate onto ball bearings.

He was the one who walked by Evan's room.

Which could only mean he went into the master bedroom. Dad's room. "Daddy," as he referred to Clifford in that chocolate-covered-ball-bearings accent of his. What did he want, looking in Clifford's bedroom? Who gave him the right to walk around this house?

"You did," Evan mutters to himself.

Then he kicks off his bedclothes, gets dressed, and goes to face the music. To save the old man any need to reassess his grandson, he wears the same clothes he was wearing last night. *He'd be used to that,* thinks Evan. *Soldiers wear the same thing every day, don't they?*

Griff is in the Dockyard, staring at the shelves of ships in bottles. Evan glances nervously at the worktable, as if the yellow book might have left some memory of itself there. But his father's worktable has been transformed back into the desk it was, a desk now stacked with file folders, papers.

On the right side is his father's old Packard Bell, voted one of the ten worst PCs ever. The screen saver is on. Psychedelia. Griff must have followed Evan's eyes.

"I was searching for something like a spreadsheet," he says.

"Steam-driven," says Evan.

"What's that?"

"Dad used to say he had the last of the steam-driven computers." Then he looks at Griff. "You know about spreadsheets?"

Griff acknowledges his surprise. "I may be old, but I'm not intimidated by technology." Evan nods. "And good morning," Griff adds, then turns to look at the wall of bottled ships. "I was just admiring the fleet here."

"Yeah. It was his hobby."

"Not surprised. He was one for making model airplanes when he was a boy. Had 'em all arrayed on shelves, just like this."

Drawn into the room, Evan looks at the boats. Thinks of telling Griff that it's not a fleet — it's a flotilla. He wants to say hands off. He is suddenly possessive of the flotilla. But it isn't that. He's just uncertain of this man who has appeared out of nowhere.

"He's good with his hands," Evan says.

Griff nods. "He sent me one of these here things," he says.

"He did?" The incredulity in Evan's voice makes the old man smile.

"Yes, indeed. Surprised the hell outta me. But it fell a little short of being what you might call a gift." Evan sticks his hands in his pockets, waiting for the story — wanting to hear any news of his departed father — just not wanting to beg for it. "It was the USS *Chesapeake*," says Griff. "Pretty little three-master." He picks up one of the boats, tilts the glass to see it better. "Only thing is the *Chesapeake* had, shall we say, a spotty career." He puts the bottle back on the shelf, sniffs at the memory, and shakes his head. "You see her first commander, he surrendered that ship to the Brits in an action that started the War of 1812."

Evan's not quite sure he gets it.

86

Griff's expression is wry. "It was a little piece of history your daddy knew would not be lost on an old soldier."

Oh. Now he gets it. "Nice one, Dad," he mutters.

Griff reaches to an upper shelf. "Here it is," he says.

For a moment, Evan is confused. Then he gets it. "You sent it back?"

"I did," Griff says sternly. "I don't like games." He turns to look at Evan, to make his point perfectly clear.

Evan nods. *No jokes.* Check. *No games.* Check. *And not easily intimidated.* Check.

Griff finds his way back to the chair behind the desk. Evan grits his teeth, not wanting to see this man sitting there — not wanting to see *anyone* sitting there. No, that wasn't it at all. Wanting so much to see one person sitting there.

"You no doubt are cognizant of . . . of your father's and my . . . problem with each other."

Problem, thinks Evan, *as in "scornful intolerance." Got it.*

He nods his head, even as Griff shakes his. "It seems foolish now," he says. "The two of us going on like that." He pushes the chair back from the desk, knots his hands together in his lap. The liver spots on his broad hands look like lichen on granite. "Acting like . . . well, like a hippie son and his grunt of a father. The dove and the hawk — that's what he called us back when he was your age." He casts his assessing eye over Evan again, as he did last night. His eyes say shabbiness.

"So you don't have a summer job, son?" he says. "A boy your age?"

"I *had* a job. But no, I don't *have* a job."

The old man nods as if he'd have guessed as much. "Getting up early too much for you?"

Evan is stunned. "Excuse me?"

Griff taps the face of his watch. "I thought we had a date," he says.

"Are you kidding me?"

Griff shakes his head. "I'm not a man who kids. What are you?"

"Excuse me?"

"Your age, boy."

"Seventeen in November."

"That's what I thought. When I was seventeen, I had already signed up. It was 1941. There was a war happening in Europe, and although we weren't in it yet, we were going to be and I wanted a part of it. Had to lie about my age, mind you, but I was big for my age and the marines were hungry."

Evan crosses his arms and leans against the door. He's fuming. He wants to say, *Stop with the lecture, already, school was out five weeks ago.*

"I spent my seventeenth birthday on a firing range in California. They had bundled us into cattle cars that morning and took us one hundred and seventy miles up the coast to this range near San Luis Obispo. Bundled into those cars like so much cattle. But that was the marines for you; that was boot camp."

Now Evan has this terrible urge to clap. He resists.

"I had this M1 Garand, clip-fed, semiautomatic. It still reeked of Cosmoline, the gunk they greased 'em up with for shipping. I tell you, I'd sat for hours on my bunk scrubbing that damn rifle to make her fighting ready."

Evan's pulse is beating like mad. His breathing is getting ragged, but the old soldier hardly seems to know he's there.

"Some wag pinned a lizard to my target. Dead center. I reduced it to lizard dust." He smiles to himself, then pins Evan with his gaze, just as if he were a lizard on a bull's-eye. "There

88

were five possible results on the rifle range, Evan," he says. "You could, one, not qualify; two, qualify; three, prove yourself a marksman; four, a sharpshooter; or five, an expert. That last result was what I was aiming for: expert. It meant a lot. It meant five dollars more pay, for one thing. A lot of money, back then. And it meant respect." His eyes tell Evan that, in case he hadn't noticed, there is a point about to be made. "You see it was what my daddy expected of me — nothing less. And in my day, you didn't disregard what your daddy expected. His respect was your aim and your honor to achieve."

Here endeth the lesson. Evan wonders if he's supposed to say amen. Instead, he's tempted to yawn. He shifts, stands straight, drops his arms to his sides, squeezes his hands into fists. "Why are you here?" he says, his voice hanging on by rubber bands.

"Because you asked me, I believe."

"And why did I do that? Ask some guy I never met, who never so much as sent me a birthday card? Why would I want to see him?"

Griff lowers his head but not his gaze. "I seem to recall you were needing some help settling things around here." His hands open like a magician's over the folders before him on the desk, the screen of the computer now a swirling galaxy far, far away.

"Why?"

"What's this about, son?"

"Just answer me. Why?"

Griff looks well and truly pissed. Good! "Because your daddy passed on."

"Exactly!" says Evan, jabbing the air with his finger. "And *that's* why I don't have a job. That's why I *quit* my job! Not because I can't get up in the morning. Which is none of your fucking business, anyway!"

"Mind your tongue, Evan."

"No, you mind yours. You've got way too much to say!"

The sergeant major sits up straight and leans forward, his huge hands resting on the top of the desk, his fingers splayed, ready to leap. "Is this how you talked to your daddy?"

"No, sir. It is *not* how I talked to my daddy. Not ever. And you know why? Because I loved him like fucking crazy." His voice has pretty well given up the ghost, but it doesn't stop him. He blunders on, his finger jabbing the air and tears springing to his eyes. "I loved him, okay? And respected him. He was the best damned father in the world. Unlike you!"

Then Evan storms out the door, heaving it shut behind him, and races down the stairs and out of the house. The Dockyard sign falls to the carpet, making no sound at all.

CHAPTER NINE

He half expects to find the doors locked—to find himself barred from his own home. It's after eight in the evening. It doesn't matter where he's been; eventually he knew he would have to come back and face the music. What's the man going to do, court-martial him? He stands just inside the kitchen door, listening. He hears the sound of the television funneling up from the den. Judging from the volume, the old soldier must be hard of hearing. All those bombs bursting in air. Ninety. Evan has done the math. Griff is ninety years old; Clifford died at sixty-two. Evan shakes his head at the unfairness of it all. He looks at the muddied orange clogs of his father, his decomposing Birkenstocks. He looks at his own torn-up Emerica Heretics with the yellow laces, piled with his soccer cleats, one flip-flop embalmed in spiderweb. And there beside them sit Griff's shiny black outdoor shoes. Even his shoes stand at attention.

Evan heads down the stairs. He knocks on the cracked-open rec room door. There is no answer. Evan pushes it open. *Shhhh.* The old man is sitting in the green wingback chair watching a baseball game on television. The infamous Griff does not look amused. Evan checks out the TV, the Dodgers and the Cardinals. He returns his gaze to Griff. He wonders if it's only the game that is making him frown. Evan pictures the old aluminum baseball bat sitting in the corner of the carport and wonders why he didn't grab it on his way in. Just in case.

There is a newspaper on the old man's lap, folded so meticulously it appears to have been ironed, like the olive-green golf shirt and ivory chinos the man is wearing.

Evan clears his throat, his left hand still on the door, in case there's some kind of weapon hiding under that immaculately folded newspaper and he needs to beat a hasty retreat.

Griff looks up at him. Nods. He picks up the channel changer from off the side table and mutes the game. There is a tray on the hassock in front of him with the remains of a meal on it. The marines have landed and apparently made themselves at home.

"I found a copy of your father's will in his files. Apparently, it has been updated some."

Evan sees this for what it is: a chance to move on. He steps farther into the room.

"I couldn't contact his lawyer, on account of it being Sunday. I'll try phoning tomorrow. I highly doubt he'll be able to give me any specifics since he's unlikely to have my name on record acknowledging me as legal guardian."

Evan nods. "So, we'll have to go together," he says. Griff nods. "Okay, thanks."

"That will depend, of course, on your schedule," says Griff.

He can't resist it, thinks Evan. Has to get the dig in—let Evan know he hasn't forgotten the scene in the Dockyard that morning. It makes Evan glad, in a way, or at least relieved. There will be no need to apologize for what went down this morning. For sassing an elder. He doesn't need to care about this man, to feel sorry, to get close to him in any way. In less than twenty-four hours, Griff has lived up to everything his father ever said about him. It gives Evan the courage to say what he wants to say.

"My father and I had a road trip planned."

"What's that?"

At first Evan thinks maybe he's never heard of the concept of a father and son going on a road trip. Then he realizes Griff didn't hear him. He steps farther into the low-ceilinged room.

"My dad and I. We were going on a road trip," he says loudly. Griff nods. "Down to Cleveland to visit the Rock and Roll Hall of Fame." He waits, watches Griff's eyes stray back to the silent image on the television. The Dodgers are up to bat, two men on base, tied three to three in the top of the ninth. Griff shakes his head.

"We were thinking of catching a Blue Jays away game there. You know, sometime when they were playing the Tribe. "

Griff's eyes find him. "The A.L.," he says. *"Pfhu."*

Evan's jaw drops a little, and then he catches something that might actually be described as a twinkle in the old man's eyes.

"You got a problem with the American League?"

"I most certainly do."

"Let me guess. You don't buy the whole designated hitter thing?"

"You can bet on it," says Griff. He sits up a little straighter in his chair. "A pitcher's got to be able to step up to the plate like the rest of his teammates. No sitting it out." He stops, his thin old lips tight. "No running away," he says.

Evan rolls his eyes.

Just then the old man groans and switches the sound back on. Gonzalez has hit a line drive to right, bringing in the runner from second and ending the tie.

The Dodgers are beating the Cardinals.

The irony of it suddenly occurs to Evan. "Boy, those *Dodgers,* huh? I mean they really are something, aren't they?" he says. "Gotta love those *Dodgers.*"

A rusty scraping sound comes from deep in Griff's throat, vaguely recognizable as being of the same species as laughter. He turns off the sound again. Then turns off the game.

"I took Clifford to a game up in Baltimore once. Not Camden Yards, the old Memorial Stadium. A road trip, as you call it. Quite a hike from Camp Lejeune, North Carolina, which is where I was stationed at the time. Took 'bout eight hours in those days."

"Baltimore's in the American League."

"Baltimore was the closest venue. There wasn't a team in Atlanta back then. The Braves were still up in Milwaukee."

"Was it a good game?"

"Can't rightly remember the *game.* The boy went on and on about wanting this and that, cotton candy, Coke, and whatnot."

"That must have been tough," says Evan. "Kids, eh?"

He meets Griff's eyes. They look like a bull's eyes, a bull that just noticed the matador's pants are down around his ankles. Evan is surprised at what is coming out of his mouth. *This is suicidal.*

"He loved the game," says Griff. "Never played it, mind you. Not the sporting type."

"Not the sporting type" comes out sounding like his dad was some kind of a Froot Loop in a tutu.

Evan is not going to put up with this. But another scene right now just seems too hard to deal with. "Yeah, well, he's . . ."

Why is it so hard to say it? ". . . was . . ."

There. Done.

"He was a big-time Toronto fan. We never got, like, season's tickets, or anything, but we'd always catch a few games."

Griff nods. He looks as if he's about to say more, but Evan interrupts him.

"I'm going to get something to eat," he says.

"You do that, soldier," says Griff.

Evan turns to leave. Then he turns back. "I haven't been sleeping so well," he says. "I'm usually up by about nine."

Griff has turned the game back on, but now he turns to Evan, his gaze level, giving nothing away. *Marine blue,* Evan's father whispers to him. *Griff got his eyes issued along with the rest of his kit.* Now the old man squints as if he has seen something unexpected. He sticks his old head out on his wattled neck, waggles two fingers, beckoning Evan closer, never taking his eye off him. Evan hesitantly approaches, stops just out of arm's reach. The soldier is staring at Evan's neck, frowning.

"What happened to the .44 caliber love letter?" he asks.

For a moment Evan feels like he just stumbled down a rabbit hole. Then he remembers the tat. "Oh, yeah. That." He feels his neck. "It was just a transfer. There was this concert . . ." He stops himself. No need to explain. As if the old man would know Alexisonfire. "I rubbed it off." He stares at his grandfather. "I'm amazed you remember what it said."

Griff smiles. "I never forget a caliber, son."

95

Chapter Ten

There's a text from Rollo on his cell phone.

—How goes the battle?

He sits on the side of his bed to answer.

—I think I've found a use for that pit in the back garden

—Lol—do it *soldier*

Evan almost phones, but he's talked out. He'd spent most of the day with Rollo, on Rollo's last day of freedom before he starts work at the Pulse, the new health food store in the mall. "Making the world a better place for vegetables," Rollo has taken to saying at annoyingly regular intervals.

There was, however, some news about making the world a better place for Evan: a girl. Specifically, a girl who wants to meet him. A friend of a friend of a friend. "She saw us play," Rollo said that afternoon. "She thought you were somewhat cool."

"Her exact words?"

"She might have said 'moderately cool.' No wait, I remember. She said 'not entirely a douchebag.'"

"Sweet."

The idea of a girl who actually saw the band play and *still* wanted to meet him was within spitting range of astounding. He is supposed to phone her. He has her name and number somewhere on his phone. He starts scrolling, when suddenly the landline starts ringing the place down. He jumps to his feet and tears to the door.

"I'll get it," he shouts. The game is still on downstairs. He doubts Griff would hear the phone anyway; there's no extension in the rec room. Breathlessly he picks up the receiver on his dad's bedside table, standing in the darkened room. It's Leo Kraft. He asks after Evan. Evan says he's fine.

"It's not too late, is it?"

"No, sir," says Evan, catching his breath. He keeps his voice low, despite the fact that Griff is two floors away.

"I'm sorry to bother you, again, but by any chance is —"

"Listen," says Evan. He sits on the bed. "There's something I've got to tell you." He swallows. "My father ... uh ... My father passed away."

Evan counts: one steamboat, two steamboats, three steamboats —

"Did you just say what I thought you said?"

"Yeah. I'm ... I'm sorry I didn't tell you when you phoned the other day."

"Oh, jeez. I'm ... I don't know what to say."

Welcome to the club, thinks Evan.

"God. I feel ... I'm so sorry. I won't bother you anymore."

"No, wait. It's all right," says Evan. "I mean I'd like to help, if I can." What he wants to say is that he'd love to have some

97

task to perform that there was actually a chance in hell he could accomplish.

"That's generous of you."

"Except I don't really know what you're after."

"It's . . ." Again, Leo's voice falters. He's really shook up. "Under the circumstances, it's —"

"I'm reading the book," says Evan. "I'm a few chapters in."

"Oh?"

"It's pretty amazing. I mean kind of crazy."

Leo doesn't speak at first. "Evan, forgive me if this seems tactless, but are you in touch with your grandfather Griff at all?"

Evan actually laughs, although it's more like a seal's bark. Then he has to quickly put a lid on it for fear he'll go ass-over-brain-stem hysterical and alert the troll in the rec room. "There has been this very weird development," he says, as steadily as his voice will allow. He looks at the door, sees the light in the hallway, no looming shadow. Dimly he hears cheering from the tube.

"He's here."

"He . . ."

"Griff. He's here."

"Jesus!"

"Yeah, well . . . He came up to help me with, you know, the legal stuff . . ."

"Right. I see. Oh, boy." Evan can imagine Leo shaking his head. "Excuse me, but I was under the impression your father and grandfather were not on speaking terms."

"They're not. I mean they weren't. Maybe they talked about this thing . . . the book. I don't know. Anyway, people had been telling me I should get in touch with him — my grandfather — since he's about the only relative I've got and I didn't know what else to do, so . . . That was before you called. Before I found out about the book."

"Amazing. And you're reading it?"

"Yeah."

"Was there a letter with it?"

"Uh-huh. I read that, too." Evan looks up anxiously at the bedroom doorway again. "Mr. Kraft—"

"Call me Leo."

"Leo, what's all this about lawyers? What is it you want to do?"

There's a pause. "I don't think I can talk about it," Leo says, dragging the sentence out as if he is removing a really sticky Band-Aid.

"Okay," says Evan, but it's a long way from okay. "You need Griff on side, right?"

"Yes. But it's . . . it's complicated." More Band-Aids.

"I get that," says Evan. He can't help sounding peevish.

"Evan, listen. Griff's got his own lawyer in on this. His latest curveball is that the book actually belongs to him — to Griff. That he only sent the diaries to my father for him to have a look at, and my father had no right to publish the thing, in the first place, without written permission."

"Yeah, but only twenty copies."

"That's not the point."

"So what is?"

"Griff claims that when he sent the diaries, his cover letter said, 'I thought you'd like to *see* this,' not 'here, I'm giving you this.'"

"And that makes a difference?"

"It does to lawyers. We don't have that original cover letter, if there even was one. It's nowhere in my father's files. So we're on shaky ground."

Evan tries to sort out what this means. Can't. "Okay, so how did you want my father to help? Like getting Griff to talk to you? Maybe I could—"

"Evan." Leo's voice is firm. "I'm sorry to cut you off, but I don't think Griff would be pleased that you have a copy of the book—that there is one in the house. Do you hear what I'm saying?"

"Yeah. I mean I hear you, but I don't get it."

Leo sighs. "Don't worry about this, okay?"

"That's easy for you to say."

"No, really. I'm sorry, but I don't feel comfortable about you getting involved."

"I do," says Evan, and surprises himself with the urgency in his voice. "I mean I'm not comfortable with it, but . . . It's hard to explain. It'd just be good to have something to think about other than, you know."

"Yeah."

"And my dad—this was on his mind."

"He talked to you?"

"No, not really. It's hard to explain. He was pissed about something . . . confused, I guess. And I think this was it."

The line goes quiet. Evan wonders if he's lost the connection. "Hello?"

"I'm still here. And I won't lie to you; we could use some help. But if you don't mind me saying this, your grandfather doesn't strike me as someone to mess with. I only talked to your dad once. It was a good long call, but it was before he'd received the book. Then there was an e-mail or two. Anyway, he certainly didn't have anything good to say about Griff. My own father admired Griff—was grateful for Ōshiro's papers. But he didn't like the man. Sorry for being so blunt."

"Hey, you'll get no argument here."

"Gave Dad the heebie-jeebies," says Leo. "And he was damn sure Griff wouldn't have sent the diaries to him if he'd known what was in them."

"I get that. I mean Griff isn't even in the story yet, but—"

"Do you think Griff knows your father had a copy of the book?"

"I don't know."

"Because I'm wondering why he's there."

"Like I said, I asked—"

"Yeah, Evan—and sorry to keep interrupting—but think about it."

"What are you saying?"

Leo doesn't speak, but there is a whole freight load of unsaid words in the silence. And Evan wonders about Griff arriving early, like that—a whole week early. *The earlier the better . . .* Wasn't that what he said?

"Evan, Griff does not want this to go public."

"But there's only, like, twenty copies. How public is it ever going to get?"

"That's the whole point of the exercise." Evan waits as if there is more—has to be more. He can almost hear the wheels turning at the other end of the line. And then, "The thing is, Evan, I'm not supposed to be talking to you about any of this. Your grandfather has had his attorney draft up a letter demanding that we, quote, 'cease and desist with any further allegations.'"

"Allegations of what? I still don't understand all these lawyers getting involved."

Leo chuckles. "Wherever there's money, there are lawyers."

"Money?"

"Yeah. Potentially."

"Okay," says Evan with a sigh. "I totally have no idea what you're talking about."

It's Leo's turn to sigh. It's a sigh-off. And when Leo speaks again, his voice drops to the level of a secret. "The cease-and-desist letter from Griff's people didn't come until after I'd contacted Clifford, so I wasn't in breach of any regulation. But talking to you with him around—Griff right there in the house . . . It's just not a good idea. For us. And most certainly not for you."

Evan can hear the finality in Leo's voice. *Don't fight it,* he tells himself. The truth is this whole thing is freaking him out. But there's one thing he can do—has to do. "Got it," he says, reluctantly. "But in case you need to reach me, can I give you my cell number? I mean it's best you don't phone the landline."

"Right. Good." Leo sounds relieved. Like he wouldn't have asked for it but was glad to get it. So Evan gives him his number. Then he gives him his e-mail address as well, just in case. He says good-bye and is about to hang up when he hears Leo say something else. "Pardon?"

"I wanted to say that your father sounded like a really nice guy."

Evan feels the stricture in his throat, overcomes it. "He was," he says.

"So was Derwood. My dad. He died back in . . . Oh, it was over five years ago. The thing is . . . what's happening with the Ōshiro book—what we are hoping to do? It's supposed to be a kind of testament to him. That's why I went ahead with it." *What?* Evan wants to shout. *What?* "That's why we're at loggerheads with Griff—at this impasse. It was something I wanted to do for my dad. I still miss him a lot. You know?" He waits for a reply, but Evan can't speak. His whole head is suddenly

102

filled with nothing else in the world but missing his father. "I am sorry for your loss," says Leo, as if he has tasted Evan's loss at the end of the phone. "You look after yourself, okay?"

"Yeah. Thanks."

Evan stands for a good long moment in the dark, thinking about the call. Then slowly, slowly, as he lets the world back in on his thoughts, something dawns on him. He becomes aware of something he hasn't noticed until just this moment. The TV is no longer blaring.

Quietly, he makes his way along the hallway to the top of the stairs and, kneeling on the broadloom carpet, sees Griff standing in the kitchen. From this angle, he's headless, but Evan doesn't need to see his face. His hands are enough. They're clutching the back of the blue ladder chair pressed up hard against the cluttered little kitchen table he and his dad never ate at. It's littered with notes, rubber bands, and stumpy pencils; the kinds of things you pull out of your pocket and leave there for no reason when you come home. There's also a cordless phone. Griff's hands hold on to the chair back so tightly that even from this distance Evan can see the knuckles are white.

Chapter Eleven

Back in his room, Evan races to his bed and drops to his knees.
The book is still there, nestled in a herd of dust bunnies. He
needs a better hiding place, fast—a less obvious hiding place.
He grabs the book, blows the fluff off it, stands up, and looks
around. His eyes land on the closet door. There's a poster of
Albert Einstein there with the quote "Reality is merely an illu-
sion, albeit a very persistent one."

"Thanks for that, Albee," Evan says, and heads to the closet.
On the shelf there are boxes. Neat containers of past obsessions,
and he knows the one he wants. He puts down *Kokoro-Jima,*
and then, on his tiptoes, he pulls down a black box big enough to
ship a cat in, if you had one. He opens it.

Ah, yes. Pokémon.

He's forgotten now how many cards he's got, approximately a gazillion, all neatly stacked in piles, organized in some order that was intensely important to him once upon a time. Neat piles bound with rubber bands. "Winner and still champion of the Tidiest Kid Ever competition," he murmurs to himself. On his knees, he unpacks the cards, then shoves the book in and piles the cards back on top of it. He looks to see if any yellow shows through. He's about to close the box when paranoia jabs him in the gut, and he stops. He takes off the band holding one of the piles and sifts through the cards until he comes to one he wants. He puts it on top of the pile, rebands it, and then places the pile right in the middle. Slowking, with his headgear: one of the cards banned from general competition. What'd they call that head thing? Right, "Shellder," not a hat, but a symbiotic creature latched on to the head of — Hell! He doesn't have time for this now. He straightens up the cards. Done.

Just in time.

The knock on the door is sharp — expected, but it still makes him jump.

"Just a minute," he says, shoving the box as quietly as possible onto the shelf. He closes the closet door, steps back. And the bedroom door opens.

"Jesus!" says Evan. "I said I was coming."

Griff stands in the entranceway, his hand on the doorknob. "I didn't hear you."

"Yeah, well, then, you shouldn't have come in!"

"Keep your shirt on, soldier."

"And stop calling me that!"

Griff nods, stiffly. But the look on his face says he's not a man used to being ordered around.

Pull in your horns, Evan.

"Sorry," says Evan. "What do you want?"

The old man scans the room. Evan sidles away from the closet until he's near enough the desk to lean on it, about as nonchalant as a terrier on speed.

Griff is nodding appreciatively. "You keep this place spick-and-span."

"Thanks. Is that all?"

Griff ignores the question — the surliness, despite Evan's promise to himself to play nice. "You must have gotten that from your mother," says Griff. "Your daddy's room was an eyesore when he was your age."

"So, I'm borderline anal. I just like to know where stuff is, you know?"

"I do know," says Griff, and stares at him hard. "So maybe you got this trait from me, after all. Skipped a generation." Evan just stares. How do you tell a man that if you thought you shared a trait with him, you'd rip your own DNA apart, by hand, helix by helix?

"I like to know where stuff is, too," says Griff, his eyes hardening.

He knows!

"It's a lesson you learn living in barracks. You want everybody around you to know that what's yours is yours."

Evan looks down. Can't match the deep blue hardness in those eyes. He leans his backside against his desk, rubs his hands down the front of his jeans, in case there's any Pokémon magic dust on his fingertips. He looks up. "Is there something you wanted?" He tries to make it sound casual.

Griff turns off the killer death ray. "We're out of coffee," he says.

For a moment Evan wonders if this is some kind of really weak joke. "You burst in here to tell me we're out of coffee?"

"Out of butter and eggs, too. A lot of things: salt, ketchup."

106

From the look on his face, patience is the main thing Griff is out of. "I thought I'd take the car up to that all-night place I saw on Don Mills. If you don't have further plans for it."

Good, thinks Evan. *And as soon as he's gone, lock him out and call the cops.*

"Yeah, sure."

"Anything you need?"

"No, I'm good."

"Well, then. I shouldn't be long."

Griff closes the door with a feigned salute. Evan doesn't breathe until he hears the click of the latch.

CHAPTER TWELVE

Evan sits at his desk, his legs apart, his elbows on his knees, the iPhone cradled in his palms, waiting for Leo to text him or phone. Waiting for more. Nothing. He sighs and puts the phone down, turns to his computer and Googles "Kokoro-Jima." He's not sure why, but when in doubt, ask the mother of all search engines.

There is lots of stuff in Japanese, some drumming group, a mail server for a domain called kokorojima.jp that doesn't seem to have anything to do with anything Evan can comprehend. There's also a TV show, which catches his interest for a moment, before he realizes it's not Kokoro-Jima; the search engine is just riffing on the word "kokoro" by now.

So he Googles "Leo Kraft."

Turns out to be a real estate agent. Nice face, sort of chubby, losing his hair, tanned, dark features, dark eyes, and high-quality real-estate-agent teeth. There are letters from happy home buyers and sellers. Evan scrolls through them, looking for . . . what?

He sits back in his chair, the fingers of both hands raking his hair, scratching at his scalp. Dandruff sifts down, a minor July snow flurry. Right. He should have asked Griff to get shampoo.

Money. Lawyers.

Maybe Leo is building a resort on the island? Evan imagines people lounging by a pool surrounded by ghostlike children in bathing suits. He imagines *jikininki* as hotel bellhops and waiters. Lifeguards.

Not satisfied, he returns to Kokoro-Jima and scrolls through several pages before remembering what the words mean in English. So he quickly types in Heart-Shaped Island and . . . well, there are lots of them. Angelina even bought one for Brad for his birthday, or so it says. There are heart-shaped islands in Polynesia, Turkey, Australia, Germany—even Canada.

But not Isamu's island. Nothing that big.

He scrolls on, because what else has he got to do? And then on page six, finally something:

"The Heart-Shaped Island: A Story of War and Healing."

Breathlessly, Evan opens the site but there is nothing there but a message:

404. That's an error.

There's a cartoon drawing of a discombobulated robot trying to put himself back together and the explanation that the URL he was looking for cannot be found on this server. "That's all we know," says Ma Google.

Evan shakes his head. What does it mean? *Was* there a

site called "The Heart-Shaped Island: A Story of War and Healing"? Was it closed down? Was that because of Griff's lawyer? But if there was a site, what was it about? Evan wants to smash the desk, have himself a good hard two-fisted tantrum. He holds off. No need to break stuff.

Then his phone dings. A message. He grabs it.

—Phined yet?

It's Rollo.

—*Phined*?

He waits.

—Phoned, douchebag.

Did Evan tell him about Leo? No. Hmm. Then it comes to him. *The girl.* The girl who didn't think he was entirely a douchebag.

—Yes. We're getting married. Invite is in the mail.

—Ha ha ha. do it!!!

Evan goes to respond and stops himself, closes the window. He doesn't have time for this right now. He's exhausted. And it's not just that. He senses that Rollo is trying too hard to bring him back from the dead. That's what it is. He wants him to think about girls and music and the stuff that makes Any Place go around. Except he doesn't know that Evan has washed up on this desert island instead, where he is surrounded by dead people . . . and one person who *should* be dead.

He thinks about the story. Griff hasn't made his entrance yet. He would have been a million years younger. Evan tries to imagine him as ever having been so young—Evan's own age from what he said.

And then an image comes to mind.

He jumps up from his desk and heads to his father's room. He turns on the light, blinks. Fights down the lump in his throat, the tears pricking at his eyes. He will never be able to

110

unlearn this room. He'll have to do something with it. Turn it into something else. Get in a lodger. Sink the fucking place. He takes a deep breath, wipes his eyes.

Get a grip, he tells himself. He's got one more year of school. Then college. He won't keep this place. No, he will. He'll rent it out. No . . . oh, it doesn't matter. He takes another big breath. He doesn't have to decide anything right now. Right now he just needs to concentrate on what is going on. Concentrate on the stranger in *his* house. He feels like Ōshiro discovering the downed plane and realizing there is this missing navigator — someone sharing his private island.

On the dresser there is wooden cigar box covered in dust. Neither he nor his father was ever much for dusting. Now there is dust on everything in the room, but the layer on the cigar box is thicker, older, white with age. In the box are some pieces of jewelry, stuff Evan's mother chose not to take when she left. She left in quite a hurry, the way his father tells it. Evan was only three; he didn't see her go. His father set her up in a catering business, and she took off with some rock star. That was the story. Evan was never sure if it was true. It didn't matter. Not anymore. He digs through the shadowy stash in the box, sniffs the faint tang of perfume that is as old as he is. Finally, he finds what he is looking for: a velvet jewelry box. He opens it. There is a silver chain inside with a heart at the end, a locket. Yes! He leaves the room, flipping off the light, enters his own room, and closes the door softly behind him. Mission accomplished.

He sits on the side of his bed and, using his index fingernail like a tiny crowbar, opens the locket's silver clasp. There are two tiny pictures inside: on the right, a soldier; on the left, a girl. The girl is a brunette with a big twisty hairdo and a flirtatious smile; the soldier's face is certified grade-A macho, hair mown short into a high and tight. You can't see the regulation blue of his

111

eyes because the photographs are black-and-white. But this is him all right: the infamous Griff. Except *before* he got the scar above his right eye. The woman must be Evan's grandmother, Mary. Evan never met her, as far as he can recall. Never heard from her, either. Evan isn't even sure how *his* mother ended up with this necklace; there must have been some communication between her and Mary.

Anyway . . .

He stares at the young face of his grandfather. This is the man who disowned his only son when "the traitorous lout" bypassed the Vietnam War by dodging to Canada. That was what Clifford used to say to him with a certain amount of pride, as if he'd fought in a different kind of war and won.

Evan closes the locket. He remembers when he was a little kid getting his eye right up close to the locket as he snapped it shut. He remembers talking to the tiny people inside, as if he were just about to lock them in a darkened room and he hoped they wouldn't be frightened. He remembers thinking when you closed the two halves of the heart together like that, the two faces inside couldn't help but kiss.

Evan's gaze drifts up until he can see himself in the mirror on the back of his bedroom door. He stands and approaches it, flattens his hair down with his hand, and tries to look tough, eyes on high beam, a nudge of a smile urged out of him by the photographer. He grimaces and makes the muscles in his neck stand out.

A blue-eyed leatherneck. A grunt.

He remembers a conversation with his father. "Your grand-daddy was a grunt. So was his father before him and so on back to the Stone Age. Which is where they probably got the name, come to think of it. 'Grunt.'"

The face in the mirror is angry. That's what was missing. Now he looks a whole lot like Griff. Angry and suspicious. And frightened.

He replaces the locket in its dusty maroon box and puts it in the drawer of his bedside table. He's about to climb into bed, when he stops and listens. No Griff. Not yet. So he turns to the closet, gets down the black box, and takes out the yellow book. Then he climbs into bed, shivering a bit from the cool breeze coming from the window. He pulls his duvet up around him and starts in again.

— V —

DERWOOD KRAFT

I have decided to insert myself into this narrative, interspersing my own recollections of the events that took place on the island Kokoro-Jima in the last year of the war, from the time when I arrived there, the time I first laid eyes on the only other inhabitant of the island. Which is to say, more accurately, the only other fully human inhabitant. The ghosts Ōshiro talks of I witnessed myself, both the flesh-eaters and the companion spirits. I understood these phantasms—if understanding isn't too lofty a term—as the manifestations of an unhinged mind, a mind high on painkillers. That was my condition, at first. Reading him, I find myself taken back to that extraordinary time, recalling it all too well.

I watched the man climb the hill, scrabbling on all fours, out of the ravine. I kept watching even when I'd lost sight of him and could only hear him crashing through the underbrush. I was only lucky he had made as much noise coming down the slope as he now did leaving. It was all a matter of who saw whom first. I had been lucky this time. I would have to make sure I was more than lucky in the future.

Was he a soldier? It was hard to tell at the time. His uniform looked remarkably like American olive-drab army fatigues, severely bleached by the sun. Had he killed a GI? The rifle was an American issue M1. He had not arrived there with it, and I knew well enough where it came from. Still and all, the man carried the rifle like a soldier. On the other hand, he had taken off from the wreckage like a scalded cat, as I'd have thought he might once he saw the remains of my crewmates. Laski and Ramirez. I hated to leave them to the elements, but there was nothing I could do for them. Not in my condition.

That there were ghosts on this island had been a frightening revelation. Hideous things, they were, too. The old-fashioned word for such visions was "ectoplasm": the gunk that supposedly oozed from a spirit, making it visible to the living. I was not a man who indulged in such fantasies. Even as a boy, I had a logical mind, was not taken up with fantasy, preferring to read the true stories of explorers and medical pioneers, science and such. But I could not deny the existence on this island of ghosts, the walking dead men, as I supposed them to be — zombies. And the other ghosts, who huddled near me and had, for days, been my only friends. Friends though they were, they were hardly more than vapor. I thought of them as hallucinations. And although I did eventually accept them as companions, I didn't expect that they would prove reliable; certainly, I doubted that they could protect me from the creatures that Ōshiro called *jikininki*. One of these revolting zombies had been mere inches from my face when I first awoke from my coma. It looked flensed, the colorful word depicting the stripping back of the flesh that New England whalers did of old. The ghouls seemed stripped of their skin, covered with weeping sores and yet possessing teeth like a hyena and eyes like warning lights on a cockpit console. There was another, only slightly more rational explanation for these phantoms, of course, and that was that I had *not* really awoken from my coma; I had only *seemed* to wake up into a series of nightmarish levels of Hell. But no matter my condition, I knew that the man scampering from the plane was not one of those mutilated creatures, whatever else he was. He was as much a man as I was. But he was a man who knew how to keep the ghosts at bay using smoke. Which told me what? That he had presumably been there awhile.

When I was quite certain Ōshiro—though of course I did not yet know his name—was gone, I lumbered down from my hiding place to where he had dropped the transmitter. I had watched him trip over it. I'd seen him shake his fist at the crows, sharing my own disdain for their rapacious appetites. But they were only surviving as nature had equipped them to, just as the ragtag soldier was doing. Just as I, Flight Officer Derwood Kraft, was attempting to do.

It had been a near thing.

I picked up the yellow box. It was a BC-778, known to the troops as the "Gibson Girl" for its shapely figure. It was a simple-enough machine to operate. A round door in the front of it opened to reveal a ninety-two-meter antenna wrapped on a spool mounted on the back of the door. This was to be raised by a box kite or alternately a helium balloon; only the kite had survived the crash landing. There was a crank embedded on the back side of the transmitter, which you attached to the top and turned with enough vigor to get the voltage up and to maintain it, as indicated by a light on the top. The transmitter then sent out an SOS for up to a two-hundred-mile radius. It was a lot of work to operate the crank. You had to sit with that gal between your knees, strapped to your thighs, to hold her in place. I'd tried one out, stateside. I'd never been much in the muscle department, but I managed well enough. That was when I was healthy, when I hadn't been lying half dead in the jungle for who knows how long.

Back when I still had two hands.

I had lost my left hand from just above the wrist. Not lost it, cut it off. It had been crushed on landing, broken so badly that I hadn't had much cutting to do. Thank God for small mercies.

My survival was a miracle, a multifaceted miracle. I had been the only one to parachute from the plane when it was hit by enemy fire. Getting out was miracle number one. I landed on the same island as the plane, which was miracle number two. Except that was only because I had jumped too late to really benefit much from the parachute's drag. So I landed in a tree and fell through many slashing branches until my downward fall finally stopped. That's when my arm got wedged in the crotch of a branch, wedged and snapped.

Miracle three: I didn't croak up in that tree. I was able to climb down—mostly falling—and, fainting numerous times on the way, find the Gooney Bird, thanks to the flames that briefly engulfed the forward end of it but mercifully never reached the fuel tanks. Was the rain the fourth or fifth miracle? Anyway, it was yet another miracle that there were enough bandages, gauze, iodine swabs, and other antibiotics, not to mention morphine tartrate, to get me through the ordeal. Endorphins from my traumatized body got me to the morphine, and then the drug took over the job of holding the pain at bay.

The fall had done most of the amputation for me. Digging a shiny new bayonet from one of the boxes of rifles, I slashed the muscle and tendon still holding my poor dead hand in place and then folded the skin and tags of flesh over the opening as tightly as I could. It wasn't easy to stitch it up. Like most American lads of my day, I had never learned how to sew, although I did remember watching my mother sew the stuffing into a turkey at

Thanksgiving. I remember leaning on the counter at her elbow, licking my lips, little realizing the use that homey lesson would later serve me!

When my arm was as closed up as I was going to get it, I poured a whole bottle of disinfectant on it, screaming the whole time. Then I wrapped it up as tight as I could manage with one hand and my teeth.

Then oblivion.

Who knows how long I was out? I had come to, once or twice, enough to douse the wound with iodine, take some more morphine, and keel over again. In the euphoria and dysphoria brought on by the drug, I remembered observing my lower arm for signs of rot. If infection set in, I knew I would be done for, because there were neither enough medical supplies nor will-power left in me to attempt a further cut.

And I survived.

I had never been one for praising the Lord. Mother was a good Christian soul, a Congregationalist; Dad not so much, as they say these days. He was a farmer back in Plainfield, Vermont, and the only bit of religion I heard coming out of his mouth was some variant of "the Lord giveth and the Lord taketh away." I myself hadn't seen much to indicate anyone was in charge up there—certainly not at Saipan or Tinian or Guam. And from what one heard of the war in Europe . . . God, if there was one, clearly had too much on his plate. But maybe this tiny island had its own smaller deity who had seen fit to bless a young flight officer and give him a second chance.

Until an hour before Ōshiro's arrival, I had thought I was the *only* living human there. This was going to be a problem. I had all the rifles and ammunition you could want, but only one usable arm. I couldn't even bury my dead comrades. I was emaciated from the ordeal, wasting away. Ōshiro had looked fit, quick, and strong. I'd be no match for him in any kind of hand-to-hand combat. So I would have to match wits with him.

I did have my handgun, but not much of the right-caliber ammo.

The first thing I needed to do was find a new home. And then I needed to get the Gibson Girl working for me. There was no point trying to raise the aerial down in the depths of the gully. There was little in the way of a breeze, for one thing. So I'd never get the box kite up. Besides, I would need all of those ninety-two meters of aerial to get a crack at transmitting a signal, and I was below sea level, as far as I could tell. So I would have to cart the contraption to some higher or more open place. Get it out to the beach, at least, get the kite up and the crank working, send my distress signal, and keep it going. All with an enemy soldier sharing the same few acres of land. The odds weren't promising.

I was a Green Mountain farmer's son. Farming wasn't what I intended to do with my life, assuming I got out of that pickle, but I had a pretty good eye for acreage. I would guess the place wasn't much more than four miles long and a mile and a half wide, narrowing to a point at its southern end. I would later learn Ōshiro's name for it, the heart-shaped island. That it was. There were cliffs at the bottom pointy end of the heart, which was a lot closer to where I was. Now that he knew he wasn't alone, the south end also offered the benefit of cover. I was living in a cave on the southern slope of the jungle and could see the hills rise up behind me, but had never had the energy to scale the heights. Now it seemed I was going to have to, and I hoped there would be more caves at the rocky south end, assuming the geomorphology was anything like it was on Saipan: volcanic rock, limestone. I had done little exploring at that point, being too busy just staying alive. Now I was going to have to work a little harder at that!

I sank to the ground and leaned my back against the

grounded Gooney Bird. That's what we affectionately called the Douglas C-47 Skytrain. The Brits called it the Dakota. It was essentially a DC-3 airliner stripped down for military transport. This one had carried its last load.

I was exhausted, worse than ever, at the thought of all I had ahead of me to do. It was going to be the Devil's own work just to hoist the transmitter to higher ground, let alone get the damn thing working. I remember closing my eyes and listening to the sound of the night gathering around me. I'm not sure if it was my mother's faith or my father's practicality that gave me the strength to go on. Both, I guess. But tired as I was, I remember opening my eyes and smiling. I was alive. No, I felt *newly* alive. Spurred on. Somehow, in some strange way, I owed my enemy for that. I was going to have to outsmart the other man, or think of a way to render him inoperable.

— VI —

ISAMU

The Brown Snake

I scrambled up the path to my hilltop haven. It was already growing dark, and the woods to either side of my familiar route were a patchwork of shadows, any one of which might contain an armed stranger. I clutched my new rifle at the ready, my finger on the trigger, my eyes peeled. When I reached my compound and saw it was as peaceful as I had left it that morning, I breathed a sigh of relief. I took the flight manual from inside my shirt and laid it down on the low table I had made for myself. I sat cross-legged and took the strange pen from my pocket and laid it ceremoniously beside the book.

A small treasure. But at what price?

Hisako-chan, how I longed to make my first entry, but my mind was like a hive with a honey bear nearby. I was too full of uncertainty, night was coming, and now the night concealed an adversary. Was he only waiting for the cover of darkness to make his move?

No, this was foolish! I had been on the island for over two months, and the plane had crashed some time ago, judging by the state of the crew. I had made no effort to hide, thinking myself alone. A soldier with a plane full of rifles could have picked me off a hundred times over as I combed the beach. I had to calm down, think this through.

My familiar ghosts came to me. I had paid little attention to them, and now, suddenly, for the first time I actually spoke to one of them, the ringleader.

"There is someone else on the island," I said. "The enemy."

His ghostly head seemed to nod. Of course he knew! "What shall I do?" I asked. I had no reason to believe they could talk, but then I hadn't expected the *jikininki* could talk, either. I looked at him closely. He has such a sweet face, Hisako. He must have been a lovely boy when he was alive, I thought. His head continued to nod until it occurred to me that this "gesture" was only brought about by the breeze. "Ah," I said, waving him away. "What good are you?" Then he seemed to smile even more brightly. The smile itself might have been caused only by the tugging of the wind at his facial muscles, but it looked real enough, for all that. It reminded me of how when a newborn baby smiles, everyone other than the parents thinks it is just gas. The parents know better.

It was a sleepless night, but sometime in the hours before dawn, I fell asleep only to wake up with a start at the raucous squawk of some bird. Peeking around the flap of canvas, my heart pumping, I resolved that my first priority must be to secure my position.

I spent the morning circling the hill to see how well the compound was concealed from view. As I had expected, it was hardly visible at all until you were within twenty yards or so, and then only the peak of the roof. Better still, the roof was really visible only from the steep southwest side, a blocky limestone cliff that a person would be unlikely to climb unless he already knew what was at the top, and even then he'd make a noise doing it. I cut more palm branches to camouflage the sharper edges of the shelter until I was quite sure it was impossible to tell that anything man-made was there.

Unless you were looking for it.

Over my midday meal I contemplated making a fort, but it seemed a great deal of work and all that construction itself might attract undue attention. I pounded my head with my fists, as you have seen me do sometimes. It was as if I had become my own father trying to knock some sense into me! What proof was there that anyone else was alive on the island? The blood-smeared cargo bay of the plane suggested a great struggle to stay alive. To be sure, there was no body, no corpse, but so much blood spilled. Ah . . .

The survivor had obviously taken himself off into the jungle, like an animal, to crawl into a burrow and die. But then I recalled the yellow box, the box I had tripped over. I had no idea what it was, but how could it be outside the plane unless someone had carried it there?

I boiled myself some tea, which I drank from a coconut shell. Whatever the yellow case was, I could not ignore it.

Which is when I decided to rig up an alarm system.

I got to it right away, pleased to have something to do with my hands. My hands have always worked a lot better than my brain! Ah, Hisako-chan, I can almost hear you laughing.

I wove together coarse Manila fiber into long lengths of twine, which I strung, at knee level, across every pathway, every means of access to the compound. The twine was attached to small platforms, packing-case remnants precariously balanced in bushes, loaded with good heavy stones, ready to tip with the slightest nudge. When an intruder tripped the switch, the platforms would tip the stones into a variety of tin basins, hubcaps, suspended sheets of metal—anything clangy that I could find in my store of flotsam and jetsam. I had quite a stockpile of useful material at my campsite.

It took me all of that day to engineer my early warning system, but after a couple of dry runs (without the metal containers in place so as not to make a noise), I stood back, sweaty and pleased at the result. Now all I had to remember was not to trip one of the ropes myself!

I didn't count on the local wildlife.

I awoke that night to a terrible clattering din, as first one and then a second and then a third of the alarms went off. Was there an army out there?! What a frightful few minutes I went through! But no, some creature that didn't stick around had tripped the ropes. Probably as frightened as I was, I thought, when I could think clearly again. I imagined a skittish deer running wildly in circles trying to escape a noisy monster that seemed to be everywhere at once.

If the enemy didn't know where I was before, he most certainly did now!

Again, I hardly slept and woke up knowing there was only one option: it was either the navigator or myself. We were at war, after all—what choice did I really have? And yet how hard it was to imagine hunting this unseen enemy down, matching my wits against an invisible adversary. The truth is, I had just escaped from the war, and I had no desire to go back to it again.

I would look for signs. Yes. Now that I suspected there was someone on the island, I would look with intention, from my platform in the coral tree. There would have to be signs. For that matter, I could always sleep on the platform.

With my binoculars, I could not see down into the ravine, only the thick canopy of that low place. It was in the deepest part of the island, where the island seemed to curl in on itself, like some secret bodily cavity, another chamber of the heart that has become my home. I could not see down into its shadows, but I could see a lot. If there was a survivor, would he not have had to rely as did I on the bounty washed up on the beach? The fact that we had never run into each other might mean that the other had seen me first, but if he had done so, he had not taken advantage of the occasion. It was a mystery.

I looked and saw nothing, and so I took the flight manual up into the coral tree with me to begin this diary. On the cover I wrote out your name and address in Saipan so that if I did not survive and the journal was found, my story and my many protestations of love could be delivered to you.

Slowly and painstakingly, in the neatest and tiniest script, I began to relate the tale of my arrival here and everything that has happened since that fateful day. It was miraculous that this strange pen had so much ink in it. It was splotchy at times, but I prayed it would hold out.

Oh, I looked up at regular intervals, let me tell you. I scanned the island with the naked eye and with the binoculars as well, and then, satisfied that there was nothing worth attending to, I went back to my writing.

This is what my father called procrastination but my grandfather called *ikigai*—my reason to get up in the morning. My grandfather always thought something grand would come of me: that I would write books or make glorious pictures. Well, perhaps he was right after all, for although I am an auto mechanic by trade, I did begin to write this book. And since I had time on my hands stretching out before me at such a luxurious length, I could take the time to think carefully before I wrote anything, not wanting to spoil the limited pages before me. Ah, you are thinking now, if only I had learned how to think carefully before I spoke! In any case, if it is only for your eyes, Hisako, I will tell you that I am pouring into it everything I have learned or felt and all the patient hours *Ojiisan* spent reading with me and teaching me the ways of the written word.

From here on, everything changes.

Over these several days, I have caught you up to this very moment, and I will write henceforth in the present tense. It will make me feel closer to you.

The air is still. I have been writing and watching. When I am in my lookout, the family ghosts cannot get to me. They tend to congregate at the bottom of the tree, looking up, waiting for me to come down. And perhaps because I am in a tree, I have been thinking of a family tree, a diagram, and wonder whether these friendly spirits really are my family, those that have gone before: the ghosts of my ancestors. Then why are they children, I ask myself.

"Why are you children?" I asked the ringleader, just now, before I climbed up here.

He didn't answer, but he reached out to me, so tenderly, Hisako, I was almost brought to tears. And as I sit here now, a rather extraordinary thought has come over me. I wonder if this family of children I am dragging around with me is *not* made up of those who have gone before but those who are yet to come!

It is later now. Time has passed. I look at the ghosts quite differently. For one thing, it fills me with joy to think that there *might* be a time yet to come: that I will survive and you and I will make a real family one day. A big family!

Is this a foolish idea? Perhaps. I wonder if it is the threat of another being on the island who might at any moment steal my life from me that lends to my musings over this sentimental idea. I can't be sure. I do know that having this adversary here or even imagining him here brings a new urgency to my writing. I want so much to put my thoughts in order, to tell my story. A simple man thrust into an extraordinary situation.

But isn't that the story of every war?

As you know, I have not had much schooling, but I learned much at my grandfather's knee and have read, or tried to, the books that Grandfather lent me. With no motors to tinker with here, I find myself tinkering with ideas, trying to see how they fit together. I allow myself to write upon the page thoughts I would never dare to express to any living soul other than you, who are endlessly patient with me and do not judge me. I know you would be glad to hear whatever nonsense I have to say. Am I not your favorite chatterbox?

The writing pleases me, even more, now that I have told you everything that has passed and we can be here, like this, in the moment. But I cannot pretend to have shaken the idea of the *other*. It works on me, under my skin, an irritant, an unwanted burden. I have survived, found a paradise, only to have the tranquillity of it compromised by this cagey *gaijin*. As the days pass, I can only picture him as very evasive and clever. When I go foraging for food, I feel the presence of him. I feel I am being stalked—stalked even in my dreams, for the kingdom of sleep has been usurped every bit as thoroughly as my island kingdom. I wake dispirited and angry. I try sleeping in the coral tree, but my sleep is interrupted by the terrible fear of rolling off.

Nowhere is safe.

There is a bird building a nest in a tree that I pass every morning on my way down to the lagoon for a swim. I have watched the little golden white-eye fly back and forth with casuarina needles, grasses, and vines. I have watched her settle in her nest, have bid her good morning and wished her good luck with her family. One time, when she was off hunting for food, I even dared to shinny up her tree to take a look: there were two pale bluish-green eggs with red splotches there.

Then, this morning, a dull gray morning, after a particularly bad night of dreams, I saw the golden white-eye not foraging or on her nest but flitting about above it, crying with alarm. I stopped in my tracks, for I saw right away the cause of her distress: a brown snake was gliding up the trunk of the tree toward the nest. No! The snake was too high up for me to do anything but watch it slither out onto the branch and over the lip of the nest, where it devoured her eggs, one by one.

I stood seething with anger, my fists clenched. It is later and I have calmed a bit and have had the time to think about the incident more clearly. I have this to say: the brown snake must eat, too. But nonetheless the event is surely a sign. I know that my rage is not simply for the golden white-eye's loss, but for my own predicament. I have let an unseen enemy slither into my nest! I am so filled with apprehension that I cannot sleep at night. I have avoided acting out of cowardice, pretending it was only caution. I know I must find out now, once and for all, if I am master of this place. I cannot put off a confrontation for one more day. Tomorrow, Hisako-chan, I will track the navigator down. If this is my last entry, then you know what happened.

— VII —

ISAMU

Tengu

Tomorrow is now yesterday, a day of surpassing strangeness. I must try to recall every detail beginning with a tragedy.

I stared at the carcass lying across the sandy path. I was heading to the Pond of Sweet Water to fill my canteen before heading into the jungle to find the navigator or his remains. I was filled with resolve. I was determined not to put off what must be done for even one day longer. I was a warrior, refreshed and ready for anything.

And then this.

It was the sambar doe, or what remained of her, for she had been savaged. Her neck had been slashed, her belly torn open. Few innards were left to be seen. Her belly was concave. Whatever had done this to her had feasted on offal, nothing else. Flies gathered on her lifeless eye.

In a nearby grove, several *jikininki* gathered, watching me.

"Did you see this happen?" I demanded.

A curious sound emanated from the wounds in their heads where a real person's mouth would be. Sniggering. They were sniggering at me. "What? You find this funny?" I shouted at them, my fists on my hips.

"It washed up on the beach," said one.

"Large," said another, holding out its arms. "As large as the largest bear."

"No, a great cat—a tiger," said still another.

"Tigers are striped," squalled one of them, cuffing the last speaker across the chest. "I ate a man who had seen one, once. This . . . this thing was black as mud."

"Brown."

"Claws," said the first. "As long as a human's hands."

"And the beak of a mighty sea eagle."

"Pah!" I shouted, striding toward them angrily. "It was him, wasn't it—the American. He is the monster that did this?"

They all shook their heads; they agreed on that, if nothing else.

"Pah!" I said again, spitting at their feet. "I will find him. He will pay for this!"

One of them dared to approach me. "This is good," it said. "We are pleased to see you filled with revenge." That should have been a clue, but it is only now in writing this down that I see what I could not then see in my rage.

I spit again, and turning on my heels, I tramped up the path, only to stop again. My hands flew to my mouth in horror. The fawn. A young buck by now, with little bumps of horns coming in. He also had been mutilated.

The *jikininki* sniggered and howled at me.

It had to be the *gaijin*. The monster the *jikininki* described was like nothing at all—they couldn't agree amongst themselves on what it looked like. Nothing else had changed on the island but for the American's arrival! So, in a way, their stories were true; there was a monster here.

As I departed, I looked around, expecting to see the flesh-eaters descend on the corpses of the deer to clean up. They made no move. Obviously, they only dine on human remains. And that reminded me of my only other conversation with one of the *jikininki*. If it was memories they were after, did this mean that deer have no memories? I cannot say. They remember where the water is sweet and the twigs are tasty. I said a silent prayer for the dead deer and then pushed on through to the pond, where I filled my canteen and ducked my head in the clean water to cool down the heat of anger that burned my cheeks. I had to be cool: keep control over the intense emotion burning inside me. Focus it.

I knelt at the pond's edge, my sopping hair falling across my face, until I smoothed it back with hard hands, strong and browned by the sun. Yes, Hisako, my hair is long now after so many weeks, and if you had seen me there kneeling by the pond at that moment, you would have probably gasped, for I must look like a wild man. There was something evil loose on the island—my island!—and I had let myself be distracted from it. I was distracted no longer.

I was a soldier again.

I had to root out this foul thing and destroy it. And then I must somehow contact the imperial forces. There was a plane-load of arms, ready for use. How could I have ignored this fact for so many days? What's more, there was probably a radio on the plane. I knew little about radios, but, as you know, I have a way with machinery of all kinds. Yes! I would make contact with whatever was left of my compatriots. I would be a hero.

Ah, you will have noticed, Hisako, with your sharp eye, that I have drifted into the past tense again. These are things I was going to do. That's what I thought at the time. But life can be strange, indeed. Read on.

I bounded to my feet and set off. My ghosts hovered near me. I saw fear or even panic in their eyes. They understood and although they could do nothing to help me in my quest, I felt better to have them there. They were my family, and I would need to be brave for them!

Silently I found my way into the gully to the downed supply plane. It was early, and the silver fuselage was draped in shadows and wet with dew. Fearlessly I approached it, my every sense alert. I noticed right away that the yellow box was gone, and days of pointless speculation were resolved in a moment. I had whiled away my time writing to you, and in the meantime a monster was out here, only waiting for Isamu to come to life, to act, to do what had to be done. It was now only a matter of following its path, tracking it down.

I hurled open the hatch to the plane, explored it from stem to stern, no longer afraid of anything, filled with holy wrath. When I left the plane, the carrion crows were gathered in the trees, unable to carry out their ravaging of the crew due to the barricade I had put in their way, but drawn to the smell nonetheless.

"Go ahead," I said. "Shriek at me as much as you want." Then without thinking, I raised my new rifle to my shoulder and fired into the trees. The crows flew up again, enraged. I only laughed. I no longer cared if my quarry knew where I was. Let him! Let him shake in his boots! Waiting and hiding had achieved nothing. Frighten the enemy into making a mistake, I thought: that was the way of it. Show no fear. Show no mercy.

I searched the ground outside the plane, my vision sharpened by grim determination. And sure enough, I found a path, recently used. I followed it up the shallow southwest side out of the gully that led to high walls of limestone. I peered up through the canopy. The walls were pocked with holes, caves. He is hiding there even now! Oh, the navigator might be rapacious when it came to defenseless deer but petrified to face a man. Did he have a scope trained on me that very minute? I no longer cared.

132

It was suddenly all so clear. No wonder I had seen hide nor hair of this monster. I pictured him now, a fearful, simpering, timid thing. The very thing I, Isamu, had become but was no longer. It was good to feel this fury. I felt more alive than I had for ages.

I climbed a rugged path between the rocks.

Stooping, I found a torn length of shoelace. A hundred yards on, my fingers plucked a ragged scrap of bloodied bandage caught on the thorns of a twisted, leafless tree, growing out of a crevice in the rock face. I sniffed the bandage. It was rank. I looked ahead to where the path met the sky. If I listened hard, I could hear the wind in the rocks ahead, and was that . . . yes, waves; this path must lead to the lower southwest flank of the island, a part I had not explored because it was so rocky and probably would yield little in the way of anything I needed. Now this barren place harbored the *only* thing I needed.

I climbed on. Stopped. Listened. There was another sound now, a whirring, mechanical sound. I slid my hand along a steep wall of cliffside, looking down at my feet with every step, so as not to dislodge a stone, and then quickly up again, feeling the wind cool on my face as I neared the trailhead. The whirring grew louder as I crested the hill. Then it stopped. Had he seen me? I flattened myself against the rock, cold at so early an hour. Then I inched forward. When I was not fifteen feet from the cliff's edge, something fluttered into my view, bobbing on the wind. A kite. A yellow-and-blue box kite. I blinked.

A kite?

I slithered back along the stone face and peered down upon a beach at low tide, a long strand trailing out into the ocean, the very tail end of the heart. My eyes followed the kite's string down, down, down to where it was lost to view behind a rocky overhang. The trail turned back on itself and carried on toward the sand, maybe sixty or seventy feet below. Edging along the path, I reached a place where, by crouching, I could see the kite string again and now the man at the base of it.

He was sitting below me, with the strange yellow box between his knees. He was turning a crank on the top of the box. His left arm tried to keep the box from jiggling, and I could plainly see the filthy-looking bandage at the end of his arm where the man's left hand should have been.

Aha!

Such a revelation! The man could not shoot. Not a rifle, anyway. Not with only one hand. He stopped cranking and wiped his forehead with his useless arm. The *gaijin* was lean, almost skeletal. I could count the ribs and vertebrae on his sunburned back. Several familiars gathered near him, shivering transparently in the low sun, watching him like mourners at a funeral ceremony. I turned to my own ghosts. They trailed behind me on the path, waiting. I looked into the eyes of the nearest one. Did he shake his head? It was hard to tell. When the sun is flat on them, they are hardly there at all. But it did not matter, in any case. I moved farther down the path until I could see the man in partial profile. He was bearded, with sunken cheeks, and ragged hair bleached to a dull tan by the sun.

This was my enemy? This helpless wretch disemboweled a sambar and her child? It could not be so. But this was no time to ponder such improbabilities. I had to keep my mind sharp and my mission clear.

The scarecrow man was completely unaware of me. I raised my eyes and looked up at his kite high out over the water, buffeted by breezes, straining at the line. Then he started to turn the crank again. In a flash of inspiration, I realized what it must be: some kind of emergency signaling device.

I had to do something right away. I raised my rifle. There

134

was a scope. Closing one eye, I brought the man into focus with the other. The muscles of his stringy neck were strained with the effort, his face grimacing. How long had he been at it? Was it already too late?

I could feel my resolve slipping away. He had only one arm. Yet I had to stop him. That was all. Stop him and then take him as a prisoner. But how was I to look after a prisoner? Indecision was tearing my rage apart at the seams.

I ran down the narrow path toward the beach, recklessly now, for the real man did not fill me with fear the way the idea of him had. I kept my eye on my quarry, still quite a way below me and well out on the sand. The path hairpinned again and then fizzled out altogether, never a real path to begin with, so I leaped from rock to rock and doubled back behind him. Finally I reached the beach and stood on the sand, my rifle raised, ready to fire. The outcrop shielded me from the sun. I stood in its shadow, cool and collected. Through the scope, I could now see a belt and holstered handgun lying on a knapsack beside the man. So even with one arm, he could still prove deadly. Surely he had no idea of my presence, or he would have tried to shoot me already. One of his ghosts lazily turned its head and saw me. It kept its eyes on me but made no effort to warn its host. Even his ghosts see no hope of his survival! I sank to one knee, the rifle raised again at a target less than thirty feet away. A target that had no idea he was being marked. He would be dead before he heard the rifle's report. He would never know what hit him.

But I stopped, again. My breathing was ragged from the climb and the excitement and from the dreadful purpose of my assignment. If a message had already gone out and if the *gaijin* could somehow make their way here, when they found no one, would they not search for him — the sender of the signal? I imagined the island swarming with troops. That would never do! But if I could take him as a prisoner, I could use him to ransom my own life.

Behind my bared teeth, I let out a silent roar of frustration that would have rung out against the steep cliffs like an air-raid siren had I given it voice.

I raised the rifle again, took aim—

And it was then that the creature jumped.

He must have climbed onto the overhanging rock above my head and out of my line of sight, because suddenly there was a black blur before my eyes and in front of me landed a monstrous thing, larger than a demon bear, completely unaware of me, loping toward his unsuspecting victim only a scant few yards away.

The man must have heard something. He turned and fell to one side, while his one good hand tried to escape from the contraption between his legs. He shouted just as the creature jumped.

And I fired.

Chapter Thirteen

He's back. Evan glances at the time on his phone. He was miles away, years away, across an ocean, on the outskirts of a war, on an island that was half dream, half nightmare.

"Demon bears?" he says to himself. "Really?"

But the story is getting under his skin. He can't think of anywhere farther away from Kokoro-Jima than this place, and yet something of Ōshiro's fear is in him. It's not as if Evan is there on that faraway shore; more like the demon is *here*.

He listens to the night, the cicadas, the distant drone of the expressway, the distinct sound of a car door slamming. He waits, concentrates. Imagines more than hears the back door open and shut.

He closes the book, closes his eyes, and leans back on his pillow. He can almost hear water lapping against the sides of the house. As if they've upped anchor and sailed away from civilization. He feels totally out to sea.

He has this weird feeling about the island: the jungle, the wide beach, strewn with bits and pieces of the war, the cliffs and caves, the impressive bamboo fort overlooking the lagoon. He has this feeling that he knows it—not what's going to happen in the story—but the island itself. He feels almost a sense of déjà vu. Is that possible? He thinks about the ghosts, the good ones, Ōshiro's companions. Ōshiro considers them children yet to come. Such a strange and kind of cool idea. And if it happened to anyone who landed on the island, then when Griff lands there, will it happen to him? Will Clifford become one of his attendant ghosts? Would Evan be there, too, one of those hopeful hangers-on? He shakes his head. Way too weird.

Then out of the crackly darkness behind Evan's eyes, a word comes to him: preincarnation. Does such a word exist? He opens his eyes and pushes the book aside, throwing the duvet over it as he climbs out of bed. He's about to check Almighty Google when he hears something. He cracks his door, listens. Music.

He makes his way down the silent hallway, drifts down the silent stairs, peeks around the wall at the bottom. A memory comes to him of sneaking down at Christmas to see if Santa Claus had been there yet. But it's not Santa Claus; it's Griff. And the music isn't "Jingle Bells." It's the same album his dad was listening to, that last night.

Evan can only see the back of Griff's head, sitting in Clifford's favorite chair in the living room. The sweet spot.

Jazz. Miles Davis. "Something Blue."

Did Clifford leave it on the turntable? The idea troubles

Evan; it wasn't the kind of thing his father would normally do. He was crazy careful about his vinyl. But then that night was going to be the least normal night of his whole life.

Or Evan's.

If his father left the album there, that was one thing. If Griff found it and put it on — the same album his dad had been playing — that was just plain eerie. Or maybe what bothers Evan is the old man sitting in that chair. The old man touching his father's precious records.

He has a glass of scotch in his hand; the bottle sits on the side table next to him. The amber contents are an inch or two lower than the last time Evan saw that bottle.

"I guess he changed," says Griff. Evan pulls back, freezes. "This isn't the kind of thing he used to listen to." Evan's face is pressed against the cool plaster of the wall. The old man is talking to himself, he thinks. And then Griff says, "Come on out, son. I know you're there."

Evan steps from behind the wall.

"I wouldn't consider espionage as a career path," says Griff.

"I thought you were hard of hearing," says Evan.

"If I'd had to rely on my ears, boy, I'd've been dead a hundred times over."

Then Evan sees his own reflection in the darkened picture window, his eyes meeting the reflected eyes of his grandfather, keen as an eagle, despite the scotch. Evan had put on pajamas when he went to bed, not sure if the old man was going to make a habit of walking in on him. He stands there feeling vulnerable, his scrawny legs hanging out of his cotton shorts. The jazz fills in the silence between them.

Then Evan says, "Well, good night," and turns to go.

"Hol' your horses," says Griff.

Evan stops but doesn't turn.

"You're up. I'm up," says Griff. "Stay awhile. Talk to me."

He turns his head, but only enough for Evan to see his profile, his broken nose, his jawbone hard under his leathery skin. "We haven't exactly been hittin' it off, have we, son."

It's not a question, so Evan doesn't answer, not even so much as to shake his head.

"Oh, for crying out loud," says Griff, exasperated. "Get your sorry ass in here."

Reluctantly, Evan finds his way around his grandfather and sits across from him—perches on the couch under the picture window. It's leather and cold on the back of his thighs. He has no intention of making himself comfortable. He has a feeling Griff doesn't either.

The old man casts a bleary kind of smile his way and then stares off into the semi-darkness of the room. There's only the one table lamp on, beside Griff's chair, and the array of lights on the console of the stereo unit. Evan sits mostly in shadow. Griff's eyes are closed. Evan thinks the old man is wrapped up in the music, but he's not, not really.

"Rock and roll," he says. "That's what your daddy listened to. Day and night, night and day." He pauses. "What was that one band called?" Evan doesn't answer; doesn't really think the question was meant for him. "The Doors. That was it. The damn blasted Doors." Griff shakes his head. "God, what a racket." He opens his eyes only long enough to make contact with Evan, who refuses to make the slightest gesture that might be interpreted as agreement. "I swear he'd put that band on the minute I walked in the house, just to get my goat."

Griff closes his eyes again, and Evan thinks about escape, assessing his chances of getting out of the room without the old man noticing. They aren't going to talk. Griff will just riff on his differences with Clifford. And Evan is too tired to rise to his father's defense tonight—too wary, knowing what he knows. Not that he really knows anything yet, except that there is suddenly a monster in the book—one that Evan left Ōshiro and Kraft stranded with.

He should go, but he decides against it. Why be on the defensive? So the old man knows that he has the book? Fine. Maybe he can get him talking. He clears his throat.

"He still has all the Doors' albums," he says.

Griff opens one eye under a steel-gray eyebrow arched like a pup tent. "Ha! Must have bought them all over again when he got here. Damn well didn't take 'em." He maneuvers himself upright in his chair. "Didn't take much of anythin'." He sips his drink, crunches on an ice cube. "Took just enough to let us know what he thought of us—thought of me." Griff pokes himself in the chest. Then he shakes his head and stares into the middle distance at something only he can see. A red light, on the stereo console, fires up in his eye like a small and angry planet. Then he snaps out of it, leans back again, and the planet veers off into darkness. He swivels his head on his stringy neck until he has Evan in his crosshairs.

"You know what I did, Evan? When he left?"

Evan doesn't answer. Three leisurely, four/four bars float by.

"I got all those records together, all those albums—the whole stinking lot of them—and took them out to my workbench in the garage." His eyes almost twinkle. He's enjoying this. "And then you know what I did?"

Evan doesn't acknowledge the question with so much as a gesture. He knows where this is going. Recognizes the cadence of the story without knowing exactly how it ends.

"I'll tell you, son, since you're obviously so interested. I took each one of those records out of its . . . whatever you call it . . . sleeve. And I broke it over my knee."

141

He mimes the breaking, bringing his fists down hard on either side of his bony knee. Evan can almost hear the crack.

"Every dang one of 'em."

Evan feels the anger welling up in him, pushing aside the weight of weariness. He feels it pulsing through him. He doesn't like this. It's not the anger he doesn't like; it's the lack of control. The old man is staring at him as if he's just made a move in some chess game from hell and he's waiting for Evan to clear the pieces from the board in his fury.

He's playing me. He's testing me like this is some kind of fucking boot camp.

Evan swallows. His mouth is dry—too dry to respond, at least not in words. But he's not going to bite. He's not going to clear the board with his arm. He's not going to run. He's going to make his move. What move is that? Then it comes to him. Something he had wanted to do in their very first run-in. He claps.

Three. Slow. Times.

The old man shakes his head. He waves his hand in the air as if at a fly buzzing around his head.

"You finished?" says Evan, his voice betraying him, frayed as a rope about to break.

The old man shakes his head. Then suddenly he puts on the full-out glare.

"What'd your father have to say about me, son?"

Evan clocks the change in Griff's voice, the focus, the intent in his eyes. If the drink seemed to have mellowed him a few moments ago, he's dead sober now.

Evan shrugs. "Nothing much."

"I'm serious, now, boy. In case you didn't notice."

Evan dares to look Griff directly in the eye. He's serious, all right. *You're a murderer,* he thinks. *That's what he told me.* He looks away.

"Throw me a bone, son."

Evan swallows. The game has changed, just like that. Here he was congratulating himself on making a strong move, and Griff's gone and replaced the board game. More like Chutes and Ladders, now. Just when you think you've climbed to safety, down you go.

"You see, I'm at a disadvantage here, Evan. I feel like I've landed on this hostile island, and I'd kind of like to know what the odds are. Where the snipers are hid. You know what I'm saying? Where the trip wire is."

Evan swallows again, clears his throat. "We didn't talk about you at all," he says.

Griff chuckles. "Aww, shucks. Why, I am truly hurt to hear that."

"Not once."

Griff glares at him. "Well, isn't that somethin'." He sniffs, takes another sip of his drink. Refuses to be dismissed. "You see, boy, a marine coming ashore on a hostile island doesn't need *much.* You learn to live with whatever intel you can get. The quality of it."

"'Intel'?"

"Intelligence, son. Information: the stuff that gives a soldier the drop, the ability to understand and deal with a new or trying situation. You hear what I'm saying?" Evan nods slowly, feeling as if he's being led toward some hidden trap. Griff holds his hand up and points at a corner of the room up where the walls meet the ceiling, as if there is something there. Evan turns to look, sees only darkness. "You spot a glint up in the trees," says Griff. "That might be the sun reflecting off the lens of a pair of binoculars. Just that one little glint. See what I mean: quality intel."

Evan shrugs again, but inside he shivers. He's thinking of Ōshiro up in his tree on Kokoro-Jima. He shakes his head. "I don't know what you're talking about."

Griff levels him with an expert marksman's gaze. "Y'all do. Y'all know exactly the hell what I mean."

He was listening. He heard me talking to Leo.

"What does any of this have to do with 123 Any Place?"

Griff looks taken aback. "Where the hell's that at?"

"It's this place, the address Dad and I gave it."

Griff sits up higher in his chair. "It is, is it?"

This seems neutral territory. Evan sits up a bit. "Dad used to laugh about how everything around this neighborhood was, like, 'crescent' or 'drive' or 'circle' or 'close'—you know—all those fancy-sounding words. Thought it was pretentious."

The old man nods. "Well, I gotta say, since you brought it up, this place sure surprised the hell out of me. This room alone, for God's sake! It's straight from the catalog of that damn chain store . . ."

"Ikea."

"Right. I-kee-yuh." Griff manages to make it sound like something you need to take a week's worth of medicine for. "The way Cliff talked when he was your age . . ." He shakes his head. "He was this high-minded somabitch. A radical. A hippie, a 'Student for a Democratic Society,' or whatever the hell they called themselves." Griff makes quote marks in the air with his free hand. "The whole nine yards. He thought he was going to set the world on fire, and instead he ends up in this clapboard, ticky-tacky backwater."

"Thanks," says Evan.

"You're welcome."

"But you know, it's funny," says Evan.

"Is it, now?" Griff rivets him with his eyes. "What exactly did you find funny about what I was saying?"

"The thing about Dad setting the world on fire. He always told me it was you who was doing that. Literally."

The old man has his glass halfway to his mouth, but he stops and glances at Evan, a dark look under his lowering brow. Then he takes a sip, which becomes a slug, and downs the glass. "So you did talk about me? Thought as much. Knew you were lying. But that—what you just said. Now there—that's exactly the kind of thing I was after. What he told you about me. He thought I was the enemy, didn't he? He thought America was the enemy."

"What does it matter?"

"It matters one helluva lot to me, soldier," he says, pounding himself in the chest with his fist. "I spent a lifetime defending my country—and yours, too, for that matter."

"Whatever. Dad looked at it differently. But listen, he's dead, okay. In case you hadn't noticed. And all that political stuff . . . that was, like, a long time ago. By the time I was born, Dad was this civil servant working nine to five for the local government."

"Okay, okay." Griff wipes his lips and leans forward, pulling at the knees of his chinos so as not to spoil the knife-blade creases. "We've gotten off track here. Ancient history. What I want to know is what he told you recently."

Evan suppresses a shiver. He leans slowly back on the couch, covers his chest with his arms. "I'm kind of tired," he says.

"Oh, well, pardon me for asking."

Evan gets to his feet. "No, really. It's been a long day." Griff sneers. "I'll see you in the morning," says Evan.

"And away he goes," says Griff, his palm zooming off the

runway of his knee and into the air like a wobbly plane taking off. Evan hadn't noticed that before, the way Griff's left hand wobbles.

Evan stops. There is no more strategy left in him. "You and my dad didn't get along. I get it. It's got nothing to do with me, okay?"

"Well, it should."

"Why?"

"Because you were a subject we had words about, your daddy and me." Evan makes a face. "I tell you true. He wouldn't let me near you, son."

Evan stares at the old man. "What's that supposed to mean?"

"Exactly what I said. I tried to see you any number of times."

"Oh, really?" says Evan, but it's the kind of "really" you say when some kid at school tells you they drank a two-four and washed it down with a thirty-ouncer of Grey Goose.

"It's the Lord's truth."

"That's sure not how Dad remembered it."

"I can just bet it isn't. But the truth . . . well, that's another matter."

"Is that right?"

"Damn straight. It's bigger than the stories people tell themselves. Bigger than the lies they live with. So out with it: What'd your daddy have to say?"

Evan can't stop himself. "When he wrote to tell you I'd been born, you didn't even reply."

"There you go," says Griff. "Ancient history again. But a perfect example of what I was saying there about the truth. Perfect!" His eyes are all sparkly again. "Maybe he didn't tell you what exactly was in that letter of his, announcing your joyous arrival into this harsh and inhospitable world. Yeah, there was a letter and, yeah, there was a picture of this ugly little critter with a knitted hat on his bald head."

"Jesus!"

"Oh, don't get your shorts in a knot; every newborn is plumb ugly — something only a parent could love. That's not the point. There was the picture and the 'good news' that he wanted you to have the family name. Clifford Evan Griffin IV. Why it might almost have been a letter of reconciliation, except for the part in the letter . . . Let me see if I can recall the exact words." Griff rests his head on the back of the chair. He raises one finger. "Yeah, I got it. Your daddy wrote, and I quote: 'My fondest hope is that this beautiful boy will grow up without the tyranny that shadowed my childhood, knowing he is free to have his own thoughts and follow his own dreams.' End quote."

Evan stares at the man with the smug grin on his fleshless lips. In this light he might be a *jikininki*. "There's only one thing I can tell you for sure that you and my father had in common," says Evan. "This big, fat, ugly hatefest."

"Ooh, I am feeling the disgust."

"Can't you just let this go?" says Evan. "The war is over. You won. My father is not only out for the count — he's dead. Isn't that enough for you?"

For just an instant Evan almost thinks he sees a flicker of something in Griff's eyes. Something like confusion — like maybe nobody told him the war was over.

Or is it something like grief?

Not likely. Evan shakes his head wearily and starts to leave.

And the old man grabs him.

Grabs him by the wrist. So fast, Evan doesn't see it coming. So tight, Evan actually yelps.

"Tell me," says Griff, his voice low, his eyes sharp as lasers.

"Let go of my fucking arm!"

"Sit!" Griff says.

"I'm not a dog!" says Evan. Then he whips his arm free, steps back, trips on the corner of the coffee table, and almost falls. Collects himself and rubs his wrist with his hand.

"Tell me what you know."

Evan sees it. Sees the difference. He's not fishing for what Clifford might have said to him. He's asking straight out. Well, fuck him.

"You're crazy," he says, his voice on the brink of tears. "That really hurt."

"Sorry."

"Yeah, sure you are! You want to know what Dad said about you? That you're a bully."

"Nothing new in that."

"Then why'd you ask?"

Griff leans back. His left arm falls into his lap, covered over by his right, but not before Evan notices how badly it's shaking. The hard hand that grabbed him, shaking.

"Because you're hiding something from me," says Griff. "Hiding something important."

Evan looks down, afraid to give anything away. Really afraid now. "I'm going to bed," he says, his words not much more than a hoarse whisper. He makes a wide circle around his grandfather, his arms held high so he won't get grabbed again.

"And there he goes, folks. Truly, his father's son. No *cojones*."

"Fuck off."

"Yes sir, when it comes to fight or flight, Clifford could always be depended upon to choose the latter."

Evan stops. Stares up at the ceiling. "I'll tell you something Dad said. He said he had fought all the battles he ever wanted to in this world just living under your roof for seventeen years."

"Is that so?"

"Yeah, that's so." Evan turns. "We never fought, Dad and I. You probably can't believe that, but we never, ever once fought."

Griff turns to look at Evan, the smirk gone from his face. "There are things you can't run away from, kiddo. There are things a man just has to do." Evan shakes his head and leaves. "You hear me?" Griff raises his voice. "Things you can't begin to understand," he says, and that soft-edged, hard-hearted voice follows Evan all the way up the stairs, along the hall to his room.

"You wanna know who made it possible for y'all to live in such blissful peace? It was soldiers like me. That's who."

Evan's at his room now. He stops, not because there's anything in the old man's words but because he wants him to go too far. Say something that would justify caving his cankerous old face in with some blunt object.

And as if he knows that Evan is listening, Griff drops his voice. Not so low you wouldn't hear it, but low enough that you have to listen.

"You might *think* you know what happened, but you don't know it all, soldier."

Evan enters his room and slams the door ineffectually. Wall-to-wall carpeting doesn't allow for worthwhile displays of temper.

He stands there a moment, breathing hard, trying to calm himself down. He thinks about blocking the door with his chest of drawers. Thinks about leaving altogether—heading over to Rollo's. No. There is no way he is going to give up this place— this "hostile island"—to the old man. He climbs into bed. Switches off the light.

You might think you know what happened, but you don't know it all.

What do I know? Evan thinks. *Not enough.* He switches the light back on. Finds the book where it has fallen on the floor. It opens right where he left off. He looks up at his door again, too edgy to read. He puts aside the book and slips out of bed. At his desk he looks for something, a weapon. This is not a house of weapons, but there must be something. Yes! On the bookshelf beside the desk is something his father brought home from a government business trip to Ponds Inlet in Nunavut.

A walrus penis bone.

It's the length of a small baseball bat and about as heavy as one, too. A weapon: something to keep nearby, just in case. He holds it down at his side and turns to face the door and the mirror there looking back at him. He wills the door to open. "Go ahead," he says to the darkness. "Make my day."

— VIII —

DERWOOD

Taken Prisoner

It was so long ago, and yet reading Isamu's story, I am drawn back down into it, a nightmare so vivid it defies explanation. Delusion? Perhaps. But there is a riddle here: what is a delusion shared by two people? The answer: reality.

I felt the weight of the creature plow me into the soft sand: felt the dampness of its rough hide, the rocklike firmness of muscle sliding under its pelt. I gagged on the swampy odor of the thing. Then came the report of a rifle. The great creature rolled over me, raking my cheek with the claws of its forepaw. I wanted to howl at the pain of it, but the wind had been knocked out of me from the impact. My hand flew to my face, felt the warm blood seeping out through the bristles of my beard. I looked up. The box kite was swirling away into the blue, the aerial snapped and snapping like a manta ray's tail in the wind as it blew away.

Another shot rang out and the mottled creature recoiled, its massive shoulder bleeding out something black and as viscous as tar. Its body was taut, back on its haunches but rearing, slashing out.

Again the gunman fired and I watched the cheekbone of the creature shatter, but still the thing would not leave. It screamed, opening its wicked beak. Yes, beak—for the face that glared at me from between its hunched shoulders was birdlike: a mammoth quadruped with the beak and fiery eyes of a raptor! I fell back, throwing my arm out toward my pack, scrabbling to pull my service revolver from its holster. But then the gunman was stepping over me where I lay, shouting and firing the semiautomatic at the creature, shot after shot, missing most of the time, the sand exploding like tiny mines going off. But the shots that landed finally drove the creature back, until it took a shot to the eye and reeled, falling on its shoulder, before recovering and bounding off twenty feet or so.

The soldier followed it, screaming some more, his back to me, his entire attention on the monstrous animal, which squealed and squawked, shrill as the grinding of some infernal train wheels breaking on a track. The man fired again and again, and at last the thing took off down the beach, shaking its head as if trying to throw off the dreadful wounds it had taken. It hobbled, then regained its loping gait and at surprising speed took toward the rocks while the gunman aimed and fired again.

A steely rationality grabbed hold of me. The man's back was to me, not fifteen feet away. I could shoot him with a very good chance of a direct hit and time to fire again if the first shot didn't kill him. Any second now this man—my champion!—was going to turn around and see the gun in my hand, at which point the odds in my favor would be drastically reduced.

Were we enemies or allies? In a split second I had to decide.

At the sound of the revolver sliding into the holster, the gunman whirled around, his rifle at the ready. He was breathing hard and his face was filled with the same repugnance and fear as I'm sure my own was. My right hand was already thrust into the air, empty, the fingers splayed. The holstered gun hung from the stub of my left arm. I cringed behind this offering, turning my head. Not wanting to see when he fired.

It was a horrible risk to take. When no shot came, I dared to glance at him. This soldier who had saved my life had been firing in frenzy at the monster. His eyes still looked possessed, his chest heaved with the exertion; the adrenaline would be coursing through his bloodstream as mine was. He could have easily fired at me without thinking, and who would have blamed him. But he did not.

Mercifully, he did not.

My arm shaking, I pushed forward my left arm, to make certain the gunman recognized my intent. *Take the damn gun!* Did he understand? Yes. With his rifle held at his side, he cautiously approached me and slipped the belt and holster off my arm. With the holster clenched in his fist, he scrabbled back a few yards, but he had spied the knapsack lying on the sand behind me. He gestured to it, yelled something in Japanese. I turned and carefully took the pack by the strap and pulled it toward me.

The man barked another command. I dropped the strap. I could only guess what he must be saying. *Be very careful!* With two fingers, I gingerly gathered up the strap of the pack and held it out for the man's inspection. He shook his head. With his chin he gestured for me to open it and show him the contents. I flipped back the flap and held the maw open for him to see. The man nodded. *Go on,* he seemed to say. And so, with the sack lying on the beach, I produced, item by item, what was in the bag: fresh bandages, a tube of ointment, a water canteen.

I held up the canteen. "Water," I said. "Water."

The ragged soldier nodded. He threw the belt and holster behind him, well out of my reach, shoved my handgun into his waistband, and then wiped the wild hair out of his face. He looked back down the beach to where the creature had run and was no longer in sight, then quickly returned his gaze to me. He patted the canteen hanging on his own belt.

"*Mizu,*" he said.

"*Mizu,*" I said. We both nodded.

So. We had something in common.

Each of us took the top off our canteens — I used my teeth — and took a long restorative swallow. Then I remembered something. I placed the canteen on the beach, hollowing out a hole for it to sit upright in. The soldier had slung his rifle over his shoulder and was taking another long drink, with one eye on me. I pointed questioningly again at my knapsack, and the man nodded at me. *Go ahead.*

From a front pocket, I slowly drew out a chocolate bar. The man's eyes opened wide.

"Chocolate," I said.

"Choco . . ." said the man.

"Choc-o-late, yes?"

"Cho-co-latu," said the soldier. He might not have had a word for it, but from the look on his face, he knew what it was.

I handed him half the bar. And while we ate, both of us scanned the cliff for signs of the creature, not quite believing it was gone, and, in my case, not quite believing it had ever been there. A terrible hallucination — a new layer of Hell.

But I was beginning to expect the unexpected. Like myself, this soldier had a little troop of child ghosts, buffeted by the onshore breeze. I had reached the point of not really noticing my own followers, the way you don't notice blackflies in Vermont in May. They're just there. Then there were the other critters with the red eyes, although none were around just now. And finally, this . . . this *thing* with hair as oily and matted and as odiferous as a beaver, but *twice* the size of one of my dad's prized hogs and

154

with a raptor's beak and claws. Scarcely believable. More like the imaginings of a sick mind. Yet the claw marks on my face were real enough. Tentatively I touched my cheek. The slashing claws had not cut too deep. The bleeding seemed to have stopped.

"*Daijoubuka?*"

I could interpret the look on Isamu's face, curiosity, cautious concern.

"It's stopped bleeding," I said, holding up my fingers to show him. Then he looked down at the Gibson Girl strapped to my thighs. I pointed at it, indicating I wanted to get out of it, and said as much, for what good it was worth.

Again my captor nodded. As quickly as I could with jittery fingers, I loosened the straps. The machine had dug into my ribs when the creature fell upon me. There would be bruises, but as far as I could tell nothing cracked.

I climbed shakily to my feet. When I was standing, I touched my index finger to my breastbone. "Derwood Kraft," I said, bowing slightly.

"Isamu Ōshiro," said the man, bowing back.

I held up my dog tag for him to see. He nodded. I placed my hand on my heart and bowed again. "Thank you, Isamu Ōshiro," I said. "You saved my life."

There was nothing to suggest in his face recognition of anything I had said other than his name, but I hoped he had gotten the gist of it. And then I remembered that I did know one word in Japanese.

"*Konnichiwa,*" I said.

"*Konnichiwa,*" said Isamu. And then he said something else, excitedly, to which I could only shrug, not having understood a word. His moment of elation passed.

And now what?

Isamu must have been thinking the same thing. He looked up

toward the cliffs again, then back at me. He scratched his scalp with his free hand. Then he waggled his rifle at me, and I understood well enough what the drill was: I was his prisoner and it was time to go. Where, I had no idea, but I was not the one calling the shots. I gave myself over into his hands. Something told me that this act was the lesser of two evils. No, it was more than that: it was the right thing to do. A man saves your life and you give yourself to him.

I closed the knapsack and threw the strap over my shoulder. Then I disengaged the crank from the top of the Gibson Girl, clipped it in its slot, and hoisted the now-useless machine. Why? The light on the top had come on only intermittently while I was working it. Had I gotten through to anyone? Only time would tell.

"*Oite ikinasai!*"

Again, a gesture made the meaning clear. I lowered the machine to the sand. Then I looked back at the sea and, turning again to him, I asked with a lot of gestures if I could put the machine under the overhang and on a shelf of stone above the waterline. For the tide was coming in.

— IX —

ISAMU

The Emperor of the Island

I listen to the creature howling to the night—in its death throes, by the sound of it. I hope it is true, but it gives me little comfort and I cannot sleep. I try to concentrate on the proper sounds of night, the breeze, the crickets. But it is as if the crickets are inside me, Hisako; crickets in my liver, my bones, my lungs. I am so angry—angry and frightened. And it is all Derwood Kraft's fault. Of that I am sure. There was no monster on the island until he came. It must be some kind of witchcraft that this man has brought with him—some *gaijin* necromancy. I try to shake the idea from my head, try to settle down, and then the monstrous creature howls.

Tengu. I have heard of the monster in the old stories but never seen one. The island provides . . .

While Derwood Kraft snores.

I have rigged up a hammock for him that is also a cage. I wrapped the fisherman's netting twice around the man after he was settled and then tied it where he could not reach the knots, on his left side, where he has no hand. Very ingenious, yes? The American did not struggle. He almost seemed to welcome it, like

I was knitting him into a womb. And sure enough, *he* sleeps like a baby!

Meanwhile his little tribe of ghost children gathers around him, like a mist with many eyes. Sometimes I see my own ghosts turn to look at his ghosts, examine their features. Though they do not venture near, they are like real children in this way, shameless in their curiosity, their eyes filled with wonder at the strangeness of these foreign faces.

What is the man up to?

I feel as if I have made a terrible mistake. Had I left the monster to kill Derwood, it would have saved me the trouble. Because that is what the man is, Hisako, trouble. What do I need with a prisoner? The island provides everything I could want for, and now this . . . this pestilence has arrived, and I, Isamu, have brought it into my house! The very house I tried so diligently to hide from his view! I must be the fool my father took me to be!

Mind you, if I kill Derwood Kraft, I would still have the creature to contend with. I wonder about that. Could it be that without its master, the monster would perish? If I were to slash Derwood's throat, would the howling stop? I can tell you, I do not feel comfortable at all with such ideas. I have killed men in the war but never hand to hand. I look over at him, my "catch" in his snug net. Would he be any help in defeating *Tengu*?

At least we are somewhat prepared. On the way back from the strand at the tail of the island, we stopped off at the plane and loaded up with ammo and another rifle. I don't suppose the American could fire one. I trusted him to carry one, although I carried all the ammunition.

Another howl pierces the night.

That is not a thing dying. It is a thing wanting us to know it is there and we will never be free of it; a thing that will keep us in its sights even if only with one good eye. A thing that will somehow recover—pluck the bullets out of its grotesque hide with its beak!

And then what?

The wind picks up. I cannot sleep at all, Hisako. And so I write by the light of one slim candle. The canvas I have rolled down against the cold slaps against the bamboo posts. It is a north-northwest wind. A cyclone wind. How quickly paradise has been thrown over. I am so full of loathing for this uninvited guest, it is like the flu coming on, making me hot and weak and jittery.

I tried to lie down again, just now, but couldn't sleep. I wrapped my jacket—another jacket from another dead soldier— around my shoulders and tried to make myself comfortable: as comfortable as a man can get with a handgun and a loaded rifle in bed with him. My cheek lay against the mesh. I was miserable. Oh, how I miss you, dear Hisako. I feel lonelier than I have felt in the whole time I have been here. What sense does this make?

I pick up my pen again, quiet my raging thoughts. Derwood Kraft could have shot me. I need to remember that. Was it only that he lacked the courage? No, it took great courage for the man to sheath his revolver and hand it to me. For when I think back on that terrifying ordeal, I recall seeing the man draw his weapon. He might even have shot at the beast, although I can-not be sure of that for so much was going on! But this I know: Derwood did have a gun and he did have my back as a target. Either he could not or would not bring himself to do it—to kill a man. He is a navigator, after all, not accustomed to combat. Is that it? I don't think so, for did I not also hesitate when I saw the *gaijin* for the first time? How long did it take me to reach the beach? Many minutes. I'd had a good shot for much of the time, but I did not take it. We are at war! My superior officers drummed that into me. But is there to be war on Kokoro-Jima as well? And if this *isn't* war, then to kill a man would be murder. Ha! Such distinctions. Thousands upon thousands of soldiers have died already. It is kill or die — kill *and* die. What makes it different now?

You see how I have changed, Hisako-chan? All this writing in the flight book has made me a great and mighty thinker. I shall no doubt write profound things with my pen stolen from a dead pilot. Ha! My lofty ideas. *Sleep, Isamu,* I tell myself.

And the beast roars back, *If you dare!*

It is late the next day, and what a day it has been. I awoke to sunlight. The flaps were rolled up.

What!

I sat up, turned. The other hammock was empty!

"Tea, Isamu?" said Derwood Kraft. He had found the stash of black tea, started a fire, boiled water . . . The American smiled as if sharing a grim joke with me, his captor: *I could have slit your throat,* his eyes said, *but chose not to.*

And so we have come to know each other. I drew a long thin heart shape on the sand with a stick. Then I pointed at the island all around and said, "Kokoro-Jima." Derwood repeated the words after me. I pointed at the sand and said, *"Suna."* Then I picked up a handful and let it fall between my fingers. *"Suna,"* said Derwood, at which point I strode across the sand and said, *"Watashi wa suna no ue wo aruite iru."*

Derwood tries to teach me English words, but I refuse. Am I not the captor? The official language of the island will be Japanese, as befits its master. Derwood calls me "Mikado" and bows to me. Where he found such an archaic word, I cannot say, but he is right: I am the Emperor! I tap myself on the chest and teach him the proper word, *"Ten'nō"*—Emperor, the Emperor of Kokoro-Jima.

But there is work to do. The pilot and copilot must be sent on their way, I declared, because I am not only Emperor but also chief mortician of Kokoro-Jima. I explained to him that we must deal with them before the *jikininki* did, if they hadn't already. But not by fire, it seemed. Once we arrived at the plane, Derwood explained, as best as he could, about burial in his country. I bowed to his wishes. But it was the Emperor who had to do the digging! Then Derwood, with his eyes closed and his head bent, said some words of prayer. I bowed my head as well, but I kept one eye peeled. Not just for any trickery from my prisoner, but for *Tengu*.

More important is the fortification of the hilltop house. Knowing what we were up against, I felt that a palisade of sharpened bamboo poles would be the best thing, and so, between us, we have cut and sharpened many, many stout poles, which we have lashed tightly together with wire and rope and Manila twine—whatever we could lay our hands on. The bamboo points outward at a sixty-degree angle on the three sides of the enclosure that are open to attack. The angle was Derwood's idea. He drew pictures in the dirt with a stick to show me his design. Although he is no older than I am, as far as I can tell, he seems a man of learning, and I listen to him when his ideas seem to make sense. Luckily, he has some ability with pictures.

The fourth side of the enclosure, the steep rock face, I feel sure the creature cannot climb, but we have strung noisy metal things along the length of it just in case. These "wind chimes" rattle discordantly in the night with every breeze. They were *my* idea, and Derwood grumbled at the rattling and jingling, but it was my belief that were the creature to try to climb up that way, the chimes would make a more significantly alarming sound.

161

At night the creature howls.

It is moving, first here and then there, although never too close, wary of these two-legged animals that resist it with noisy fire. Is it my imagination or is its voice growing stronger?

We work hard, work together. Derwood cannot do some things, but he is learning how to do a lot, and he never shirks from a task or knocks off early. He is not strong, but he is willing.

He sings as he works sometimes. One day I had to drop what I was doing and dance a jig that seemed to fit the crazy sound of the words he was singing — although everything he says sounds crazy to me, anyway. We both laughed. And so the Emperor learns his first English, though I have no idea what it might mean:

Skidimarink a-dink a-dink,
Skidimarink a-doo,
I love you.

There has been no mention of the strange yellow contraption. I have seen Derwood looking at some lightweight wire in the impressive collection of supplies that I have carted up from the beach. The thin cord that attached his box kite to the yellow machine was no ordinary twine but shone like wire. If that is what Derwood is thinking about, he makes no attempt to retrieve the thing, even though it is pretty clear that his "prison" is unbounded, except by the ocean. The ocean and *Tengu*. He can come and go from the compound as he pleases. Well, that was obvious from the first morning when he freed himself. But still he seldom wanders away. Maybe for an hour or so and then I fret until he returns.

"If you are killed by *Tengu*, then I will have to bury you and that is a lot of work. Maybe I will just burn you," I threatened one day when he had been gone for a long time. Derwood laughed—laughed at me. He did not know what I was saying, but I was very animated in acting out what would happen to him. Ah, I can see you smiling, Hisako. What, me animated?

I suppose that he is too frightened to face *Tengu* alone and will not go too far or take unnecessary chances. He wears his handgun on his hip like the cowboys in American movies, but surely a pistol would be inadequate to stop the beast. So he stays near and the yellow contraption has made no appearance. "Gib-san-gurlu." That is what he calls it. If it were meant to be some kind of distress beacon, it has not worked; weeks have passed and no one has come, no one alive. Now and then a body washes up on the beach to be cremated or buried. Ah, Hisako, how I mourn with each new corpse. Surely, the Afterlife is not big enough for all the people who are dying.

I do not show him my watchtower. I do not want him to know of it, and, thankfully, the coral tree is so thick with leaves that one cannot see the little platform sixty feet up. I have a good reason for keeping this secret. I do not want the American to know that Tinian is so close—that American forces are so close. I doubt Derwood could climb, anyway, with only one hand.

— X —

DERWOOD

Cyclone

I found Isamu's "watchtower" within the first three days. I called it the crow's nest. I had grown up in Vermont and had been lord of many tree forts. And I had been drawn to the tree for the very same reason Isamu had been; it was the tallest thing on the highest point of the island. When I circled it to see where best to get a grip, I found that the thorns had been cleared away in one particular place and smiled to myself.

The Mikado keeps his secrets, I thought. That is what I called him to myself. In his presence I called him by his name unless he was acting in a high-and-mighty way, and then I would bow deeply and call him *Ten'nō* Ōshiro, which I guessed was the proper word for emperor. Anyway, I could keep a secret just as well as the next guy. And so, laboriously, I made my way up the tree, a Green Mountain boy again. After all, I was only reduced by the loss of one hand, and the lad in me could still get a grip on a good solid branch. My body — and there wasn't much weight to it — knew how to fling its weight around to find the right balance for scaling things. I got a fair number of scratches, but it was worth it.

The headland was relatively clear of tall trees, and you could see for quite a way, so there was no fear of being surprised by the beast. That was the first thing I looked for when I got up there. The next time I came, I brought Isamu's binoculars with me. It did not require much in the way of deception. Isamu would go off to fish from his raft on the coral reef. That's what he said he was doing, at least, but more than once when I was up the tree with the binoculars, I saw him swimming out in the lagoon. The first time he was lying on the water, his arms spread like some naked Jesus on a transparent blue cross, casting a shadow on the sand below him. Moving the binoculars closer to shore, I saw his ghosts huddled at the edge of the water waiting for him to return. Such a strange phenomenon. My own attendant ghosts waited for me at the bottom of the tree. Though they were childlike, they obviously did not have a child's gift for either swimming or climbing.

Other times I would see Isamu sitting in the center of his raft, cross-legged, writing in a book. I never saw the book at the compound. It was something else the Mikado kept under his hat — or under his shirt.

The binoculars were good, M 36 × 30 field glasses. And what a surprise, when I held them to my eyes and looked eastward, focusing in on the green blur in the distance: Tinian. I had landed there more than once since the invasion and recognized it right away. But that is not entirely the truth. The runway construction that had been under way when I last touched down there was far advanced by now. Tinian had always been a strategic target because it was within bomber range of Japan. That was what the Army Air Force was all about in the Pacific, strategic bombardment of the Japanese home islands.

Those were my people over there!

I wanted to yell and wave my hands. Not a particularly

rational thought. In any case, the island did seem close enough that I could take the fishing raft and be there in a few hours. If I'd had two good hands to row with. The elation of seeing the island withered away as I remembered my predicament. You might ask how could I have forgotten it even for a moment! I suppose there was a store of optimism in me somewhere just waiting for a chance to jump up and shout hooray. They don't hand out optimism as part of your kit when you're a flyboy in a war. You've either got it or you don't. I looked at my incomplete limb lying in my lap. It still ached a fair bit, though not all the time. But my native optimism refused to take a hike, just yet. The island was close enough to sail to, I thought. I'd have to rig something up on my own, obviously, and in secret. It was then, as I tried to wrap my head around all of that, that I came to my senses.

Getting there was a hopeless proposition, for now. But I did have the Gibson Girl. The island was well within the radius that she was capable of, if I could get her operable. That, I supposed, was not going to happen under Isamu's nose, and I had to admit there was no way I could imagine returning to the southern beach to reclaim the beacon just yet. To be perfectly frank, the idea scared me to death, what with that monstrous angry thing out there. Nor did I want to fluster or otherwise agitate my host. Every now and then, the Mikado would strut around exerting his command, insisting that I was his prisoner, but he was incredibly industrious and good company, quick to laugh at some amusement and with a beguiling smile.

Skidimarink a-dink a-dink.

Isamu loved the song and sang it with me. He also enjoyed watching me trying to do anything one-handed. It made him laugh and slap his thighs. Derwood Kraft, vaudeville clown. I have to admit, I hammed it up a bit sometimes, just to watch him laugh at me. He might be the enemy, but he had saved my life and not just that terrible day of the attack. I shuddered to think how I would have survived here without his knowledge of the local flora and fauna. We had shelter. We ate well. And we had ourselves a little castle. Fort Ōshiro! We had a lagoon to swim in at the end of the day, although always with the raft nearby and a rifle aboard it. Who knew if *Tengu* could swim! I knew it was Flight Lieutenant Derwood Kraft's duty as American Army Air Force personnel to get myself back into action. I suffered some misgivings about shirking this responsibility—let alone fraternizing with the enemy. But I will admit freely here, so many years later, it was Derwood Kraft, the man, who knew that I would make no attempt to return to action if by doing so it would risk Isamu's security here. He was, after all, my unlikely savior, this emperor of the heart-shaped island.

I was in the crow's nest when the storm came. I picked out the greeny-gold light across the sound, watched as darkness subsumed the southern reaches of Tinian, watched the sea surge, whipped by winds I could not feel—not yet—but that were coming our way. A cyclone. A typhoon: a warm-core storm system, nothing like the nor'easters I was used to back home, blowing in off the Atlantic seaboard. A typhoon in these seas could be two or three times that size. The cyclones in the Mariana Islands were among the biggest in the world. It was something I'd learned about flying these waters. And one was coming our way.

We had to take shelter. Fort Ōshiro might be perfect as a position of strength, but it was completely exposed to the weather. With a typhoon there might be winds of ninety knots or more. I'd seen it over the Philippines from the cockpit of a plane. Even a modest cyclone might have a radius of two hundred miles.

I hurried back down the tree, fell the last ten feet, tearing my

167

arm on the tiger's claw thorns. One of my waiting entourage of ghost children reached out to the cut as if to stop it, his young hand poised over my arm. He smiled but, seeing my expression, grew wide-eyed, frightened.

"I don't know how the wind affects you folks," I said, "but we're going to skedaddle." I didn't stop to see his response. They seemed to show emotions, but it was difficult to tell if they understood anything. I raced back to the fort, calling Isamu's name as I ran, praying he was not down on the lagoon or, even worse, out beyond the coral reef. From the calm stillness of the north end, he would have no idea of what was coming our way, sneaking up from behind.

"Storm!" I yelled. Isamu didn't know the word, but I was swinging my arms around over my head like a crazy helicopter and my eyes must have told the rest. I held up the binoculars, pointing southeast; that was all Isamu needed to know. He snatched the field glasses from me and raced away from the compound, his anxious ghosts in swift pursuit.

"Where the hell are you going?" I shouted after him, but Isamu didn't stop. I guessed he was going to look for himself. Well, I wasn't hanging around to wait for him. I shoved some food and water into a backpack, tried to think if there was anything we could do to storm-proof the camp, but gave up in despair. Luckily, Isamu was back quickly, and he joined me, grabbing some supplies and of course a rifle and ammo.

"My cave," I said, pointing toward the south end of the island. The typhoon was coming from the southeast, so it seemed insane to be running toward it, but with any luck the cave in which I had holed up would be in the lee of the storm, with the spine of the island, a towering limestone wall, at our back. I didn't need to explain it to Isamu, and we took off. The rains came before we were halfway there. Driving rains and winds bending the palm trees on the high hills so that they looked like the flowing mane of a racehorse. We descended into the jungle and had some protection from the worst of it. But when we climbed up the cliff to cross the ridge, we were buffeted something fierce—almost knocked off our feet.

I remember looking southeast as we climbed, shielding my eyes from the needles of rain. The real storm had not made landfall yet; this was just the warm-up act. We scrabbled up the path, slipping on the wet rocks, one arm up protecting our faces, while grabbing at handholds on the limestone wall. It was a time to wish dearly for two hands. But whenever I faltered, Isamu was at my back, pushing me forward, grabbing the back of my shirt with his fist to hold me up. Then finally we reached the top of the southern rise—completely exposed to the storm. Isamu lost his balance, punched by a sudden draft, and I grabbed him with my one good arm just before he fell. Then we dropped six feet—threw ourselves down onto the western side, where the wall of stone protected us from the wind. By then the rain was torrential.

The cave was spacious enough and dry. I had not returned to it since my capture, but something had been in there, foraging for food; the floor was a mess of crumbs and cans flung about, not to mention animal scat. I had built a great pile of leaves and grasses in a corner and thrown a tarp over it as a bed—a nest, more like—not a very comfortable one. I fell onto it when we arrived, soaking wet and exhausted. Isamu sat cross-legged by the cave's mouth, staring out at the ocean pounding the rocks forty feet below. He sat, backlit by the shimmering, almost supernatural light. The sky to the northwest was clear, and yet behind us the island was being pummeled. Then I drifted off to sleep to the sound of the sky turning itself inside out.

* * *

169

It was light when I awoke. Isamu was leaning against the wall by the opening. Behind him the foliage dripped, but the sky was blue beyond that. He was looking at something. It took a moment for me to realize what it was. My sketch pads.

"You?" said Isamu, pointing at the pad when I joined him.

"Me," I said, nodding. I sat down on the wet lip of the cave, my legs dangling. The sea had settled, sloshing in the pockets of seaweed-covered rocks below. Seagulls circled, full of babble about the storm, I guess, and scanning the roiling sea for anything tasty it might have churned up.

Isamu held up a page to show me, pencil drawings of planes: a Gooney Bird on the tarmac. He turned the page to a B-29 Superfortress from a low angle, so that the mighty bomber loomed above its charcoal shadow. I flipped the page to reveal a Sikorsky R-4B "hoverfly" helicopter, as well as various attempts at drawing a pilot friend. I never got very good at people.

"Good," said Isamu, using the English word. Despite his reticence to learn the language of his prisoner, he showed great aptitude at language acquisition.

"Good," I said, laughing at my own expense. "Yeah, sure."

"Yeah, sure," echoed Isamu, and laughed too. He flipped another page. I pulled the sketchbook around so I could see it: a pencil sketch of the Gibson Girl in detail. Isamu cast me a look of unease, suspicion. He closed the book and handed it to me. I flipped through the densely covered first few pages, glad to have it back.

"Time to go," said Isamu, hopping to his feet with an agility that made me feel old by comparison. I gathered together some things I'd been wanting: the pack with my few art supplies, various drawing implements, a small watercolor kit, another sketch pad, filled, and a brand-new one. There wasn't much else.

Time to go.

When we got back, the fort was gone.

Chapter Fourteen

Evan drifts off, drifts away, circling, circling drunkenly—a cyclone in his head—whirling and snatching up bits of the days—words and objects alike—and hurling them about so that there are monsters and there are men and beaks and claws and hard words and grabbing arms and pages flying and ships in bottles on stormy seas and bits of phone calls and words funneling down the line . . .

He wakes up. Dizzy.

There is the beginning of something like light in the room. He turns toward his window. Not dawn but false dawn. He looks at his cell phone: 3:23. He rubs his eyes. Picks it up. A text message:

—Do orphans eat cheese?

What the . . .

It's not a number he knows. Orphans . . . cheese . . .

He falls back onto his pillow, too tired for riddles.

Start again. He looks again at the cell phone. Nothing from Leo. What had he been expecting? He thinks back to their conversation. There was something Leo said. Evan tries to piece it together again. A clue. He can feel the excitement of it—that was what woke him up. The feeling that he knew something he didn't think he knew. Something hidden somewhere, but somewhere he had access to.

E-mail.

Leo and Clifford had e-mailed.

He goes to roll out of bed and—

"Ouch!"

The walrus penis bone.

He pushes it onto the floor, where it thunks on the carpet. Gross! He actually slept beside that thing.

On wobbly legs he makes his way to the door. Opens it. Listens to the dark hallway. There is no light downstairs. He tiptoes to the Dockyard, the first door on the landing. He listens again. Nothing. He tries the door, pushes it open. *Shhh.*

The room is empty. He doesn't turn on the light. He goes to the desk and wakes up his father's ancient computer. The light from the screen blinds him. He types on the clunky keys in the dimness, goes to his father's e-mail account. There's no password. Too bad. He goes to his father's in-box. Types Leo's name into the search function. Double clicks. No items appear. So he tries the out-box. Nothing sent to Leo, either—nothing, anyway, that is still there. Finally, there is only the trash left to search. He doesn't expect much by now. And that's exactly what he gets.

172

He leans back in his father's chair. It squawks and he goes cold all over. He holds his breath. Nothing. The old man must be sleeping it off.

Whatever was in those e-mails, Griff didn't want him to see it.

— XI —

ISAMU
Tengu's *Return*

I pulled away the wreckage of broken bamboo and torn canvas and knelt before my little shrine of flat stones in the far corner of the compound. I have led Derwood to believe it is an altar, a holy place. He is a gentleman, and I know that he will keep his distance. But in truth, it really is a shrine, in a sense, for I kept my story hidden there. This story. I hoped the heavy rocks had been enough to protect what was inside. The rocks have fallen in on one side, but when I carefully lifted them off, there lay the flight manual wrapped in oilskin, dry and safe.

I turned as Derwood joined me and, seeing the concerned look in his eyes, I made an important decision. I unwrapped the book and showed it to him. I must admit I was slightly afraid he would think it inappropriate that I had taken the flight manual for my personal use. Might it be a sacrilege to use a dead man's property in such a way? I had no idea and I watched him closely for his reaction. I saw only avid curiosity.

I stood and took the book from him, pointing at the cover where I had written your name and address. I underlined the kanji characters with my finger, explaining who it was. Derwood nodded, though obviously none of the words made any sense to him. His vocabulary by now includes much of the natural world around us: the names of fruit and seafood. He knows a lot of the language of work and survival, but this does not extend to such abstract ideas as wife or love or devotion. I handed him the book and pulled my *omamori* from inside my shirt, where it always stays, and from it I took the picture of you.

"*Watashi no tsuma*," I said. "My wife."

Derwood looked at your picture and smiled. "Your girl?"

"Girl," I said. Is that what you are? So be it. And having some-one to finally talk to about you, I went on and on and tried to explain to Derwood that we had been married only a few weeks before I enlisted. Oh, I was hungry to talk about you, Hisako. And although I knew this American gentleman could not under-stand a word I was saying, he nodded his head appreciatively, smiling, I suppose, at my enthusiasm. There we stood in the ruins of my house — our house — our shattered stronghold, talk-ing about the only thing left to me, other than my own little life.

Derwood nodded. Then he pointed at the photo again.

"Your *wife*," he said.

"Wife." This was something different from "girl"? It didn't matter. "Wife," I said again.

"*Tsuma*," said Derwood. Language has to be like this, a nego-tiation with no text to turn to, no teacher. I glanced at him again, and the smile had slipped from his face. He was looking around at the mess left behind by the typhoon. The golden moment was over. I slipped your picture back into my *omamori* and the *omamori* back inside my shirt. I replaced the book in the oilskin and back into the altar and moved the stone into place. I held out my hands to indicate the devastation.

Derwood nodded, cheerlessly. "Come," he said. And we made our way through the mess to the table where we eat, the low table I built, low enough and heavy enough, made from rock, that it had been left in place but not untarnished by the events of the day. There was a hideous heap of stinking yellowish-brown excrement there.

It is clear that we have to rebuild. Quickly. We have survived the typhoon, but *Tengu* has left a reminder that he is still here and healthy again!

So, where is he? Why does he not take advantage of our lack of defenses? I have heard of such demons: harbingers of war. And is it not just like war that this creature wreaks havoc and then pulls away, so that you run the risk of going mad with waiting?

We work hard in the humid weather and then take turns standing guard by night. We built a fire and kept it going until daylight — certainly there is enough kindling around!

Among my finds have been several forty-two-gallon oil drums, although I've never found a use for them. They stood on the beach, too large to bring up to the fort. Derwood came up with the idea of wrapping long branches with cloth and drenching them with oil. There are six of these torches, standing sentinel around us, stuck into the ground, far enough away from the newly reconstructed fence not to be a hazard — not to us, at least. We have spent most of a day rolling two of the heavy drums uphill to the fort.

"Come, *Tengu*," I murmur to the night.

I dream of *Tengu*.

His hideous face becomes the very face of war. I dream of dipping one of those torches into the flames and jabbing it down the monster's horrible throat, or at least blinding him. After all, he only has one eye left after our first encounter. "Come," I whisper. And for a moment, I actually think I see the flames reflected in the eye of the creature.

But *Tengu* does not come, although the *jikininki* do. They hover well back from the flames, ghastly in the flickering light. They hiss and fart, as usual, but they also cackle in a way that sounds extraordinarily like laughter. One night when Derwood was asleep, I got up and walked toward the nearest and boldest of the creatures, holding one of the flaming torches in my hand. It was scared but did not withdraw, only cowered, raising its wretched arm up to cover its face.

"Go!" I said, poking the fire at it. It withdrew a few feet but kept turning toward the bamboo fence, as if waiting for something. I could guess well enough what. "You want *Tengu* to come, don't you?" I said. "There will be lots of leftovers for you and your kind."

"Yes," the creature hissed. "A feast of stories."

I looked closer. Was this the same character I had talked to so many weeks ago? It is impossible to tell with them, because one can barely look at their faces without revulsion. "You still say it is just stories you are after?"

"Yes. Stories. You cannot understand."

No, I do not understand, but I wanted to. Because as horrible as the countenance of this thing was, with its sunken glowing eyes and ravaged cheeks and yellow teeth, there was something that disturbed me about its manner, something that struck me as pathetic, whereas up until then I had only looked upon the *jikininki* as carrion eaters, scavengers.

I squatted and then sat cross-legged on the dirt, the burning torch beside me. "Tell me. Make me understand."

The *jikininki* looked through the slits in the bamboo, out to where the wind off the lagoon rustled the leaves of the forest. Then it turned its attention to me.

"You," it said. "You have your own ghosts. They hover near

you, protectively. They have no strength to help you but can only look on from their world of waiting. You see the hope in their faces? They are the ones waiting to be born."

"What do you mean?" I said, though I had come to this same conclusion.

"The children you will have and the children they will have." I turned to look at them, at my familiars, the ones who were always there. The torchlight seemed to glow inside them, but their features were lost to me. Then the nearest, a boy, reached out a hand to me, and some of the flame seemed to sit on his palm. He was seated like I was, and he reached out and, though I am ashamed to admit it, I did not reach back to him. It was all too strange.

"They were here waiting in this place for only you," said the *jikininki*. "And because you came ashore alive, they have found you and wait with you for deliverance."

I nodded. As I said, I had reached much the same conclusion and was only surprised to find confirmation in this mutilated creature. "Then, what are you?" I asked. "In the stories you are the restless dead. You were human once, yes?" The *jikininki* shook its head. "So you are unborn as well?"

This time it nodded. "Yes, but not like them." The creature stared at my ghosts. "You see, the fathers we might have had were washed up on this shore already dead. So we will never be. We have no one."

It was a startling idea to me. I tried to reconcile it. "But there, just now you said 'we.' There are many of you. You are a tribe, yes?"

"You are wrong. We are not a tribe. We are not 'we,' though I have used this word for lack of a better. We are one and one and one." The thing gestured behind me at my huddled ghost children. "They are what *will* be. The *jikininki* are what never can be."

It was such a strange idea, Hisako, illusive as fire, a bright thing flickering that I could not grasp. I heard a loud noise from beyond the walls of the fort—a rustling that was louder and clumsier than the wind! The zombie straightened, a hideous smile lighting up its face, then shuffled off, and right there, behind where it had been standing, *Tengu*'s eye appeared, staring through a crack in the bamboo wall. I jumped to my feet and grabbed the torch. The *jikininki* cackled at me, its teeth glowing in the light. I looked at *Tengu* again. The eye pressed up against the crack in the wall was the monster's right eye. The one I had obliterated with gunfire. It had grown back.

I am not sleeping well. Too often I am in a foul mood. We work together, but tempers flare from time to time. Derwood cannot work as hard as I do. He is weaker and crippled. We are both frightened and, I admit, I am irritated and prone to mistakes and injury. After four days of intense effort, the fort is now completely rebuilt, stronger than ever, but our nerves are badly frayed. And I can only think that the monster has been waiting for us to reach such a state. They say a crocodile kills its prey and then drags it down to the bottom of the river, where it traps it under debris to rot. Softening it up. This is what *Tengu* has been doing with us. Derwood Kraft and I are trapped at the bottom of a dark river of fear.

— XII —

DERWOOD

Opening the Gates to Hell

I wasn't sure what woke me. I gripped my service revolver and peered toward the bamboo wall. There was a tipped teacup of moon in the sky that did not spill enough light to make out anything. I listened, heard a rustling in the bushes that could have been an errant breeze. No. There it was again, and there was no wind to speak of that night.

Isamu spoke of how our nerves were frayed. It is true. I was a wreck. Had we been able to really communicate, I feel we might have been able to boost each other up. I had no idea of his conversation with the *jikininki*, although he might well have tried to tell me about it. It frustrated him to no end that I could not speak his language. I have never been particularly talkative, but he was a man, I think, who thrived on lively conversation. I could see the frustration growing in him. He was hungry to talk. I grew up in a family of sisters and quickly learned to keep my thoughts to myself. Whatever the reason, Isamu and I were at odds with each other. We were prisoners because of *Tengu*. But we had also made ourselves prisoners.

I lay the revolver down on my lap and rubbed the stump of my left arm. There were phantom pains there; fingers itching to act that were no longer there at all. Such treachery. The mind plays such tricks. None of this seemed real, and yet it was the realest thing I had ever experienced, a fear so visceral it made my insides churn.

Did we trust the fence? We had buried the stout bamboo stakes deep in the ground, reinforced them with heavy rocks, lashed the wood tightly together. The stakes angled out as they had before, the sharp points seven feet above the ground. Could the creature jump so high? I remembered its escape from us on the beach. Despite its many wounds, it was nimble on the rocks as it scaled the cliff. Perhaps we should build a trench on the other side of the wall? A moat? But I was not about to suggest any more digging to Isamu. That was part of the problem. Much more of the work fell to him. I tried my best. Even rigged up a wire contraption that fit over my stump and could grasp a shovel. But it was a poor substitute for a hand, and increasingly I felt myself to be a poor substitute for a man.

That night I heard the thing growl. How could a creature with a raptor's beak make such a sound? It was the low rumble of a big cat, deep-throated, utterly intimidating. I felt I should wake Isamu, but his sleeping was so haphazard, I was loath to disturb him. Meanwhile, I became increasingly nervous.

It was planning something.

I heard the sound again, a growl that ended in a kind of clicking noise. There was no denying how close it was. I swung up out of my hammock and in my bare feet made my way to where the torches stood in the ground. The fire was not lit, but there were matches nearby. Fumbling in the dark, I found the box, shook it, heard the comforting rattle, then heard the growl again, sounding so close I feared irrationally the creature had somehow entered the compound. I lit a match, yet another one-handed trick I'd mastered, and with a trembling hand raised it to the dark, turning slowly around in a full circle before lighting one of the torches just as the match was at its end.

The torch swooshed into flame. Gripping it tightly, I approached the barricade. In order to hold the torch, I had stuck my gun in the waist of my pants. If the damn creature broke through the wall, I could only hope to hold it at bay with the torch. I thought I should wake Isamu, but by then I was afraid to say anything out loud—wasn't sure I could. My throat was bone dry. Were I to try to speak, I imagined only a peep would come out.

For God's sake, wake up, Emperor!

By now I was at the wall. I tried to peer through the cracks as I slowly walked the perimeter, holding the torch as near as I could without burning the barricade down.

Then I saw it and stopped dead in my tracks: an eye, gleaming with firelight. A hawk's exophthalmic eye staring directly at me, pressed up against the bamboo. I jumped back, waved the fire in front of it to scare the thing off. It didn't flinch. Instead, I heard the three-inch-thick bamboo squeak and watched the thick twine tauten. *Tengu* had pressed a bulky shoulder against the barricade. Hypnotized, I leaned toward the crack only to see the dark, mottled body slide along the fence toward the gateway. The sturdy door, reinforced by thick planks at the top and bottom, was hinged with wire wrapped round and round many times. I followed the creature, not two feet away, with only the fence between us. I could smell the fetid odor that rose from its flanks. I wondered if it was one of those creatures that likes to roll in its own feces. It smelled as if it did.

Again it leaned its muscled haunch against the fort, but this time against the door, testing it! Then it raised its beak and began to tear at the Manila twine, shredding it. There was wire as well and nailed boards, but the astuteness of the creature made my blood run cold.

"What are you?" I said, my voice cracked and desperately small.

Tengu eyed me, and then its beak opened wide and a screech came from it as loud as the squeal of a jet engine. It was so sudden — so powerful — I fell backward on my backside, dropping the torch. Just as a shot rang out.

Isamu had jumped from his hammock and fired into the air. He joined me at the fence, where I was groping for the handle of the torch lest it roll into the wall.

"*Tengu?*" he asked.

I nodded. But when we looked again, each of us at the crack in the wall, there was nothing to see but the vague form of the underbrush across the clearing and the moonlit shimmer of hungry ghouls, hovering nearby, expectantly. One of them was soundlessly clapping its hands.

It was sometime later we heard a different kind of cry. Some animal dying.

The dead deer lay halfway down the hill path that led to the lagoon. It had been eviscerated, a thread of entrails leading off into the tall grass that bordered the sandy route to the beach. To me it seemed a message to us written in blood.

"We have to do something," I said. Whether Isamu understood me or not, he nodded. We couldn't go on living this way.

Later that morning, I showed Isamu a series of small drawings I had made in my sketch pad, a plan view of Fort Ōshiro II, showing the shelter, the kitchen and dining area, the shrine, and the place we stored supplies. A large area inside the entranceway, directly before the gates, was marked by a dotted line. Below the drawing there were diagrams and section drawings indicating my plan. Examining the page carefully, Isamu nodded. It would be a lot of work, but it was something.

If the creature came to the compound that night, neither of us was aware of it. We had worked all day behind the walls, worked feverishly at backbreaking labor. Now we lay sleeping—or at least Isamu was—dead to the world, trusting in our handiwork, but with a weapon or two near at hand.

I was quite certain the animal had some kind of malevolent intelligence beyond anything one would expect to find in nature. *Tengu* was toying with us. Had I been asked before *Tengu* came, I would have said that I did not believe there was evil in the natural world, only survival. My childhood reading had included Darwin. I read books on how things worked and the biographies of scientists, inventors, Arctic adventurers, men of discovery. I wasn't much for stories; my imagination tended toward the mechanical, the factual and prosaic. But despite all that, I was quite certain that simple survival was not at the heart of *Tengu's* nature. I had lived on a farm and seen barn cats play with mice, catch and release them only to pounce on them again. The cruelty we perceive in our human naivety had a purpose, I gathered at a young age, student of nature that I was: the cat keeping itself sharp, working on its skills, its quickness. We didn't feed the barn cats, other than a bit of milk if they were lucky. They depended on their hunting skill. What *Tengu* was doing seemed to have some darker purpose that was unfathomable to me. And what we don't understand we have to ascribe to either God or the Devil, don't we?

Survival was very much at work in what Isamu and I were cooking up. We had been on the defensive, but now the creature was stalking us, tormenting us. It was as if it had been put on the island to drive us crazy—to drive a wedge between us. And it had been succeeding for a while. We had snapped at one another, sulked, and eaten separately.

Until we came up with this plan.

The beast did not return, not that night nor the next. It was a form of torture. Could a beast be that sly, that premeditated? If it was possible, then we would have to fight fire with fire. So the next day, we acted as if there were no *Tengu*. We went fishing, swimming, foraging. We played baseball with a small coconut and a stick. I marked out the bases on the beach and tried to teach Isamu the rules. We put on an act for the demon. If *Tengu* was watching, the thing saw two men with nothing to fear. We bathed in the lagoon just before sunset. To me it felt like some ritual thing a warrior might do—a gladiator before entering the Colosseum. And maybe this prolonged and showy tactic worked, for it was that night the creature returned at last.

We heard it prowling along the perimeter of the fence, heard the low growl deep in its throat and chest, the ticking sound; heard it pick at the Manila twine, heard the bamboo click and creak as it tested the strength of the wall. Finally it got to the gate. We waited under a breathless thin rim of moon, heard the creature press hard, find some give in the door, and press again. There was silence. Retreat? No, not that—not after all our work!

But it had only retreated far enough to charge the door. Suddenly, its body crashed against the reinforced bamboo! Once, twice, and then it broke through. And there we were, two men sitting side by side, waiting across the yard directly before the thing, lit by torchlight. It roared at us, a victory roar, and charged.

And the pit opened under it.

We held one torch each high above our heads as we looked down into the six-foot-deep hole Isamu had dug in the sandy ground. A pit we had rigged with sharpened bamboo stakes.

The squealing was horrible, the raging, writhing creature pierced through and through. But even though it was pinioned there, I never let my revolver stray from the thing's misshapen head. Isamu stood transfixed by it.

"The oil, Isamu," I cried.

He didn't move.

So it was I who put my torch and gun down and tugged, one-handed, a large vat of oil, spinning it on its rounded edge, trying to keep it from tipping, all the way to the edge of the pit. I kicked it over and the thick liquid poured over *Tengu*. Exhausted, I looked at Isamu, expecting him to throw his torch on the howling monster. But Isamu only watched, his eyes blazing in the reflected light from his torch, his body immobilized by shock. So, badly shaking now, I recovered my own torch from where I had stuck it in the ground and threw it into the pit. The howling didn't end until the flames did.

There was no celebration. Not that night. The creature was finally dead; I was able to grasp that, but it was harder to let go of the fear it had engendered.

The rain helped.

It came sometime in the predawn. A light rain but continuous. After a bit, I sought the shelter of my bed, wrapped myself up in bedclothes, and fell into an exhausted sleep. When I awoke, Isamu was sitting cross-legged at the edge of the pit, his body as still as a Buddha, his hands curled in his lap, but with nothing of the Buddha's serenity on his tired, rain-soaked face. His eyes were open but unseeing, looking down into the hollow place where the charred and soaking remains of our tormentor

186

lay. Isamu was so still that I wondered if he was actually dead. I knelt beside him.

"It's all right, Isamu," I said. "We did it. It's over." Tentatively I touched his arm.

Finally, the other man acknowledged my presence. He nodded. But his eyes were full of a sorrow that I couldn't understand.[1]

---

[1] Curiously, Ōshiro does not write about the incident, only mentioning *Tengu*'s demise after the fact, as you will see. It seems from what he writes that either he wanted to protect Hisako from the horror of it, or that he repressed the event entirely.

The Jikininki *Speak*

I left the fort this morning. The door was open wide. Derwood was at work shoveling dirt into the pit we had excavated. He probably still is. So much work, using the wire hand he has made himself. Hard work. Too hard for him, but I did not offer to help. I did not want to be there. *It* was there. The horror. We had dug a pit and filled it with sharpened spears, and *Tengu* charged to its death into it. The siege is over. I should help, but I do not. I feel weak—weak as I felt when I first dragged myself up onto this shore from my raft. I feel, Hisako, as if it is all catching up to me: the war, my flight, the months alone, the uneasy time with an enemy who has become a friend, the terror that he brought with him that is now past.

Except I cannot quite believe that.

I sit down on the beach by the gently lapping tide, writing this. Trying to explain to you what I cannot understand myself.

"It will come back," I said to him as I watched a shovelful of sand fall across the blackened corpse.

He seemed to understand me and stopped his digging, and with his good hand patted my shoulder. "No, we've done it, Isamu-san. It is over." I nodded because I knew the words "no" and "over," and because he expected me to agree with him, but I was full of uncertainty. That is when I left and walked down the hill to the beach. It is as if something of me died in the night.

I look out to sea. It is a dull day, the sea calm, exhausted, tired of the moon always tugging at it, not wanting to always be coming in or going out and never getting anywhere. I stand at the lip of the tide and feel my feet sink a little into the sand with every halfhearted sip of the waves that slips by my ankles.

I'm not sure how long I have been standing here, but I suddenly become aware that I am being watched. I expect it is Derwood—that he has come for me. For one terrible moment, I even think he has come to kill me, now that the danger of the monster has passed. The terror is exhilarating. So I do not turn right away, confident that after all we have gone through, he will not shoot me in the back. I want to look out upon the weary sea, drained of its color, not even made lively by the squawking of the gulls on this strangely quiet morning. I close my eyes. Some small dark part of me almost wants him to pull the trigger.

When I do finally turn, my ghostly children are waiting patiently just beyond the water's edge, and beyond them is a small cadre of *jikininki*. *They have come for me*, I think. They seem to know something I don't. But I am not afraid.

"What is it?" I say. I fold my arms impressively and stand as straight and tall as I can, not wanting them to get any fancy ideas. "Have you come to make a petition to the Emperor of the Island?"

One of them, the nearest, says, "Our own emperor wishes to speak to you."

"Ho! So you have a leader? I thought you were one and one and one?"

"I am not the leader," says another of the creatures, coming forward but not closer than the gentle lapping of the tide. Water,

189

it seems, is another element that does not agree with them. "We borrow words from the stories of those who have died so that we may converse with those who are living. If we must. I am first among the dead you see before you."

"So converse with me, first of your tribe!" I say to the creature in a jaunty voice. My depression of earlier has lifted a little. As dark as my depression may be, at least I am more alive than these miserable creatures! It is almost entertaining to watch them pulling away from the tide with their faltering steps, not able to bear even the frothy hem of the incoming water. It has risen past my ankles. The tide is turning, and I half think I might stand here and watch these miserable fellows have to withdraw farther and farther from me up the shore, as the sea climbs inch by inch up my body. I will stand there unmoved by them or by the sea until I am claimed by it.

"A word with you," says the one who calls itself the first. "But I cannot raise my voice so loud as to be heard above the tide." I relent. I unstick myself from the suction of the wet sand and march up to where the *jikininki* congregate. My diary and writing implement sit on the sand. I move them farther up the shore and put a rounded stone on them so they do not blow away. Already, I am hungry to write this scene in those pages. I shall write it as if it is happening before your very eyes.

"What is it you want?" I say it in a most regal voice so that they hear I am not anywhere near ready to become fodder for their ravenous appetite.

"Perhaps, if you knew more," says the first, "you would look more kindly upon our . . . our needs."

I know what their "needs" are and cannot help but turn up my nose. Still, I would speak to them. "Go on, king of the ghouls," I say imperiously.

The ghoul king, or whatever it is, looks around at its ghastly companions. "I am the first. Not the king, not the leader, for we have no leader, no followers. I arrived in this place before anyone else, that is all. That is all that distinguishes me. I have been here the longest."

At that moment one of my ghosts, the boy who always ventures nearest, suddenly slips his hand in mine. I look to see if he is afraid, but he does not seem to be. It is hard to tell if he has any sense at all of what is going on. The first of the *jikininki* glowers at the ghost boy, flinching. They seem to find the companion ghosts distasteful.

"There was a first body to float up on this island," says the *jikininki* spokesman. "A fisherman whose boat had overturned in a storm."

"But if he was dead," I say, "how did you learn how he died?"

"Dying was among his memories," says the *jikininki*. "His last thought. His topmost memory."

I should have known better than to ask.

"His body lay there for a great long time, for there was no one here to attend to him, to do what *you* do and send him on to the Afterlife, or to do what we do and consume what he had been, taking up his story and making it our own.

"He lay there long enough that I grew from him. Not his ghost, you see, but the ghost of what would never be, though I had no sense of that, at first. I stood looking down on his rotting corpse, abandoned on the beach, picked at by other scavengers — the crabs that had come ashore with him, the gulls and carrion crows, but still not entirely decayed. And something in me, some instinct, led me to understand what I must do."

"Please spare me the details!" I say. The demon bows slightly, as if I truly am an emperor. "And in time other corpses arrived?"

"Other corpses, yes. And with each corpse fresh memories. And it might have stayed that way, with just me here — the island

all my own, alone, providing many stories for my consumption —
but then there was a war at sea and the dead floated in, too many
to count. And while I feasted, there were so many corpses —
more corpses than I could get to — so other *jikininki* came into
existence as had I, rising as a dreadful need out of the corpses.
The need for their stories not to be lost."

The thing bows to me and says no more.

"That's it?" I ask. "This is supposed to win me over?"

But the first of these monsters seems to have forgotten I am
there. Its nose is raised in the air, and when I look around, it is
true of the others as well; seven or eight of them all sniffing and
turning this way and that, until finally one of them starts marching in its ungainly gait along the beach in a northward direction,
and soon enough the others turn that way, too.

And a horrible thought occurs to me.

"Derwood!" I call out. Something must have happened to
him. He slipped while he was filling the hole and fell, skewer-
ing himself on one of the bamboo spears. The boy child clutching my hand stares up into my eyes, smiling, unconcerned about
anything, not of this world and free of all of its horrors. I gently
extricate my hand from his so as not to disturb the wraith, and
bowing slightly to this glowing child and to each of his kindred,
I take my leave, pick up my diary and pen, and race after the
jikininki, soon passing them and dashing up the hill toward my
home and my only friend on this strange and impossible island.

— XIV —

DERWOOD

The Aftermath

I filled in the pit we had dug, which was now a grave for *Tengu.*
The work was hard and my improvised prosthesis was next to
useless. I ended up kicking dirt into the hole as much as shoveling it. By the time Isamu returned, I was sitting cross-legged on
the ground, rubbing an unguent into my aching and bruised
stump. The contraption I'd constructed as a metal hand had
chewed my forearm up something terrible. All that was visible
of the pit was a square-shaped depression of churned-up sand, a
few inches lower than the surface of the ground. I had decided
that I would shovel or kick sand into the hole on a daily basis, a
little bit at a time, and then roll one of the steel oil drums over it
to compact it. In time, I hoped, weeds would grow in and grass,
until no evidence of the hole could be seen at a casual glance and
the blasted thing in it might gradually be forgotten.

Isamu seemed distant, as if something had snapped. I
called to him and smiled, glad to see him back—glad of some
company—but my greeting barely registered on his face. He
took the shovel without seeming to notice the work I'd done and
headed from the compound without a word. I could only assume
another corpse had washed ashore. I'd leave it to him; I was too

tired to bury anything else right now. I stood and stared down at the square of sandy soil that marked *Tengu's* resting place. I smiled grimly to myself. Burned and buried. We had granted the creature both rites, as if he were both Eastern and Western.

Sadly I watched Isamu withdraw into himself over the next few days. My own relief at being free of the monstrous creature buoyed me to no end. I cooked nice things for Isamu that he ate but without delight. I sang his favorite songs to no apparent success. My voice is not much, I'll readily admit, but it used to get a laugh out of him and now he seemed not to hear.

One evening, after we had eaten, he tried to talk to me. I listened intently but, knowing so little Japanese, I could only make out that he was talking about *Tengu* in relationship to the two of us. He would point at the monster's grave and then at me and himself. His eyes would inquire of me if I understood, and when I shook my head, he would throw up his hands and go off by himself.

He slept late a lot, which was not at all like him. Then one morning I awoke and found his hammock empty. I went about my morning ablutions trying not to worry. *His spirit will come back once the horror has truly passed,* I thought. I had watched men wander around after a battle, seen the same vacancy in their eyes. They were alive but what was there to celebrate? I'd flown supplies into Guam that past August, after the Americans took back the island. There were more than seventeen hundred men to bury and some six thousand men officially injured, but I saw injuries in the eyes of men who wore no bandages. It was as if being alive was an affront to the dead. As if being alive only meant there was going to be another opportunity to die; that they had been saved only to prolong the agony. We have a name for the illness now: post-traumatic stress disorder. It was called shell shock back then. Whatever you call it, it's not something you can put a bandage on.

The day that Isamu left early, I worried enough that by midafternoon I made my way up into the coral tree and scanned the island, hoping to catch sight of him. The sun had passed to the other side of Kokoro-Jima before he made an appearance. He was walking along the beach carrying the Gibson Girl.

Isamu built a new box kite. He had thin wire, a whole roll of it, wire that would be perfect as an aerial. He had hidden the wire from me, but now he produced it, and together we set about making the distress beacon operable. In the end it was Isamu, the stronger of the two of us and certainly the most dexterous, who cranked it enough to get the light on the top glowing. He cranked it like a man possessed.

This is good, I thought. *He is ready to get out of here. Ready to go home.*

Then we waited. Isamu wrote; I drew: plants, flowers, rock formations. It was as if the Gooney Bird had been my own personal *Beagle*, bringing me to this tiny island, and I must record the flora and fauna here just as Darwin had done a hundred years ago on his grand tour. I wasn't sure what Isamu was doing. I recognized his ballpoint pen as belonging to my pilot, Pete Laski. It was a new invention but tended to jam unless you held it pretty well straight up and down. Flyboys used them, because the lower pressure in the cabin made the ink flow just fine. I asked Isamu what he was writing, but what could he tell me?

He's telling the story, I decided. And I could see, as he must have been all too aware of himself, that the story would have to come to an end quite soon, for there were only a few pages left in the flight book. So I gave him my second sketch pad and one of my last pencils. Isamu stared at the pages and pages of blankness and smiled for the first time since the death of *Tengu*. But it was nothing like the smiles I had come to know. It was as if the monster still had its claws in him, for the smile was strained and tinged with grief.

He had lost something. The monster has stolen something from him. That was as much as I could deduce. I did not know at the time about his talk with the *jikininki* and how that affected him — infected him: the horror of an abandoned body giving birth to a ghost that must forever eat the stories of others, having no story of its own.

Isamu had woven mats out of grass for us to sit on when we ate at the low table, a new table to replace the one that *Tengu* had soiled. One night, when Isamu didn't seem quite so lost in his thoughts, I reached across the table and tugged lightly at the string around his neck. Isamu produced the *omamori* but did not open it.

"Hisako," I said. "Soon you will see Hisako."

Isamu stopped eating. He smiled and turned to stare vaguely in the direction of the island that had been his home.

"Boy, oh boy, are you going to have a lot to tell her," I said, making various gestures with my hand that we had come to understand as a form of sign language.

Isamu nodded. Then he stared straight into my eyes. What was going on down there in those deep brown depths? Did he doubt that help would come? Or did he doubt that there was anything to go home to?

We worked the Gibson Girl every day, taking turns. And every day I went up to the crow's nest to look for a sign of rescue. I would wait until Isamu had gone off fishing or on one of his long walks. What I saw on Tinian was an enormous airfield taking shape. Already the Seabees had built one runway at North

196

Field that looked incredibly long, and other runways were under way.[1] The place was a constant beehive of activity, day and night. But surely there was someone there who could spare a few hours away from the war effort to slip across the strait and pick up two lost souls.

---

[1] The first runway was, in fact, eight thousand feet in length. By the following spring, there would be three more. It would be the largest airfield in the world for a time.

— XV —

ISAMU / DERWOOD

Rescue

I saw the boat first. It was early morning, first light. The sea was dead calm. The sky blue with pure white cirrocumulus clouds five miles up. A herringbone sky. The boat was anchored two hundred yards offshore at the inner edge of the heart's eastern shoulder. A small American gunship. The kind we called "devil boats."

I raced back to the fort and roused Derwood from his sleep.

"Come," I said.

I watched Derwood run forward when we reached an open spot on the hilltop where I had first seen the boat. I held back, out of view.

"We're saved," said Derwood, turning to me, his eyes huge with excitement. He had thrown out his arms, and his eyes were on fire. I knew what he meant, even if I did not know the words.

"Yes," I said. "You go."

He ran back to me, like a child at the fair, running back to grab the hand of his kind but slow-moving grandfather, wanting to drag him through the gates into the fairground.

"You go," I said to him, and touched his chest. There was no mistaking my intention.

"You, too. Come."

I could not explain to him my fear, the apprehension that had been growing in me for days now. "You go first," I said. This time I pushed him in the chest with both hands and pointed out to where the ship was.

Derwood nodded vigorously. "Good plan," he said. These were words I knew. "I'll tell them about you," he added in our complicated sign language. He pointed from himself to me. Slowly I shook my head and watched the color drain from his face.

"Go. Hurry. Quick."

Derwood started to protest. I grabbed and tugged at the hair on either side of my head with frustration. "Go!" I growled. "Go!" I shoved Derwood harder. I knew the man would not stay, for I could see the excitement in his eyes. And sure enough, he went. He raced down the hill waving his arms. He was wearing what he had slept in: pants cut short at the knee, a faded khaki shirt, no shoes.

I sit in my tree to write this, Hisako. He has gone.

I'll take over from Isamu here. I reached the beach in under three minutes and raced out onto the sand waving like mad, yelling at the top of my lungs. I needn't have worried. There was already a canvas-covered Carley float being lowered into the water. A sailor dropped into the raft and took up the oars. Someone on deck waved at me. Good. I waved back. Until that moment, I seriously worried that the PT boat was a hallucination.

The sailor turned out to be a marine, though what he was doing on a navy vessel, I would not find out right away. He could have been a tinker or a tailor for all I cared. I waded out to the raft, whooping like a kid at a Friday night football game, and held the craft steady while the marine hopped out into a foot of water.

"Fella, am I glad to see you," I said. I took the man's hand in mine and shook it as I introduced myself. The man's hand snapped to his brow.

"Lieutenant Kraft, sir," he said. "Sergeant Griffin, Sixth Marines."

"At ease, Sergeant," I said, barely able to keep from laughing. Then he saw the familiars.

And I witnessed for the first time the phenomenon of them coming into existence—his own ghosts—growing out of the still morning air. I had almost come to ignore my own flock, always obediently at hand. You have to understand that my own first experience of them was awakening in acute pain to find them hovering nearby like hospital attendants and the *jikininki* right there as well, much larger—and hungry! Talk about hallucinations! My own tribe of ghosts had come into existence while I was unconscious and so I did not get to see them "born," as I did at that moment with Sergeant Griffin's ghosts. It was as if the air coalesced before our eyes, here and there and there and there, on up the beach.

My eyes darted back and forth between the ghosts and the marine. I watched his hand reach for the firearm in his holster. Then he withdrew his hand, aware of me watching him. Our eyes made contact, and I'm sure my eyes were shining with the kind of brightness one associates with a madman. Without so much as a nod, we seemed to come to a tacit agreement. He would not say anything about what he was seeing—what was snapping into existence before his very eyes. Nor would I. We would ignore it and it would not be there.

Together we pulled the raft ashore, while Griffin explained how they'd been getting intermittent signals from the island for a few days. I nodded excitedly, but found myself strangely tongue-tied and what I suspected was way too close to the edge of hysteria. What was I to say? Where to start? The Gooney Bird, that's where.

"There's a C-47 in the jungle back there," I said, pointing southwest. "We went down back in mid-September en route to Mindanao, carrying firearms and ammo."

"Survivors?"

"Just me." I held up my left arm. "Well, most of me."

The marine gave me a stiff-lipped nod. He was not the demonstrative kind, but I could see the respect in his eyes. Eyes that had been searching the beach restlessly when they weren't looking directly at me.

"And the shipment?"

"In good shape, last time I looked."

The sergeant smiled, grimly. "Well, I'm guessing the Sixth Marines will make as good use of that consignment as the GIs would have done."

"What's the news from the Philippines?"

"MacArthur waded ashore at Palo, Leyte, on the twentieth."

"Of November?"

"No, sir. October. They seem to be doing just fine, from what we hear. They're pummeling the Japs."

And there it was. *The Japs.* Now what?

I must have given something away because Griffin looked at me with his head cocked. "Everything okay, sir?"

"Yeah. Yeah. Guess I'm just . . ." I looked up to the headland. "There's something I need to get."

"You need help?"

"No."

"You want company?"

He knows. Time to pull rank.

"No, thank you, Sergeant," I said, getting the tone of command just about right. "Give me one minute." I held up my index finger, to make sure he knew what I meant and to make a point. I turned and started to go, then turned again and said, "Make that ten minutes."

"Yes, sir," said Griffin. There was a knowing look in his eye, though what he thought he knew, I had no idea. The marine wasn't about to risk insubordination, but he was clearly suspicious. He was the sharp-eyed type. And I couldn't help wondering whether when Isamu saw the boat, Sergeant Griffin had already spotted Isamu. There was no time to waste.

Isamu was gone. I didn't dare call for him, in case the sound traveled, but I looked everywhere I could, fully aware of the man waiting down on the beach and a boat filled with sailors who had better things to do with their time than wait on a bearded shipwreck of a flyboy. I got angrier and angrier. Did the damn fool think I would sell him down the river after everything we'd been through?

On an impulse, I raced over to the coral tree. I looked up to the platform but could not tell if he was on it.

"You saved my life, Isamu," I said, staring up into the thorny branches. "Come down. I promise you'll be treated fairly. It's time for me to help *you.* Do you hear me?"

There was no sound, only some bird flitting about like crazy as if I were going to steal her eggs.

"Please!" I said. It was a word I knew Isamu understood.

I waited. I didn't dare climb the tree in bare feet, nor was

202

there time. Meanwhile his patient ghost family mingled with mine, exchanging furtive glances.

Finally, I swore, colorfully. It was a word Isamu had heard me use on more than one occasion when I'd stubbed a toe or banged my head into something. A good strong word to indicate I was hurt. Hurt bad.

Then I sighed and said, *"Sayonara, kokoro no tomo."* "Good-bye, my friend."

I turned a few yards from the tree and shouted, despite my earlier trepidation about being heard. *"Mata modotte kimasu."* "I will be back."

When I reappeared on the beach, I was in my uniform, such as it was, the jacket frayed at the cuffs, the pants oil-stained, and my garrison cap looking as if a bird had been nesting in it. I was carrying the Gibson Girl transmitter and one of the rifles from the shipment.

Sergeant Griffin saluted me snappily.

I saluted him back. "Let's get out of here," I said.

I watch the devil boat leave from my watchtower with my friend Derwood upon it. They will be back for the guns. Will I let that happen? Those guns would kill Japanese soldiers. I will have to give this matter significant thought. I will write about it, ask your advice, Hisako-chan. You are so wise—wiser than I am. It will be good to be alone with you again on our desert island. Just the two of us.

The soldiers will come, and the *jikininki* will melt into the depths of the jungle. Troops of healthy soldiers would be as intolerable to them as fire. Soldiers are only good to the *jikininki* dead. Were I to booby-trap the plane, all that I would accomplish would be to feed the undead—these gluttons of other people's memories. There would be too many to bury, and burying is hard. Harder than fire.

It is strange, but sitting up in my tree, with the devil boat racing away, only a speck on the wide flat ocean, I realize that I have ceased really to think of the war as them and us. We are all flesh and blood, together. Have not Derwood and I proved this point? We have.

Together we have vanquished war! Ha!

From my post in the watchtower, I trained my binoculars on the marine. I saw what Derwood did not see. The marine's eyes watched him run up to our headland fort, and though the marine could not have seen any sign of habitation from where he stood, there was suspicion in his eyes. Without meaning to, Derwood led the marine directly to me. I will be most careful when they return that I am not anywhere to be found.

So Derwood and I teamed up to destroy *Tengu*. But war is not destroyed. This is what I have learned, here on the heart-shaped island. And I have learned that it is good to help the dead on their way to the next world and save them from the ravages of those whose only taste of life is a bitter one, filling them with borrowed memories that fade and leave them hungry for more and never satisfied, never satisfied. Saving the dead from the *jikininki* has taught me what killing never did.

I wanted to say to Derwood I will wait for the end of the war. I wanted to say that no prison could be as bountiful as this island. I wanted to say that I trusted Derwood Kraft—trusted him with my life! But war was war, despite what we have accomplished together, and that if war was war, then one man must be the prisoner and the other man the prison keeper. That is the way of it.

It is sad I could not tell him all this. Sad that although we had learned to communicate so well in the months of our time together, we do not share enough language to speak such complicated thoughts, although I am as sure as sure that this man if any would understand. I wanted to call Derwood my friend. But in the end it is better to say nothing. To do nothing. To wait it out. Wait for the end.

CHAPTER FIFTEEN

Evan looks up, wide-eyed, no longer sleepy—beyond sleep. He is here in his room and he is there, as well! He is on the island with them. It has only just occurred to him.

Derwood witnessed *him*—Evan—coming into existence: him and his father and nameless other Griffins, the moment Griff stepped ashore on Kokoro-Jima. Who were they: the children *he* would have one day and then their children—that was who.

Preincarnation.

Evan shakes his head at the mystery of it. The desire to look up the word has left him. He just wants to believe in it. Wants to have made this journey—to have walked that white sand beach, even if he was only a little bit more substantial than the air. And then it occurs to him that if Derwood saw Evan and his father popping out of the morning light like that, so did Griff. Maybe it had undone him. What would a man like that think of such a thing?

Did he recognize Clifford when he was born? Hey, I know you . . . Then Evan remembers what Derwood said, how Griff paid the ghosts no heed. Even then. It must have been like practice for having a real family. Don't look at them. They don't count.

Evan listens to the quiet.

He lies on his side, rests his cheek on his hands. The penis bone lies on the carpet where it fell, shadowy and strange. Could he use it? He imagines the scenario: Griff stealthily entering the room in the darkness, Evan hearing him, instantly awake, but not moving other than to silently grasp the handle end of the club, miraculously back under the covers where he'd put it. And — just as the old man is at his bedside, reaching out with his murderous big hands — Evan throws off the covers in a flurry, and . . . and . . . the damn club gets caught up in the sheets and does him some serious damage. Evan, that is.

The rescue party: that's how Griff fits into the island story. Is that how he sees this trip to Any Place? Has he come to rescue Evan in his hour of need? Or has he got a whole other kind of agenda for being here?

There is a hint of sunrise in the room, as if someone had lifted the curtain at the end of the world and the day ahead had seeped out, close to the ground, a crawling kind of thing, not ready to stand on its own two feet. Not anything strong enough to dispel Evan's dark fear. He turns his lamp back on, but that's worse, somehow. It's as if the tight circle of light is no more than a flimsy and rotting bamboo fence, and just beyond it, far too close for comfort, *Tengu* still prowls. He turns it off again, abolishing those feeble walls altogether, but at least allowing him to see more clearly; to see the door, expecting it to open at any moment. He recalls Ōshiro sitting in front of the pit, like a tethered goat.

He thinks: Evan Griffin, tethered goat.

Could he hit a man? Really whack him good?

Hmm. A trap would be way the hell better. He reimagines the door opening and a very old man walking in, only to fall into a pit ingeniously covered by beige broadloom.

The house ticks. Evan closes his eyes, feels the house slow roll on the tide. Then he snaps his eyes open again, like a soldier on watch. He looks down at the book in his lap. Only a few more pages.

— XVI —

DERWOOD

The Debriefing

Writing this chapter with the benefit of having read Isamu's report from his coral tree, I am appalled at my foolishness in returning to Fort Ōshiro. He is right. I gave him away, although it was never my intention. It was a long, long time ago, but remembering it now—the sight of that gunboat sitting on its shadow in the crystal-clear water of the lagoon, I was overcome with the kind of animated, crazy-limbed happiness of a child at the fair, just exactly as Isamu described it. In my defense, may I put before the jury of whoever reads this journal that while I was a flight lieutenant, I was a very young man. I shake my head to think of it and my part in what later transpired.

Let me pick up the story on the following day in Tinian, the very island I had observed through binoculars with such longing from that same coral tree. Picture this: a bearded, scrawny, not-yet-twenty-one-year-old staring with amazement at a window. Not amazed at what I saw outside the window but at the window itself! Glass, for God's sake! There was a weedy bit of grass, a dirt road, and, across it, ragged vegetation dulled by dust. A troop carrier bumped along the road. There had been traffic all through the night, diminishing the pleasure of sleeping in a real bed.

I had been rescued for this?

I couldn't help asking myself: if it had been a Japanese gunboat that had arrived at Kokoro-Jima yesterday, would I have done what Isamu did, run and hidden? I know I would have.

I showered, reacquainted myself with soap for the first time in over two months. Then I stared into the mirror above the sink and imagined shaving. It wasn't much of a mirror; it wasn't much of a beard. It had come in red, though the ragged mop of my hair was the faded brown of barn wood. Under that scruffy beard was the skin of a boy who left his family farm in Plainfield, Vermont, to go to war. No, I liked my bearded self, for now at least. Sooner or later I would be ordered to shave. I would wait until then.

The day before, medical personnel had examined me, expressing astonishment at my health. "You ever think of going into medicine?" one of the doctors asked me, examining my stump. "Come and look at this, fellas," he added, grabbing anyone around to see my amputation. "Neat as a pin."

I stared at the stump of my left arm with a mixture of emotions. Loss, of course. Sadness. But also I marveled at how well it had healed. "Is there much work for one-armed surgeons?" I asked the doctor.

He shook his head. "A damn shame," he said.

There had followed a lengthy debriefing that I have avoided attempting to write about here because it was hours long and full of military-type redundancy, the kind meant to catch you out in a lie. There were times when I felt as if I had been captured after going AWOL rather than rescued, an officer who had been shot down and survived. The Military Intelligence Division was not quick with compliments the way the medical staff had been. But thinking back on that day's interrogation after a lifetime, I must admit that the hostility I sensed might have been more a product of my own guilty conscience. My narrative—my story—to these hardened inquisitors made no mention of another soul on my island. I owed Ōshiro at least that much: his secrecy. Enemy soldiers had to be rounded up and held somewhere safe. Sequestered. I understood that. I had seen what a lone sniper with nothing to lose could do. And everyone on Tinian knew about suicide attacks. What they didn't know was Isamu. I justified my silence to myself this way: the man was in a prison camp already and not just due to the isolation of the island. A prison seemed to have materialized in Isamu's head.

A knock on the door brought me back to the present, 0800 hours, Monday, December 11, 1944. I would have to get used to time again. Army time. Or in this case, marine time since they were the ones running the show.

It was Gunnery Sergeant "Griff" Griffin. I invited him to step inside. "Welcome to the Ritz," I said.

"Officers' quarters look pretty good to this leatherneck," Griff said in a friendly enough fashion. "When was the last time you slept in barracks?"

I smiled. "What can I do for you, Griff?"

"Folks here are anxious about the armaments on that plane. They want to move on that right away. Today, if you're up for it."

The sooner the better, I thought. "I'm hunky-dory."

"Good, then," said Griff. "We're lining up vehicular transportation. A chopper would have been best, but there isn't a big-enough one we can free up, so we've lined up a half-track."

I frowned. "I'm not sure even a half-track will get you down into that gully."

Griff nodded. "We'll get as near as we can, and then it'll be grunt work. It won't be the first we've encountered."

"I bet," I said.

"We're scurrying around to get a lighter operational to transport the M3 over there. That and an LCVP for the troops."

"Troops?"

"Yes, sir. I'm taking a platoon over." His eyes firmed up their contact with mine. "We hope to get under way by twelve hundred hours."

Troops? What was he planning? Suddenly I got cold feet.

"Why the urgency?" I said. "I mean those guns have been sitting there for over two months."

"With all due respect, sir, we get a little jumpy knowing there's a stash of rifles large enough to fuel an insurrection just off our port bow a few miles."

There was no mistaking the guardedness in Griffin's tone of voice. A day of debriefing had hardened me, and there was no way I wanted this discussion to go any further.

"Forgive me, Sergeant. I see your point. I've been out of commission for more than two and half months." *Stop apologizing,* I told myself.

Griff nodded. His blue eyes were full of accusation. Another commissioned officer might have told him to stand down, might have called him up on charges for looking at a superior officer that way, just on the edge of contempt. But this was a can of worms I was not about to open. Didn't have the nerve for it. "Let's get those arms off the island," I said, wrapping up.

"Yes, sir," he said, but I was pretty sure he had other plans in mind. And if I wasn't careful, I might find myself facing a court-martial for willful stupidity.

We agreed on a time to meet, and I closed the door on him. I had a lot of thinking to do and fast. I wanted to get back to Fort Ōshiro one last time, but I was going to have to do it without tipping off its location any more than I already had. I also had to be prepared that this by-the-rules sergeant could probably find the place without any help from me. If he did, I'd have to tell one heck of a story about how I'd managed to build such a fine habitation all with one hand.

I led Sergeant Griffin and his men to the downed Gooney Bird. There was a full weapons platoon of thirty-nine men, plus me as the token O-2 in charge and Gunnery Sergeant Griffin as the real leader, as well as three bomb experts who monitored every step of the way, sweeping for mines and then checking out the downed plane for booby traps. With an armed guard, the transfer of materials got under way and would carry on through the rest of the day, racing against the clock, because it was getting on to mid-December and the sun would set before six. I slipped away as soon as I could.

"Not much good here," I said, holding up my stump for inspection. If Griff was going to give me any trouble, I would pull rank on him, but he acknowledged the truth of what I was saying, and I made my way up out of the jungle to the beach, where a number of soldiers stood guard near the landing craft, patrolling the beach, having a smoke, waiting. I watched one of them blow smoke into the face of his nearest child ghost. The child only smiled, unaffected by the gesture or the smoke. For a moment its small head looked as if it were smoldering.

I sauntered back to Fort Ōshiro, snapping photographs with a borrowed camera and looking like a tourist. I wanted some kind of record of the place. I took a roll of snaps. Yet another thing that was difficult to do one-handed.

I had cadged a box of pencils and three ledger books from the camp quartermaster, all of which was stuffed in my shoulder bag. I did not expect Isamu to be at the camp, and so I was not too disappointed, or tried not to be, when I found the place empty. I told myself it was wisdom on his part to have made himself scarce.

It was eerie to be back. Only a couple of days had passed, and yet the place felt alien to me. I stood for a moment on the spot where we . . . well, where Isamu had dug the pit and I had badly filled it in. Down below me lay the charred skeleton of a monster. It seemed remarkable now. Being alive seemed remarkable, and I made a solemn promise to myself, there and then, that I would never forget how outstanding it was to be alive.

The compound.

If the suspicious sergeant I'd left back at the Gooney Bird was to take a gander at this place, my story would be sunk. Two hammocks gave the game away. I half thought about taking mine down and trying to give the camp the look of being a solo enterprise. But there wasn't time. I would have to trust Griff would not come this way, and the best way to assure that was to not dawdle.

I left my presents in the shelter in Isamu's hammock. There didn't look to be any chance of rain, but I didn't want to take a chance. Along with the box of pencils, I left my penknife. But there was more. I had procured — stolen — two bottles of black ink, which I left along with my Eversharp fountain pen, the one I had been given for Christmas on my sixteenth birthday. I wasn't sure if Isamu had ever seen a fountain pen, but I knew he'd figure out how it worked.

It was the best I could do. I was about to leave, when I opened the topmost ledger and wrote, with the Eversharp:

Arigatō gozaimasu. Thank you very much.

Then I wrote out my name and the date and my address back home in Vermont. The war would end. Isamu was endlessly resourceful. Maybe he would make it back to Saipan. Maybe he'd write one day. Maybe we would become friends. Right at that moment, the world was full of enormous possibilities.

I turned to go, and there was Isamu in the open doorway of the compound. He bowed, ceremoniously. I bowed back. Isamu entered the fort, his back straight, the little emperor of a little island. I waited as he approached. Saw the moment when his eyes fell upon the things weighing down his hammock. He looked at me.

I bowed again. Isamu was changed. His ghostly crew stuck very close to him. One of them, the eldest of the children, held his hand. Would any of them appear in a photograph? From my pocket I drew the camera. With my eyes I asked if I could photograph him. Isamu backed up toward the compound gates. But then he stopped and bowed, dropped the hand of the ghost child and stood at attention, like a soldier. I snapped two pictures. Then just as I was about to snap a third, I started singing "Skidimarink." Isamu's stern face cracked, and I pushed the shutter. I wanted that smile. Where or when I would dare to get this roll of film developed was a problem for another day. I would have to keep it well hidden for now. The photos, with or without ghosts, amounted to proof of treason. I hadn't quite finished the roll, but I wound it up and removed it from the camera.

I bowed again. I would have liked to shake hands with the man, embrace him, but I sensed sadly that there was no chance. It was not his custom, in any case.

Then he left, without a word, trailing his ghosts behind him. I wasted no more time. I was glad for the chance to see him once again. For, although I didn't know it then, he would never write to me, would never leave Kokoro-Jima.

I made my way down to the beach. I stopped on the trail and looked back up toward the headland. You could just make out the coral tree. I caught the glint from a set of field glasses. I almost went back to warn him that the man who had brought me here had the eyes of a hawk. But there wasn't time. I could see soldiers milling down by the landing craft. I hurried and met up with the gunnery sergeant marching along the shore toward me.

I watched him as the distance between us narrowed. His eyes were everywhere, and I tried to see the place the way he did. Without the Stars and Stripes flapping in the wind on a flagpole, he could only assume this was enemy territory. It was on islands like this that the brunt of the fighting got done. Down here on terra firma. The Army Air Force played a huge role in warfare by then,[1] but, when you thought about it, war was always about land—who had it and who wanted it—and so it made sense that this was where the line was drawn and the killing started.

This was not one of those islands, I wanted to tell him. Surely the ghosts that trailed behind him were proof that this was somewhere altogether different. But he ignored the ghosts. He had probably assessed their potential danger to him or his men upon first laying eyes on them and, finding no weapons on their flimsy bodies, did not let himself be distracted by their fawning, the way they followed, any more than a sailor pays attention to the wake of his boat. But I will tell you, it was quite a sight to see the platoon gathered together on that beach with all those spirits hovering nearby like a vast human-shaped fog.

I didn't talk about the ghosts to anyone. In a war, sanity is a difficult thing to hold on to. And you didn't want to give the other fellow any sense that you might be losing yours. I had loaded more film in the camera by then and took the sergeant's picture. When I finally got the pictures developed, stateside, there were no ghosts.

---

[1] The U.S. Air Force wouldn't come into existence until 1947.

— XVII —

ISAMU

Leave-Taking

I watched Derwood leave from the watchtower. Leave for the second time. I knew they would return, if only for the arms. Derwood had not betrayed me, nor did I expect that he would. Watching them load those crates of rifles into the landing craft, though, I felt so sick at heart that it bent me over double. The two of us managed somehow to live here on the island with no further thought to the arms in the plane. That is what I assumed. Had it been me who was rescued, would I not have done the same thing? I fear I would have. Now they are in the hands of soldiers. Hisako, I found myself shaking with self-loathing. I even cried out. It is a wonder they did not hear me all the way down at the shore.

The war must still be going strong, if what is happening on Tinian is any indication. So those rifles will end up killing my people, and it is only in seeing them leave the island that I fully understand what my failure to act will bring about. Perhaps you would ask me, Hisako, in your wisdom, what could I have done? Could I have blown the rifles up, somehow? Overnight, could I have single-handedly hidden all those crates in caves?

Where? How? Or perhaps you would say to me, Hisako, that the enemy was well supplied in any case. That nothing could stop them. That we are finished. This is what I feel in my bones. I fear it must be true. Great bombers now fly from Tinian on regular missions. Bombers that, by the enormous size of them, might fly even as far as our homeland. I watch them load the bombers, I watch the mighty planes go and watch them return, day in, day out. What are five hundred rifles in such a conflict? But no, I cannot reconcile myself to any of these excuses. I am wretched.

I am so lonely. Lonelier than before. I almost hate Derwood Kraft for crashing into my life! By the scratches on the bamboo pole I have been here now one hundred and forty-six days.[1] I am weak with longing for you, Hisako-chan. But I carry on. I fish and bathe and bury or burn the dead. There is no end of them. The *jikininki* rail at me, and I ignore their pleas.

It will be New Year's Day in just a few days. *Akemashite omedetō.* Happy New Year, Hisako-chan. I can remember the feast we had a year ago to welcome in the New Year. How strange it seems that it was our one and only holiday together. We knew then — or I did, for sure — that we would be married before the year was up. Then the world speeded up, and we were married even more quickly than we would have expected. I wonder if you regret our decision? Had we not married, would losing me like this have been easier or harder? I can only say for myself that it would have made no difference whether we were married or not, for I intended to spend the rest of my life with you. I hope you know

---

[1] I marked my own stay on the island (which amounted to approximately fifty-seven days). I say approximately, because, like Ōshiro's, my first day or two were lost in a feverish and drug-induced haze. By my estimation, this entry of Isamu's dates from around Christmas Day, 1944.

that. And I hope if you read this and I am not there, that you will be happy to know this.

I failed to tell you that I am now writing out my thoughts, as few as they are, in the sketch pad Derwood gave to me. I tried to use the ink-loaded pen he left me, but you will see that I have badly blotched my effort and have reverted to pencil. The other pen that he told me was called a "ballu-pointo" ran out of ink and none can be added, though I tried.

Such great generosity Derwood has shown to me. There are these other lined books he left, enough for me to write a novel of great length had I but the talent. I certainly have the time. But I seem to be running out of steam.

I think about Derwood. How if Emperor Hirohito himself landed on my island and demanded that I give up my prisoner, I would not have done so. Now, on the other hand, had you arrived, I would have led you straight to him. I know you, my Hisako-chan. You would not have been frightened, not as long as I was there. You like people—all kinds of people. Maybe it is because of working in your father's noodle shop. You have met so many! You are not quick to judge. Why, you even liked me when I would come in for my lunch and tease you. Do you remember? I would ask you to sing, and you would blush and then your father would sing, and we would all laugh.

I am smiling to think of those days.

I worry that the pencil marks I make will fade over time, for I have no idea how long it will be before you see this, or if you will see it. Or if you will see me again. This is a sad thought that I banished from my mind, but I can no longer pretend that it is not a possibility. Some days I feel as if I did truly die on that day on Tinian when I saw the puppet battle. Three times I awoke and who is to say whether one of those awakenings was into a new world? If this is it, then it is a good one. The air is clean; the food is plentiful. But it is now a lonely place. It wasn't before Derwood arrived. Just surviving seemed a miraculous thing in those times. Then he came and reminded me of what it is to be with people. Then *Tengu* came and reminded me of what it is to be at war. And so now what is it? Some unquiet part of me asks what is there left to learn? And there is a darker voice inside me that asks what is there left to live for? Ah, but the reason for living is before me in these words scratched onto a snow-white page. You. There is you to live for and, in your place, there are these words. How I pray that you are well. But to whom do I pray? Are there gods anymore in the world?

— XVIII —

DERWOOD

A Word Before the End

Ōshiro made only three more entries despite the extra writing material I left him. Indeed, the three ledger books I purloined from the quartermaster were sent to me, by Griff, along with the flight journal and the sketch pad. The sketch pad contained several pages of writing, but the ledgers were untouched, empty. Apparently, Griff wanted me to understand that he had sent me *all* the writing left behind by Isamu Ōshiro and had not withheld any of it. This, I decided, was just the thoroughness of a well-trained soldier. But it interested me, nonetheless. At that point the sergeant—or I should say the sergeant major—would have had no idea what the books contained, as I mentioned in the prologue. The writing was all in Japanese. He would have no reason to suppose there might be evidence in Ōshiro's writing that would incriminate him.

Of what happened to my friend Isamu Ōshiro between the previous entry above and the following entry in late January, I can only guess. He writes that he was running out of steam. There is a wistfulness that might easily be interpreted as the words of a man not long for the world. Perhaps that was it. But in truth, he was a different man after *Tengu*. There are some battles you lose even if you win.

That being said, the last entries bear witness to extraordinary happenings and, I hope, something of happiness, as well.

— XIX —

ISAMU

A Child!

I have a child! *We* have a child, Hisako. Ah, but why am I telling *you* this? Of course you will know. How do I know? Because this very day I witnessed the most astounding mystery. When I arrived on the beach, back from fishing on the coral reef, I saw the ghost children huddled in a close circle. I don't pay them much attention, for the most part, for they are always there wanting my attention but not in need of it. Something was clearly different today. You see, usually, they become quite perturbed when I go out on the water, and I swear they look as if they would whimper, if they could only make a sound, like puppies tethered in the yard while the master must go to work. So when I landed and was not met at the beach by them, I was most curious and went to where they were gathered.

Although they are translucent and some of the lesser ones almost transparent, they were packed together so tightly I really could not see right away what it was they were looking at. When they became aware of my presence, however, they moved aside enough to allow me a view. And there was the one who always stands closest to me lying on the sand struggling, as if under the force of some great pressure, a seizure of some kind. I was greatly perturbed. The poor thing looked so frightened, though the others only watched in fascination. How he writhed, clearly distressed!

The next moment, his entire head was gone.

Such a surprise!

He was squirming most terribly now—this headless boy—pushing for all his might with his feet planted on the ground, his back arched, his shoulders pressed into the bright sand of the beach. Then the tops of his shoulders were gone and then his chest, and then—with sudden and astonishing speed—the rest of him disappeared, right before my eyes. I stood there, stunned.

Behind me the fish I had caught splashed in the shallows on the string by which I keep them tied to my raft. They splashed loudly enough to wake me from my shock. The other children were not shocked or horrified at the loss of their fellow.

They danced! Their pale faces filled with joy as if a wondrous thing had occurred. Which is when I realized what must have happened.

He had been born.

A baby had been born, headfirst into the real world.

When I counted the days and weeks and months, I realized that it could be true! I decided it *must* be true. Am I not the Emperor of Kokoro-Jima? I decree it is true!

I hope my own joy reaches you wherever you are. And I hope that this boy child who has been my ghostly companion all these months will prove to be an honorable and good companion to his mother.

Tonight I have decided that I will dream of holding him and singing him to sleep. If you hear a ghostly wailing sometime in the wee hours of the morning, do not be afraid. It is only me!

— XX —

ISAMU

Is This the End?

I have written nothing for so long now. The day that marked the anniversary of my coming to Kokoro-Jima came and went without my making so much as a note in my journal. By my estimation it is now August 7, 1945. I see here before me my last entry from so many months ago. How strange it is to read it again and think about this ghost boy who was here with me and is now there with you. I have decided this is the truth. I am the emperor of this place, and my every wish is my command!

And yet it is stranger still to think of how much he must fill your life up with his coming into the world, whereas all that I have is this vague sensation of missing him. The others show no sign of missing him. They only wait patiently for their turn, I suppose. Sometimes I allow myself to think that they are our children. How can that be, you ask? Why, that I will find you again and we will be husband and wife together and will make other children, and there will be that many fewer ghosts on this enchanted island. This sweet thought I allow myself.

But only sometimes.

If my theory is right, these ghosts could as easily be the children our child will have and his children's children. There is some comfort in that.

I write today, because something has happened that snapped me out of this lethargy that has claimed me all these months. Something I must record. As I was about to head down to the lagoon to go fishing, I noticed a wave far out at sea. I had never seen a tsunami before but instantly knew what it was, for it was like no other wave in its height and breadth — its utter vastness. I was halfway down the hill, and even though the tsunami was still far off, I feared it might actually engulf the island! The top of the hill is perhaps three or four hundred feet above sea level, but I even wondered whether I had better climb the tree to my watchtower to avoid this mighty wave. But what would be the point of that? For a terrible moment I imagined myself stranded in a treetop in the middle of an ocean! I did not move. I stood there almost paralyzed and watched in grim fascination as the wave rolled over the coral reef — huge now and I would say majestic, other than the terror it raised in me. It sped across the lagoon. Never, not even on the stormiest of days, do those sky-blue waters see much choppiness, for the coral reef protects the lagoon from the raging of the sea. Not so this day. The wave churned the bright blue water into a leaden gray soup and then crashed upon the shore, swallowing it up. My raft was lifted, lifted, lifted, and then hurled into the trees! It remains there high in the branches like a strange and broken tree house, fifty feet up!

The water rose and rose but did not reach the headland upon which I stood, which is just as well, because I could not move. I was in such shock. It rose and rose, and then the waters streamed off from every side as if I were at the bow of a mighty ship cutting a swath through the ocean. I was safe, at least for the time being. I have not yet ventured from this high place lest there is another tsunami yet to come. But I imagine the low jungle might be flooded—a giant salt lake! I will have to see when I dare to walk down there. The cargo plane. I can imagine it floating, a pathetic wingless waterbird.

I wonder how many of the *jikininki* might have been swept away by the tides. I can't pretend that I will miss them, but I cannot help thinking, as I write, of what would happen to them in the turbulent waters, all their hard-won memories tumbling out of them to be lost in the ocean. Are there, even now, small water organisms ingesting little pieces of all those collected stories?

By early evening the sea was calm again, but waves splashed on the shore at the place of cleavage in the top of the heart-shaped island. The lagoon was gone forever. The coral reef destroyed.[1]

---

[1] This description of the tsunami hitting the island moved me tremendously and made me think. If Ōshiro's reckoning of the date is realistic, then it would have been the day after the dropping of the atomic bomb on Hiroshima, August 6, 1945. Might this tsunami have been a result of that cataclysmic event, some fifteen hundred miles away? I can only speculate. If there was another tsunami after the bombing of Nagasaki on August 9, Ōshiro does not say.

— XXI —

ISAMU

The Return of the Sergeant

I have not been counting off the days in this journal for some time. I make my scratches on the bamboo pole, but otherwise one day folds into the next. I mentioned the date, last month, of the tsunami that destroyed the lagoon because it is a phenomenon of such magnitude I wanted it to be recorded, in case my journal is ever discovered. It might prove of interest to the people who keep track of such things, eruption and catastrophic events. And so I will record this date, as well: the return of the sergeant.

It is September 20, 1945, by my reckoning. I was on the beach when I saw the boat approaching and raced as fast as I could up to the compound and then, forthwith, to my watchtower. With the binoculars I could see that the boat heading toward the northeast corner of my island was not a military craft. It was, at a guess, a sixteen-foot inboard that looked as if it had been rigged for fishing. However, the man who steered it into shore, as close as he could get before dropping anchor, was no fisherman. I could see by the stripes on his sleeve he was a marine sergeant, and when I watched him walk up the beach directly toward my hill, I recognized the long stride of the man who had rescued Derwood Kraft some nine months earlier. He wore his helmet despite the swelteringly hot weather, and carried his rifle and a handgun in a holster strapped to his thigh. What was odd was that he carried what looked like a picture in a frame under his left arm. He approached the compound as if he knew exactly where he was going, and I wondered whether Derwood had been tortured to give up his secret.[1]

As he got closer, he hoisted his rifle into the air, and I could see that there was a white flag attached to the end of it. Apparently he came in peace. I made no move to go and discover whether he was an honorable man or not.

As he reached the top of the hill, I lost sight of him because my platform in the tree does not permit me to see the compound through the foliage. I was quite sure that this was where he was heading. I had a weapon with me, my handgun, which I had grabbed on my way up from the beach, just in case.

I waited and in a few minutes—a surprisingly short time— I saw him on the hill again, heading down toward his boat. I watched and saw him actually wade out to the boat and hoist himself on deck. I expected him to leave, but he merely sat in the shade of the cabin. He had left the picture behind.

Curiosity got the better of me. Was this a "gift" he had brought me? A picture for my island home? How very odd. He had propped it up in a way that I would be unlikely to miss it. It was indeed framed and glass covered, but it was not a work of art. It was the front page of a Japanese-language newspaper

---

[1] I had not been tortured. By September I had already been long discharged and was living in my parents' house in Plainfield, Vermont, helping with the haying and busily sending out applications to universities, to capitalize on the GI Bill that had just been introduced. My mind was no longer on war or my extraordinary friendship with Isamu, but on college and the future. I'm not sure when I finally got over not having ghosts with me everywhere I went. It took a while, and sometimes I conjured them up out of the air even years later, something seen out of the corner of my eye.

announcing in bold headlines the unconditional surrender of Japan. There was a photograph of the Japanese foreign minister signing the peace treaty on the American battleship USS *Missouri* in Tokyo Bay. The "Instrument of Surrender," as the newspaper called it, had been signed and witnessed on September the second.

The war was over.

The next step was mine, but what was I to do? Why did I feel that this lanky stranger was not to be trusted? Yes, there was a truce flag, but it was flying from his rifle. Was I supposed to surrender to him? Why? If the war was over, why had he come himself? These were the questions that plagued me, and I decided to sit and write them down so that you would know how confused I have become.

What am I to do, Hisako? Were you here with me, you would have the answer, I'm sure. You would raise me from my torpor and say, *Come, you foolish man! It is time now. Your son awaits his father!*

Why is it so hard to leave? Why is it so hard to trust? I had learned such trust with Derwood Kraft. Where has it vanished to?

I am so uncertain about what will happen next, and I want these thoughts to be known to you, in case this soldier's intentions are not honorable. Nor is it just him I distrust. I do not trust myself.

I look up from where I write at the altar and look at my compound. It is sadly overgrown. I have lost the urge to keep the weeds at bay. The doors of the mighty fence were wrenched open one stormy night, and I have not bothered to fix them. What is the point? There is nothing on this island to fear. Not until today.

But you are shrewd, Hisako. You will want to know why I dared to sit in the compound to write this when, at any moment, this *gaijin* might return. I can only say that this is a calculated risk. If he comes and finds me here, writing in this journal, he will have the advantage over me and what will happen will happen. Is this a suicidal urge? I do not think so. Something is becoming clear to me that I have not quite understood until this moment. I have not lost the desire to live, but I have somehow lost the will to make any kind of decision. Even as I write this down, I cannot help but ponder what a strange confession this is to make. But when I sift through the tattered thoughts in my mind, I come to a dark place and in that dark place lies the answer: *Tengu.* He is still there inside me. He is my master, in some terrible, insidious way.

I can see clearly enough now that I have become unbalanced, Hisako-chan. This is a paradox, is it not? If I can state so clearly that I am sick in the head, then I am clearly sane enough to recognize it.

I need help. I need help to make the next move. How can I hesitate now, of all times, on this day so long awaited for? Is it because I fear that you have not survived? I have *made* you exist. I have ordered it and ordained it! I have decided that you have a baby — our baby, a son. This belief was based on observation: did I not see the ghost boy born out of my world? Ah, but how is such a vision rational? Saipan fell mightily. Many, many died. We only heard rumors, but there were many, and each one seemed more horrific than the last. And not just soldiers but the civilian population suffered. I have held all this at a distance, unable to bear thinking of it. *You are alive,* I have told myself. It was the only way I could stand this solitariness. Can I stand to know differently? But now . . . Now must I face the truth that were I free at last to search for you, you would be gone? That would be a fate beyond endurance.

* * *

231

I have waited now a good long time. Hours. I can only assume he too is waiting, waiting for me to go to him. I get up, more than once, with that in mind and then I balk. Clutching my diary to my chest. I cannot do it. My fear rises. It is irrational, but I cannot stop it any more than I could have stopped the tsunami that tore apart the coral reef and returned my beautiful lagoon to the wider ocean.

This above all you must know. *Aishiteru.* I love you. I cannot explain the strange feeling in my heart right now. The fear that will not leave me. But that does not change my feelings for you and for our child, if such a child exists. How I hope to see him. We shall see whether the war can let me go, or whether it will claim me for its own. I will place the diaries, just so, here under the stone in my little altar. I will go to my tree and wait.

— Epilogue —

A Mystery

Sadly, it is I, Derwood Kraft, who picks up the story at this point, for Isamu Ōshiro wrote no more. I am writing this entry from the comfortable office of my ranch house in Palo Alto. It is a whole lifetime later. Norah, my wife of many happy years together, passed away almost ten years ago. We were blessed with a son, Leonardo. Just the one child, for Norah came to me when we were both approaching middle age. Our lives had been consumed with study, with the brave new world of the "Age of Information." Assuming there is any truth to Isamu's miraculous vision of birth on the beach of the lagoon, there was a son born to him, somewhere, as well. Just the one child, unless . . . I must confess that it has only just occurred to me he might have escaped Kokoro-Jima, after all. Despite his diffidence, his apparent trepidation, the sight of the soldier may have caused him to leave the island. Did he hide and find a means of leaving on his own? If he did, he did not take his precious papers, the story you have just finished reading. That seems hard to fathom.

Then did he leave *with* Griff? It seems unlikely. Why would Griff end up with the papers? All I can say is that we do not know. Sergeant Major Griffin, having sent me the papers, remains obdurate and unresponsive to my pleas for an explanation. He will not return my calls or letters inquiring as to what happened next. He will not say how he came upon the papers. In the absence of further information, one way or the other, I am left with only conjecture, and I have been a scientist too long to jump to conclusions. Nor will I engage in inductive reasoning in such an instance. Based on the information before me, there is much that one might infer. I have asked Griff repeatedly to comment on this mystery. I have met with implacable resistance. Over a year has passed and I am not well. In order to see this publication carried through, I must leave things as they are, hoping that there may be an addendum to follow, that the mystery can be laid to rest.

As I mentioned in the prologue, we have expended a great deal of energy trying to find Hisako Ōshiro or any other living members of Isamu's family. We have engaged translators and looked in Saipan and Japan and, indeed, anywhere within the reach of our extensive search engines. I can only hope that when and if we are able to discover a link to Isamu Ōshiro's family, the mystery of his final day or days on Kokoro-Jima will have been resolved.

Let me end this book, then, with one final thank-you to my remarkable friend, the Emperor of the Heart-Shaped Island. That he saved my life has been accounted for herein. That he was a friend in the deepest possible sense of what that word might mean can only be repeated again and again.

Arigatō, Isamu. Thank you.

Palo Alto, California
May 16, 2008

CHAPTER SIXTEEN

Evan wakes to the sun streaming through his window. The clouds have passed; the air is already warm. Through bleary eyes, chock-full of sand, he checks his iPhone. Eleven thirty and another message, this one from a number he recognizes:

—Lunch. 1:00. Be there or . . .

"Be square," mutters Evan. He throws his head back on his pillow. Some time yesterday, he and Rollo cooked this up: lunch at the mall on Rollo's break from the Pulse. Good. Better than what's awaiting him downstairs. He's in no hurry to see Griff. Not after last night's confrontation. Not after last night's reading. Not after his covert trip to the Dockyard to find that Griff had erased Leo's e-mails. His father had known how to send and receive e-mails, but Evan doubted he had known how to erase anything from the trash. Had to be Griff.

Evan closes his eyes again, just long enough to see if there's any sleep he left behind in there. He could sure use some. Nope. All gone.

The phone dings.

—I was thinking of raclette in particular.

The same mystery number as earlier: the cheese person. What the hell is raclette? Sounds like a sport. But with cheese? He shakes his head.

There's a lot on his mind, and the worst of it is trying to imagine how he will keep his grandfather from *seeing* what's on his mind. Evan is not used to lying, not even white lies. There is just so much he's not used to these days. He gives a few moments' serious thought to murdering Griff, wonders whether murder would be easier to hack, practically speaking, than having to be evasive. Maybe he could whack him in his sleep. Even marines have to sleep, don't they? But since he'll probably already be awake, that would mean another whole day of waiting, not to mention a life behind bars.

His mind drifts back to the book. What is he supposed to make of it? Despite Professor Kraft's reluctance to jump to conclusions, Evan can't help jumping with both feet. Griff must have murdered Ōshiro. What other explanation can there be? It was as if Ōshiro had written, "There is this hungry tiger prowling around me as I write this. I wonder if he's going to eat me?"

But in the clarity of the morning, Evan feels an uncertainty he can't explain. It irritates him. He *wants* Griff to be guilty of this crime. And yet . . .

He has to admit to himself that it's all circumstantial evidence. There's no smoking gun. It's the kind of evidence a smart TV lawyer could get a criminal off on while you watch with gritted teeth and reconsider the merits of mob justice. It's hard to think of any other way the puzzle pieces fit together. *Which means, Sherlock . . .*

That we're living with a murderer, Watson.

Suddenly it seems to Evan as if those conversations with his father on the last day of his life had been a warning. Whatever you do, my son, do *not* let the infamous Griff into this house. He wishes his father had been a bit more forthcoming with his recommendation. Come to think of it, Dad had been evasive, not wanting to talk about it, as if despite his ancient hatred for the man, the facts didn't add up. Evan summons up his father's face and sees only unknowing in his eyes.

He rests his head on his woven fingers. Whatever happened on that island in the Pacific happened a long time ago. He has his own problems right here on this even tinier island. There's just the two of them — no ghosts, thank God.

Or are there?

He doesn't feel the ghost of his father. And that's good, isn't it? A ghost hangs around because there was something left undone in his life, some important wrong that needed righting and he can't quite make it to heaven — can't quite get into the idea of anything like tranquillity until . . . well, until the thing is laid to rest. So in a way there is this ghost, theoretically, anyway: the boy who ran away from home and spent the rest of his life hating his father, never getting the chance to make peace with him.

Yeah. Good luck with that one, ghost.

And then Evan realizes something — something halfway profound. Griff has never — not once — said anything like "Sorry for your loss, soldier." He hasn't even acknowledged that he — Griff — lost a son, for Christ's sake. What kind of a man is he?

Whatever Griff wants to think, Clifford did achieve at least one of his life goals. He might not have brought peace to the world, but he made it happen here in this house. Evan is not going to let this embittered old hawk ruin what his father did. What he and his father shared.

Okay, good one, Ev. Very noble. Now, what the hell are you actually *going to do?*

The mystery of the island churns inside him. Monsters and zombies and ghosts, oh my. It is scarcely believable, and yet he knows it is true. Feels it. He has had that experience reading, from time to time: that the story was actually in his blood. But this time it is heightened. If there is anything to what Ōshiro said—and which the *jikininki* corroborated—then he, Evan, *was* there on the island, the moment Griff landed. Didn't Derwood see the familiar ghosts spring to life around Griff? He squeezes his eyes shut, wanting to be there.

He wants to know what really happened.

No, he wants a confession, that's what. So does he ask outright? He tries to imagine that scenario. Sees himself on the floor with his grandfather's foot on his neck.

You might think *you know what happened, but you don't know it all* ...

Evan sighs, gets up, takes the book, and hides it in his Pokémon collection. Slowking looks a little anxious as Evan places him in the center of the box. Must be Shellder leaking a little venom into his brain.

Evan dresses in red jeans and a black tee featuring all the dates of the Bluebonic Plague World Tour. "The plague— coming to a town near you!" He hopes his grandfather will appreciate it.

He's going to play it cool. He will show this man that he does have *cojones*. He's not going to run away—not until it's time to meet up with Rollo, at least. This is his place. "I am the Emperor of Any Place," he says to the mirror on the back of his door. He flexes his biceps. The mirror silently chuckles.

But anyway . . .

The soldier downstairs may be battle-hardened, but Evan is younger and faster. He won't make the mistake of getting too close to him again. He is armed with knowledge now. And fueled by mystery.

CHAPTER SEVENTEEN

Evan listens at his open bedroom door to locate the other being in the house, the alpha male who has descended upon him like a plague. He hears the faint clink of china and heads down the hall, down the stairs, advances, sees the mighty warrior at the sink, washing dishes. He's as dapper as he was the day before: different chinos, beige this time, and a different golf shirt, maroon. *It's a uniform,* Evan thinks, *just one with more color combinations.* At least he doesn't look quite so alpha at the kitchen counter.

"You look sick in that apron," says Evan from the doorway. His grandfather turns and raises an eyebrow.

"What's that supposed to mean?"

"It's just an expression."

Griff stares at him. The Gorgon death stare meant to turn him to salt or some other condiment. Evan doesn't blink. Finally, Griff turns his attention back to the dishes. "Thought it was about time someone got this place shipshape and battle ready," he says.

Evan looks around. The room is sparkling. "Pretty good."

"It's a damn sight better than pretty good."

"Okay," says Evan. He's leaning against the doorjamb but feels the urge suddenly to stand up straight; if not quite at attention, then at least in a position where he could "hop to it," if commanded. It's amazing how the guy can zap you of confidence with a word or two. Even in an apron.

"Talked to Ronald Lee," says Griff.

"Who?"

"Your father's lawyer. We're seeing him Wednesday, fourteen hundred hours, if you can fit it into your busy timetable."

"Okay. Uh, what's that in human time?"

Griff turns and glowers. Then returns his attention to the dishes.

Go on, Ev. Grab a tea towel and start drying. Let's turn this into a family movie. Maybe the two of you could go out and play a round of miniature golf.

"I came across some life-forms in your fridge that might be used for chemical warfare," says Griff.

Evan nods. He knows the culprits: the Tupperware containers he had avoided, hoping his father would one day attend to them, which was obviously the same strategy his father had adopted in reverse. "Dad and I had this thing," he says. "One of us would invite someone over every few weeks or so for dinner so that we had to clean up." Evan has reason to think that this is where a normal person might actually manage a chuckle. But Griff shows no sign of doing so.

241

"Does that live here?" he says. He nods his head toward Evan's amp, in the corner of the kitchen where he left it that night a million years ago when the world as he knew it ended. The guitar is there, too. He hasn't had much inspiration to play.

"It usually lives in the rec room," he says. "I could move it down there. Maybe you'd like to give it a shot. I could teach you some chords."

"No thanks."

"Something by the Doors, maybe?"

Griff favors him with a wry expression and scrubs at a ceramic bowl so hard, Evan expects it to burst in his hands. He wonders if he's suddenly remembering what went down last night in the living room. Then Griff's hands loosen, and he looks up at the window. Not *out* the window, but at it, as if there were a secret message written there that was only visible when the light was just so. He speaks.

"When the music's over . . ."

Evan feels a chill climb up his spine. "Excuse me?"

Now his grandfather's vaguely evil grin deepens. "It's the song Clifford used to play all the time."

"Oh. Right. The Doors. Not your style?"

Griff shifts down into glare mode. "When I saw your room last night, it was hard to believe you were his son. But the truth is you're a lot like Clifford when he was a kid. Never missed the opportunity to fire off a round or two in passing."

Evan resumes his rest post on the doorjamb. He shakes his head at this whole new brand of military metaphor that's found its way into the formerly peaceful land of Any Place.

The sink empties with a resounding gurgle, but the old man doesn't strip the apron. He turns his attention to the toaster. He gets baking soda out of the cupboard under the sink and makes a paste of it with water in a saucer, then begins to scrub the

242

toaster with a toothbrush. Evan didn't know they had baking soda. Probably didn't; one of the things the house was low on and important enough to add to the late-night shopping expedition. How had they ever gotten by without it?

"You seem cocky this morning," says Griff. "Must be all the sleep you're getting."

"I didn't get to sleep right away last night."

Griff nods. "Correct. I wandered out back sometime around one. Saw your light on. Found myself wondering what you might be up to."

Evan hugs himself. "Gathering intel."

That stops Griff. He looks over, his eyes full of knowing.

Nice work, Evan. He feels like one of those stupid kids you hear about every now and then who shoves his arm through the tigers' fence up at the Metro Zoo and loses it. And then for some dumb reason, Evan feels ready to lose another.

"I'd kind of like to set up some ground rules," he says.

Griff throws him the kind of amused, sidelong glance Jean-Claude Van Damme might give a rabid squirrel.

"It was good of you to come and help out. I appreciate it. Really. Thanks for phoning the lawyer and thanks especially for cleaning the toaster. But I don't want to hear any more crap about my father. Okay?"

Griff grunts. "Yes, sir," he says.

"And you can stop with all that, too."

"All what?"

"The soldier stuff," says Evan. "'Better get some sleep, soldier.' Stop calling me that!" says Evan. "This isn't Fort frigging Sumter."

"Watch it, kiddo."

"No, with all due respect, *you* watch it. This is my house and you can call me Evan. It's your middle name, too, so you should be able to remember it." The scratching of the toothbrush stops for a nanosecond, then starts up again, but slower. Evan wonders if it's his toothbrush. He takes a deep breath. *Where is this going?* The tiger is looking hungrily at his leg by now.

"Just so you know," says Griff, not looking up from his work, "when I call someone 'soldier,' I mean it as a compliment."

"Oh, that makes me feel a lot better," says Evan.

Then Griff pushes himself away from the sink and whips off his apron.

Evan steps away from the doorjamb, ready to move — move fast — his hands out to his side as if he had a couple of firearms ready to draw. He doesn't run. And, as it turns out, all Griff had in mind was to frighten him. He stands there folding the apron carefully, a grim look on his face. It makes Evan think of all those times in movies he's seen an American flag folded over the casket of a dead soldier. He feels a renewed sense of unrest.

"You just about done?" says Griff, turning to face him. "Because I've got a pile of bills to go through, accounts to settle." Evan nods, feels a little bit proud of having said his piece, and only a little bit stupid. "At some point you need to know how to deal with the bills yourself."

Evan nods. That much is true. But it isn't going to happen today.

"I'm going out," he says. He makes eye contact with the man, daring him to have anything to say about it. Griff turns to look out the window. His mouth is shut, but his tongue seems to be busy, as if there are hard bits of words stuck between his teeth and he's trying to find exactly the right ones to express what he thinks of this disrespectful boy. He turns and looks at Evan through hooded eyes.

"Might I expect you home for dinner?"

Evan shrugs. Wishes he had some killer line to throw at

the old man. But his ammo is used up. Ammo? *Fuck, now I'm doing it!*

"I don't know," he says. He turns to go.

"We need to talk, son," says Griff.

Evan waits, his back to Griff. "What about?"

"That call you got last night."

Evan's glad he hasn't turned around, but he doesn't kid himself—Griff can see his reaction to the remark. His whole body has tensed up. "What about it?" he says.

"Like I tried to tell you around about midnight—albeit I was a little rough—there are things you don't know. Things that are none of your business."

Now Evan turns, slowly. "So that gives you the right to listen in on my phone calls?"

Griff shakes his head. "No sir, Evan. I did not do that. But I did pick up the phone directly after you got off. Tried star-six-nine. Now that's a good service, that is. Told me the last call that came to the house was from the six-five-zero area code. Leonardo Kraft, to be precise. Am I right?" Evan nods. No use denying it. "What'd he tell you, Evan?"

"He told me the same thing you just told me."

"Come again?"

Evan sighs. "Mr. Kraft didn't know Dad had died. And when I asked him what he was after, he told me it was none of my business."

Griff raises his eyebrows in surprise. Then lowers them and levels his gaze at Evan. "That all?"

Evan feels the anger rising in him again, can't resist it. "Actually, he did say something else, something really important. He said he was sorry for my loss. I mean this guy never met Dad, but he was nice enough to think his death might affect me."

He waits, his heart pounding. Is that pain he sees in Griff's eyes? Damn, he hopes so. Griff goes to speak, stops. Evan waits. Griff nods, clears his throat.

"So Clifford was talking to Kraft," he says.

Evan can only stare at the old man. Cannot believe that this bastard is so heartless. A murderer? The tiny suspicion of doubt he felt earlier dissolves into grim certainty. "I gotta run," he says, regretting the choice of words the minute they're out of his mouth.

Steeling himself, he crosses the threshold and enters the pristine kitchen. He passes Griff by, swiping the car keys off the little table as he goes, expecting Griff to lash out. At the back door he stops, waiting for some last disparaging comment, some dig meant to get his goat. It doesn't come. And so Evan takes his goat and leaves.

CHAPTER EIGHTEEN

The mall: an oasis of *got it* in a world of *gimme*. Evan's not much for the mall, but at least there's no *Tengu* here, as far as he knows.

It's certainly far from being a desert island, he thinks, as he settles on a bench. The bench looks like it was ripped off from a Victorian park and painted mauve. He squints, looks around. The floor is a sort of anemic sand color, come to think of it. There's a palm tree in a nearby clothing store, although it's only papier-mâché. And, through half-closed eyes, a lot of the people do in fact look like the walking dead. There's even a lagoon. It's about twelve feet across, complete with water fountain. A little kid is walking around the rim of it, leaning over to gaze at the glittery coins at the bottom of the pond, holding tight to his mother's left hand while she talks into a cell phone in her right. Evan checks his own cell; he's got half an hour to kill before

Rollo gets off work. Better here in Nowhere than back home in Any Place. And as if on cue, the instrument dings to announce a text message.

—Didn't mean to be mysterious, orphan boy. It was an invitation to dinner. If you're lonely or whatever. No need to reply.

Right, one mystery solved: Olivia, the Oreo girl. An invitation to dinner: what's this about? They don't really travel in the same circles. For one thing, he doesn't own aviator goggles or a bandolier. So it's just neighborliness? Whatever it is, Evan can't deal with it now. But he's touched. He tries to think of something to say. Can't. There's too much else on his mind.

What is he going to do?

He doesn't know his father's lawyer—didn't know he had one, any more than he knew he still had a grandfather until that last night, talking to Dad. What if Griff tries to talk the guy into making him a legal guardian or something? The disgust wells up in him.

There is this sorrow deep down inside him, squashed under an avalanche of anger. It's as if Griff showed up and stole his grief from him. Ha! His name even sounds like grief.

He punches in a number on his cell phone.

"Leo Kraft, here. Hello?" It's his real estate voice.

"Hi. It's Evan."

"I can see that. What is it, Evan?" He sounds busy and guarded.

"I thought I'd better tell you that Griff knows you called."

"Oh, damn."

"I guess he heard us on the phone, and after I hung up, he did the star-six-nine thing."

"What'd he say?"

"I told him you didn't know my dad was dead. And when

I asked you what you wanted, you told me it was none of my business."

There is a pause at the other end. "Do you think he bought it?"

"What's there to buy? I don't really know anything."

"But do you think he knows you've got the book?"

"Why should he?"

Leo sighs. "Oh, hell. I am sorry. There was no way I wanted you to get caught in the crossfire." *Now* he's *doing the whole warfare thing. It must be infectious.* "Listen, Evan. All I can say is what I said last night. The less you know the better."

Evan wants to shout at him that if he knew any *less* he'd be put away in some institution for morons. He sighs. It's not true. He knows just enough to be totally frustrated. And it's not Leo's fault. He knows that, too. "I finished the book," he says.

"Ah."

"So, I get why Griff is being . . ." He can't think of a polite word.

"Cautious?"

"Yeah."

"I hope you've hidden it well."

"Yeah, I think so. Anyway, I figure even if he found out I'd read the book, it doesn't rub off on you, because it was just there on my father's desk, right? I'd have found it all by myself. So I read it. Big deal. No harm, no foul."

"Right," says Leo, but he doesn't sound convinced.

"What am I supposed to do: unread it?"

Leo laughs. It has the too bright, clear sound of someone who has to laugh a lot professionally.

"Can I ask you something?" says Evan. "Something else?"

"Sure, I guess."

"The story is so surreal—so . . . I don't know—crazy—and yet your dad, he wasn't crazy, was he?"

"Not at all. He was a brilliant man. Revered—a scholar."

"Yeah, I got that. But then . . ." Evan stops. He's not even sure why he started.

"Then, what, Evan? What are we supposed to make of it all?"

"Yeah, I guess. I mean monsters and ghosts . . ."

There is a pause. "I'm not sure what to make of the monster, but I can tell you something about the ghosts. My mother had a favorite story about the first time she met my dad. She was a graduate student. She knocked on the door to his office, and he said come in, and when she did, he dropped what he was carrying."

"What do you mean?"

There's laughter in Leo's voice now—the genuine kind. "He was carrying this big honking piece of hardware, I guess, which he just dropped when he saw her."

"I don't understand."

"He'd never seen her before in person, but he recognized her."

"You mean . . . but wait . . . The ghosts? On the island? But that isn't—"

"I should tell you this, first off," says Leo. "My mother was Iranian—she'd say Persian. In any case, she had this extraordinary face. Beautiful. Big features—huge eyes. It wasn't her that Dad recognized that first time . . ." He left it at that.

Evan finished the sentence, remembering the picture of Leo he'd seen on his website. "It was you."

"Right. Exactly. He had seen *me* on the island—the ghost me—and when he met her, he knew right away, she had to be my mother." Evan doesn't say wow, but he feels it in his solar

250

plexus, feels the *wow* punch him hard and then seep into his bloodstream. "Evan, I've got an appointment. Thanks for keeping me abreast of what's going on up there."

"That's okay," says Evan. And actually it is okay, because suddenly, out of nowhere, another idea has occurred to him. "Have a good day."

"You too, Evan."

Evan hangs up. Composes himself, then opens Google on his phone.

"Evan?"

He looks up. A middle-aged woman with long hair is smiling at him over a cart full of groceries. It takes him a minute to recognize her. He's never seen her in anything but gardening clothes with her hair all pulled tight in a ponytail.

"Mrs. Cope," he says.

"How are you?" she asks affectionately, leaving her cart and coming to perch beside him on the mauve bench. "I've just come from your house," she says before he can answer, "and I met your charming grandfather." If anything her smile is wider now, and Evan has no idea what to say. Mercifully, Mrs. Cope does. "Such a gentleman," she says. "A real southern gentleman."

"Oh. Uh, yeah."

"Just like your father," she adds. She's got her hands pressed together in front of her mouth, and she looks almost smitten. "I thought I'd better drop over to cut back the petunias," she says. To Evan it sounds oddly like some kind of spy-type code. "They always get a bit straggly around mid-July. And while I was at it, I decided I might as well dig up the tulip bulbs and put them into storage. The car was gone and I didn't know anyone was there. But Griff . . . well, he was ever so helpful." Evan nods like a zombie. What's the point of arguing? Besides, there is a tear in her eye, and he's afraid of what might happen if he disturbs her story by telling her the truth. Telling her that this southern gentleman is a one-man wrecking ball. She notices him noticing the tear, and she self-consciously rubs it away with her finger, then busily looks through her purse for a little packet of tissues.

Was there something between her and Dad? She's way younger than him. Hmm. The things you don't know about a person.

Without looking at Evan, she continues to chatter, rubbing her nose, sniffing. "I'd like to come back and prune the roses," she says. "Clifford always did around this time." She chuckles, sniffs, rubs. "His rule of thumb was a quarter inch above the first leaf with five leaflets." She looks up, her eyes shiny with hopefulness, and Evan wonders if she's passing on this information to him.

"A quarter inch," he says. He can't remember the rest.

"Yes, above the first leaf with five leaflets."

"Okay. Good. Thanks. Got it."

She looks pleased. "I'll show you sometime." She closes her handbag and rests her hands on the latch. "I'm so glad I ran into you," she says, reaching out to tap his knee. Her smile ignites again.

"It's nice to see you, too, Mrs. Cope," he says. And he means it.

"Rachel," she says.

He nods. "I need to get your casserole dish back to you. It was . . . really good. Thanks."

She cocks her head to the side and smiles, her hand on her heart. "No hurry," she says. Then she stands up and straightens her dress. "Don't be a stranger," she says.

"Thanks. I won't."

And she's off, leaving Evan sitting there, stunned, wondering about all these nice people: goth girls and gardeners. But there was something he was supposed to be doing. He looks down at his iPhone, wakes it up. It's opened up to Google. Right.

"Why didn't I think of this before," he mutters to himself. He goes to his Internet server, goes to Webmail, punches in his dad's coordinates. He needs a password for this, but he knows what it is, because he was the one who set it up:

ax1sb0ldasl0ve

And up comes his father's in-box. He scrolls down and down and — *Bam!* Leo Kraft. "Damn, I'm good!" he says. He opens the e-mail. Scans it quickly. Obviously not the first communication, but a continuation of something they'd been talking about.

Yamada's work is amazing as I'm sure you'll see.

"Yamada?" says Evan under his breath. He scrolls down. There it is again. "Benny Yamada."

"Yo!"

He looks up. It's Rollo. "Just a minute," he says.

"I don't have a minute," says Rollo. "I've got half an hour, and in that time I want to ingest an enormous quantity of meat, preferably full of growth hormones."

Evan doesn't put up an argument. He glances at the iPhone, closes it. He can follow this up later. "Who's Benny Yamada?" he says.

Rollo scratches his cheek. "Second baseman for the Mariners?"

CHAPTER NINETEEN

They talk vegetables. "Celeriac," says Rollo.

"What is that?"

"A vegetable. But it would make a good name for a super-hero. It sounds kind of fast. *Celeriac.*" His hand zooms through the air. "You could do a T-shirt with this vegetable guy who's got a head like celeriac rescuing, you know, a carrot in distress."

Evan shakes his head wearily. "This job is getting to you, Rollo. You should probably see someone."

"Monica wouldn't like that."

"I mean someone in the head-shrinking business."

"Speaking of seeing someone," says Rollo, and pulls out his cell phone. He starts scrolling through a list, and Evan imme-diately takes out his own, glad for the excuse, intending to fol-low up on Benny Yamada. The name almost rings a bell. But as he waits for the WiFi to kick in, Rollo suddenly hands him his Samsung.

What?

Evan only says it with his eyes as he takes the phone. Rollo makes the same gesture he does when Evan is supposed to keep on going with a guitar solo. Someone on Rollo's phone is saying hello.

"Hello?" says Evan.

It's the girl.

The friend of a friend of a friend. He glares at Rollo, who holds out his hands like he can't help himself, he's just way too wonderful for words. Then he goes back to his fries, a contented look on his face and gravy on his chin.

The conversation that follows is generic. The kind you might have in a language lab when you're learning Portuguese. Evan feels like he's opened this box full of worn-out and dusty phrases, which he inserts into the conversation in more or less the right order. Like building something, except that there won't be anything there when he's finished. Whenever he can catch Rollo's eye, he glares at him, makes threatening gestures with his plastic fork.

"No way," he says pleasantly to the girl.

But apparently there *is* a way and the girl—*what the hell is her name!*—goes on to tell him about it. He's only half listening, but it's not her fault; she's not dumb. And it's not his fault, either; he's just numb. Still, he hangs in, recognizing the pauses, the openings where you're supposed to plug in a reply. The weird thing is she sounds nice. She's not a chatterbox; she's saying interesting stuff—what he catches of it. It's just that the part of his brain that knows how to do this kind of thing is buried under that avalanche of anger and that deep and buried sense of loss. That's all. It's like he's been away a long time on an island in the middle of nowhere and he's forgotten how you play this game.

"Really?" he says, sounding as interested as he can.

And, yes, she does mean *really*.

But now Rollo is noisily gathering up their garbage. He points at his wrist as if there had ever been a watch there.

"Hey, this is cool," Evan says into the phone, "but Rollo's got to get back to his vegetables and this is his phone. Yeah, I know. Yeah, he is totally insane. In fact, he's doing his little insane dance right now. Or maybe he just needs to pee."

She laughs. It's not a bad laugh. Maybe a seven.

"For sure," he says. "Yeah, absolutely. Uh-huh. You too."

Then *click*.

Now he can put all of his energy into a vegetable-destroying glare. "Don't ever do that to me again," he says.

Rollo throws up his hands. "You were great, Ev! Haven't lost any of that famous Griffin panache."

Evan hands him back the Samsung.

"So?"

"So, what?" says Evan.

"You're seeing her when?"

Evan rolls his eyes. "She leaves for camp at the end of the week. She's a counselor. Hey, stop the matchmaking, okay?"

"Okay, okay. I've done my work."

Evan walks him back to the Pulse. They don't talk, but it's fine. Evan recognizes it to be the kind of not talking they do together as opposed to the not talking he's been doing a lot lately.

So . . . progress?

Then Rollo is gone, and, sitting on the same mauve park bench as before, Evan checks up on Benny Yamada and begins to finally understand what is going on.

CHAPTER TWENTY

He heads home but takes a detour to Laramie Close. He's been there once, though he can't remember why: trick or treating when he was a kid, dropping off homework? Whatever. He thinks he can remember the way, which house. There are maybe ten house designs in the whole suburb, but it's surprising how you learn to find your way around by the smallest of details. It's like those king penguins coming back to the herd from a fishing trip and somehow finding their own penguin kids among the thousand other penguins all in their dinner jackets.

He rings the bell and — Yes. Got it.

"Oh, hey."

"Hey."

Olivia Schlaepfer is dressed almost normally in jean shorts, a white top, and . . . well, a six-gun strapped to her thigh. "Orphan boy," she says. If she's surprised to see him, she gets over it pretty quickly. "If you're here for supper, you're way early."

Evan shakes his head. "Thanks, though. That was nice."

"Anytime. Oh, if it's about adoption, we could talk to my parents."

For one crazy moment he thinks she's serious, but a sly smile gives her away.

"No," he says, "but again, thanks. Actually, it's about Benny Yamada."

"Oh!" Now she's interested. "What about him?"

"You know his stuff, right? You're into the whole graphic novel thing?"

"Yeah. How did you know?" Evan shrugs. But she launches in anyway. She's talking even as she leads him to her room.

Benny Yamada, graphic novelist and soon to be moviemaker.

She opens up the home page of his website on her computer. Evan had already found the site on his phone at the mall — enough to get the idea. But now he looks more closely on her big screen and listens as she fills in the background.

There's a picture of Yamada: Asian, bleached blond, cool as hell in a Lakers ball cap and a T-shirt that says WILL FIX IN POST.

"I've got the Tilt to Fade trilogy," she says. "You could borrow it if you like. *Backspatter* is the first — that's the one they're filming." She turns to him, her eyes huge. "There are rumors that Henry Austin Shikongo might play Rat Catcher."

"No, really?" says Evan. He doesn't know what she's talking about, but he recognizes how important it is.

"Totally," she says. "I can't wait."

258

Then she tells him that she liked *Alpenglow* the best and that *Collateral Spam* was pretty weak, but then third sequels always are, "Don't you think?"

Evan isn't sure what he thinks. His mind is reeling.

"I don't believe this," he mutters.

Olivia looks him square in the eye. "Why are you really here?" she says.

Whoa! He didn't think this through. But before he has to start making up some outrageous lie, he notices "New projects" on Yamada's menu bar. And when he scrolls down, there's only one project listed: *Kokoro-Jima.*

A tiny island in the Marianas not to be found on any map. An island populated by ghosts and the hungry dead. A soldier washes ashore, battered, bruised. A soldier alone and then not alone . . .

"Amazing," he says. "Freaking amazing."

Her eyes do a little Spanish Inquisition number, but he just turns back to the screen. "I know," she says. "Look at this." She pulls up four full-color spreads:

1. A Japanese soldier, his face wracked with pain, lying on his belly, parting bamboo with his fingers.

2. A wrecked cargo plane in the jungle, the sky filled with carrion crows.

3. Another soldier, an American, holding some kind of weird yellow contraption in his hand, his other arm ending in a bandaged ball where a hand should be.

4. A band of flesh-eaters standing in the long grass like a bunch of bad-ass amigos in a Tarantino movie. Amigos with torn gray skin and red eyes.

Evan leans back in his chair, wraps his arms tightly across his chest. His heart is beating out of control. He stares at the illustrations, shaking his head in stunned disbelief. Then he notices that Olivia is watching him.

"You know something about this?" she says.

He nods. "Yeah, but I can't tell you. Not right now."

She weighs his answer and he can see she's dying to press him for more, but then she backs off.

"It's really too bad," says Olivia.

"I'm sorry," he says.

"No, that's cool. I mean about the project."

"What?"

She shakes her head. "Apparently the whole project is on hold." She scrolls down to Yamada's closing remarks. How the book is pretty well complete but hung up in "Production Hell."

Back in the car, Evan texts Leo. He doesn't know much about what a cease-and-desist order from a lawyer might be, but it's a good guess that Yamada's site is in violation of it. Not that there's any mention of Griff. Not that there's any picture of him.

He backs out onto Laramie Close and then just sits there, not knowing where to go. Home? If it was hard to play dumb before, it's going to be impossible now. But where else does he have to go? He looks back toward Olivia's door. She's standing there watching him. He waves. Makes gestures like there's something wrong with the car. Then it moves — jerks — and he makes a joke of it, like he was doing something wrong, like he's just learning. She frowns and goes in. He owes her an explanation, but it will have to wait.

He goes home. Mystery solved — well, one mystery, anyway. It's not the publication of *Kokoro-Jima* that Griff's pissed off about; it's this graphic novel by a best-selling author. But what is Griff's problem? Why does he feel so threatened? They can change the name of the killer; it doesn't have to be him. Or is it the idea of it? The marines: the whole honor shtick. What's their motto? *Semper fidelis:* always faithful. Is that what's eating him up? Only one way to find out.

He enters the back door and sees the brown cordovans, sitting on the floor at attention. *Your deduction, Sherlock?*

The fiend is out, Watson.

Evan tears upstairs. In his room, he opens the closet and pulls down the black box filled with three years' worth of furious Pokémon buying and trading. Kneeling on the floor, he removes the lid and his blood runs cold. Slowking is no longer in the dead center of the box. The stacks have been returned neatly but not exactly. Evan gingerly removes one stack, then another. There's no yellow at the bottom. The book is gone.

He can't stay here. Not now. He needs to think. He needs to come up with a plan. He has to go — *now* — before Griff gets back.

He leaves. Squeals out of the driveway. Next door, Lexie Jane is standing in her driveway with two other girls with skateboards. They peer at him, their hands keeping the glare of the sun out of their eyes. Burning rubber is not what people do in Any Place. You're not supposed to be going anywhere that fast. You're not supposed to have to escape from your own home, but right now he needs to be any *other* place than here.

So . . .

Back to the mall. Or maybe to Olivia's? Maybe her folks can get those adoption papers signed up double quick. But going back would mean talking about *Kokoro-Jima* and he can't do that. Then another idea occurs to him. Something that is almost normal. It doesn't solve anything, but it *puts off* solving any-thing, and that's what he needs right now — because he has a feeling that his head might explode otherwise. He pulls out his phone. It's not a plan. It's just an evening, which is as far ahead as he can see.

CHAPTER TWENTY-ONE

The vision overtakes him out of nowhere. It's what Ōshiro described in the book, but it's real, suddenly — surprisingly real. Evan sees the soldier make his way up a sandy hill. There's a white flag hanging limply from the barrel of his rifle. The soldier has a framed picture under his other arm. He's shimmering a little in the heat haze; light bounces off the glass in the frame. He stops, raises his head. Evan sees it, too: a flash of light high in the trees.

Intel.

There are ghosts trailing him — them. Evan is one of them. If he squints he can see others, insubstantial, hovering a little apart from one another. They are spread out like a *V* of geese following the soldier. They tremble in the onshore breeze as if the wind might unwind them. In the reflection off the blistering white sand, they seem little more than a coalescence of light, a thickening into moving forms.

He stares into the hot white haze, tramping along, trying to keep up, feeling on his bare feet the heat of the sun-smacked sand, though, when he turns to look, he sees that he has left no footsteps.

Then his eyes catch a glimpse of other specters, moving surreptitiously through the undergrowth to his left, like jackals keeping their distance from a lion but wanting what the lion wants. These are nothing like children, but large lumbering things with red-hot eyes. Evan looks behind him, and they are there, too, following at a distance, just as Ōshiro described them. He hurries to catch up to the soldier — is drawn to him, pulled along. So are the other ghost children, not like geese now, but more like a pack of skittish dogs on invisible leashes.

Griff comes to a stop at the crest of the hill, smack on top of his noonday shadow. He stares out to the cool blueness of the sea. His face is covered with sweat; his eyes look grim.

Evan feels a presence close at hand and, turning to his left, sees a ghost girl looking directly at him. Her hair is almost the same color as the air, long, and lifted by the breeze, flying out about her. Who is she? She is clothed in a luminous shift. She brings a wavering hand up to clear away the ash-white blondness from her face.

"Evan," she says.

He is shocked that she knows his name — that she can talk. The familiars didn't talk in Ōshiro's story. When he tries to respond, nothing comes from his mouth.

"Evan? Evan!"

And he is sitting in McDonald's.

There is a conventionally pretty girl sitting across the table from him with several little red bird clips in her brown hair. For a moment he can't recall her name.

"Where were you?" she says.

Bree, that's her name.

"Your eyes got all, you know, far away . . ."

"It's nothing. I . . ."

"Do you want to tell me?"

Evan sighs, smiles. "Sorry, it's just been a weird time lately." She doesn't know about his father's death. It's not something you say to a friend of a friend of a friend. The whole date would get really . . . what? Awkward. Pretty well impossible, really.

Bree gasps. "Oh my God, it's not like those people who suddenly fall asleep, even if they're driving a car?"

"No."

"That would be really scary."

"Yeah," says Evan. "That's called narcolepsy. It isn't narcolepsy."

"Oh," she says. She smiles. "That's good, at least."

"That was almost what we called our band," Evan says, aiming for levity and sounding more like he's on amphetamines.

"Excuse me?"

"The Narcoleptic Bunnies," he says.

Her smile is genuine but edged with concern—*not a good expression on a first date,* thinks Evan.

Date? What am I doing on a date?

"I like your band's name," she says. "Pocket Monsters, right?"

"Uh, yeah."

"That's like Pokémon all spelled out?"

Evan sighs. "Yeah. Pokémon is a contraction, actually."

"I know," she says. "My little brother explained it to me."

He's holding a Coke. When did that happen? He puts it down on the table. His hamburger sits on its wrapper, untouched and not looking all that hot.

"So. Your little brother is into Pokémon?"

Bree nods, glad to be having a real conversation, and all Evan can think is why did the band call itself anything so memorably geeky.

"Do you still play?"

"Guitar?"

"No. You know—"

"Oh, Pokémon. No. Not for . . . I don't know, years."

Bree has a dab of something on her lip that makes her look vaguely vampirish. It's even a little sexy. Probably just dipping sauce. She looks hopeful and then sort of sad. "You just sort of drifted away," she says. "Does it happen a lot?"

"Like I said. Things have been, you know, difficult. I haven't been getting much sleep."

"I get that." Bree nods sympathetically. "Should you see someone about it?"

Tell her something. He tries on another smile from his hidden stash. This one is a size too small. He takes her hand. "I haven't told anyone this," he says, but then he's distracted again by the dab of dipping sauce.

Aware of the focus of his gaze, she licks her upper lip.

"Gone?"

He nods.

"Tell me," she says, and holds his eyes, damply, in her own. Her hands are kind of damp, too.

"I just had this weird sort of vision."

"Really?"

"Really."

She squeezes his hand a little. "You want to talk about it?"

266

"The vision?"

"Sure, if you want. But I was thinking more about how the vision is probably just a symptom of how 'weird' things are right now for you. It's like . . . you could tell me about that . . . if you want. If it would help, I mean. But you don't have to."

He shakes his head. "Thanks, though."

"Okay," she says. Her shoulders droop a little, but she tries on a smile of her own—a pretty good one, all things considered. With her free hand, she pushes back a lock of hair that's escaped from one of the red bird clips. She's got nice hands. Her nail polish is blue. Blue and chipped. Then her hand, finished with her hair, drifts toward their clasped hands and rests on top of them. "So you were having this vision?"

"Oh, yeah," he says. "I was on this desert island. The sun is totally blazing down. And . . . Are you ready for this?" She nods. "There are these ghosts."

"Ghosts?"

"Yeah. Ghost children."

"But it's daytime?"

"Yeah."

"How can there be ghosts in the daytime?" It is something Evan has not considered. "I mean how can you even see them if the sun is shining?"

"They're not kids in sheets."

"I know, but—"

"And I'm one of them."

"What?"

He doesn't say it again, lets her figure it out.

Bree's hand flies to her mouth. "You're one of the ghosts?"

He nods, wonders too late if this could be a deal-breaker. They have been together approximately three hours.

Her eyes grow even wider. "Do you mean you're dead?"

Evan gives it some serious thought. "That's the crazy part," he says. "These ghosts . . . it's as if they're the ghosts of people who *will* be, instead of the ghosts of people who used to be."

"I don't get it."

"I know. It's pretty out there," he says. Bree's hand, skittish as a pigeon, flutters back down to the pile of hands. Now his other hand joins their three hands, so that there is a knot of fingers sitting in the middle of the table.

"Preincarnation," he says.

"Reincarnation?"

"No. *Pre*incarnation. That's what's so different. They're ghosts from before a person is born. You know, as in 'prenatal' or 'premature' or . . . like that."

"Or 'preoccupied'?" she says.

"Yeah," he says.

Her eyes slip away. She looks down at the table.

"Oh," he says, suddenly getting it. "'Preoccupied.' Right. You mean me?" She nods. He's impressed in a way; she's sharp.

"You don't have to talk about it," she says. "It's none of my business."

Her face is actually kind of sweet. Or it was, anyway. It's sort of sour now. *Which is funny,* he thinks, *because she chose the sweet and sour dipping sauce.*

"It's not like a social comment or anything," he says.

"What's that supposed to mean?"

"I mean, yeah, I've got a ton of stuff on my mind, but I'm having a good time."

Her hands slowly extricate themselves and slide away along the Formica tabletop, to fall off the edge and disappear into her lap. She looks down at two sad, cold Chicken McNuggets.

"I'm sorry," he says. "Really, I mean it. Bree?"

She looks up and now there's an actual tear in her eye. "It's Kira," she says.

Oh! *That's* it! She thinks I'm pining over some other girl. Then he looks more closely at her face, at her offended eyes, and he realizes that Kira is *her* name.

Chapter Twenty-Two

Evan finds the back door locked. He hasn't a key. He never carries one anymore, since his father retired. This is yet another habit to unlearn. He pulls out his phone. It's almost eleven. He drove Kira home in silence. Then at her place, she smiled, really nicely, his slipup forgiven. "When I get back, maybe you can tell me what's going on." Her voice was different. She'd dropped the date voice. He liked how she sounded. "I'm going to do that," he said. "Kira." She laughed, and her laugh was definitely an eight this time. He looks at the house and thinks how it might be good to see her again. When she gets back from camp. Assuming he survives.

He peeks through the kitchen door—the curtain's not quite closed; the kitchen is empty. He cranes his neck. His amp is gone. So is his guitar. He remembers Griff telling him about breaking all of Clifford's records. Evan remembers how the old man had relished telling him that.

There's a light on in the hall beyond the kitchen door. He knocks. No answer. He swears to himself. Knocks louder. Nothing. *The grump must be downstairs watching TV,* he thinks. Listens. Hears nothing.

Shit.

Two thoughts tumble over one another. He's gone. He's dead. He tries to imagine finding another dead body in the house. He remembers firemen lumbering through the place. He wonders if they're going to be as supportive this time. I mean how many dead bodies can you report in one month before somebody gets suspicious?

So, does that mean he's gone? Will there be a letter on the table?

Dear Evan,
I've gone. Fend for yourself, you ingrate.
Yours affectionately,
Grandpa Griff

How great would that be? But he knows it can't be true. Griff never runs away, never backs off. And now it's late and dark, and all of Evan's misgivings are back like a bevy of ghosts huddling way too close.

He shakes them off and goes around to the front door; tries it. Locked. He rings the bell. Holds his finger on it, getting angrier and angrier.

He needs to pee. He should have gone at McDonald's.

"What is this?" he says to no one. Some lesson he's supposed to learn? Never trust anyone. He looks through the side window: the front hall is shadowy — the light he saw from the back door was from the upstairs hall, dimly illuminating the stairs. He steps back, out onto the front lawn, and looks up. There is only one other light on, the one in his father's bedroom.

Evan looks next door at the Guptas' house. There are no lights on. It's after eleven now. He could go there, anyway. They'd take him in, no questions asked. Well, no, not exactly; there would be questions asked, questions he doesn't have the answer to.

There are lights on at the Reidingers', as well, but the only light he cares about right now is the one in his father's room. He gets a lump in his throat. How many times has he come home late—way later than this—to see that light on? And it was never like he was in trouble, even if he'd missed curfew. It was just that his dad couldn't sleep until Evan was home and safe. This was different. His dad always left the front porch light on for him, the door unlocked.

Shit!

He runs around to the back garden, opens and closes the gate. Looks around and then pees in the begonias. Or are they petunias? Are these the flowers Rachel Cope just did something to?

Shit!

Okay, that's taken care of. Now what?

He could phone, he thinks, but if Griff hasn't heard the doorbell, what are the chances he'll hear the phone? And then he remembers, finally, that there is a spare key. Of course! In the days when Evan was a latchkey kid with a working single parent, there were the occasional times he forgot his key. He goes back to the carport and locates a jar of nails on a shadowy worktable in the back corner. The key is in there. He pricks his finger on a nail. *Serves me right,* he thinks.

He heads toward the back door. Stops, turns around. Sees the aluminum baseball bat in the corner of the carport gleaming with a smear of streetlight. Shakes his head. *I'm not going there,* he tells himself. *This is* not *a military operation.*

He unlocks the door and steps into the kitchen. The kettle stands glistening in reflected light from the hall. The old man had brought a shine back to its greasy sides. He couldn't stop at just the toaster. *There's no stopping him,* thinks Evan. The idea fails to lighten his mood. He crosses the kitchen and listens at the entranceway. The light above the stairwell down to the rec room is off. Maybe Griff has retired early and just left the light on upstairs. After doing what?

He climbs the stairs, his hand too tight on the railing. Silent on the broadloom, he reaches his father's open bedroom door. Griff sits on the far side of the double bed, his back to the doorway, seemingly unaware of Evan's presence. Evan checks this time. There is no mirror or darkened window in front of Griff — no way to see Evan's reflection. Besides, the old man is leaning over something in his lap. Evan waits, holds his breath, his hand on the doorjamb, prepared to push himself off and bolt.

"Are you just going to stand there?"

Must be Spidey sense.

"How'd you know I was here?" says Evan.

"I can smell you, boy. Smell the fear."

Evan goes very still. There's a bed between them — between him and a ninety-year-old man. He could take the car. Get the hell out of Dodge. Or he could reconsider violence — go to his room and get that walrus penis bone and put it to good use.

But, no. No violence. Not here in his father's room. And the bottom line is he's not going anywhere. He's not the one trespassing.

"What are you doing?"

Griff turns his head but only so that it is in profile. "I was looking for something."

"What?"

"Something your father took, when he left home."

"He took a backpack with a few clothes in it."

"Was that what he told you? Is that the fable he spun?"

Evan doesn't speak. He can feel the old man lifting the hammer of a mousetrap, bending it back against the pull of the spring. "He didn't tell you about the money, did he?" says Griff. Now he's folding the hold-down bar over the hammer, setting the cheese in place. "It was money we kept in a coffee tin for emergencies."

"He did tell me. What was it, fifty bucks?"

"It's still theft."

"So you want the fifty dollars back?"

Griff snorts. "Don't be a damn fool."

Evan waits. Gets his feet firmly underneath him. Makes fists of his hands. He's ready to smash his hand down on that mousetrap just to hear it snap!

Whatever the old man has up his sleeve, Evan is not going to get fooled into losing his shit. He takes a deep breath. Waits. Hears a clicking sound.

"There was one other thing," says Griff.

"Something Dad took."

"Something of mine." Now he turns his head enough to look at Evan. "Well?"

Well, what, shithead? But Evan knows exactly what he means. Can he resist asking? Can he resist knowing what it is that Griff is talking about — maybe even holding in his lap?

He steps into the room, stops. Waits. "Did you find it?" he says at last.

Griff nods. Then jerks his head in a come-here motion.

Evan doesn't move.

"Are you going to take all day?"

Evan cautiously circles the bed and stops five feet from his grandfather.

Which is when he sees the gun.

He gasps but doesn't move. The gun is in the old man's lap, held lightly in his right hand. It's an old-fashioned pistol with a wooden handle and a black barrel about three inches long.

This was not here! My father did not have a gun in this house!

"It's a Nambu," says Griff. He lifts it slightly for Evan to see, and Evan immediately steps back. Griff grins, turns it a bit so that the flat black barrel catches dull glints of lamplight. "A Type fourteen," he says. "They were issued by the Japanese army to every NCO—that's noncommissioned officer. Oh, sorry. I know you don't like me using military terms."

He glances up at Evan again, and in the lamp-shaded light, his eyes seem rheumy, glazed over. *Not tears,* thinks Evan. *Something else—some disease that clouds the eyes of the very old.* It makes him look more monstrous than ever.

"It's a semiautomatic," says Griff, his voice quiet but firm. "Takes a clip of six." He does something quick with his hands, and the bottom of the stock opens; a slender magazine falls out into his left palm. He holds it up. It's empty of bullets, as far as Evan can tell. He realizes suddenly that he has stopped breathing. It occurs to him it might be a good idea to start again.

"You're lying," he says.

Griff shakes his head.

"Why would my father steal a gun?"

"Maybe he had plans for it."

"You mean using it? I don't think so."

Griff looks up at him, and there is something like

begrudging respect in his eyes. "You're right," he says. "He'd have never had the guts to shoot me."

Evan has the overwhelming feeling he should not be here. The message is very clear in his head, a flashing light going on and off, sirens wailing—the whole early warning system of firing neurons working perfectly, except for the part about getting the message to his legs. He is transfixed. That little black gun, even without any bullets in it, even without being aimed at him, has him in its grasp, more strongly than Griff's hand on his wrist the night before. It's a kind of seizure. And from the look on Griff's face, he knows it.

"He took the gun because it was something I prized," Griff says. "That's why. Something small enough to carry that would inflict the maximum amount of pain on his old man. That's what a handgun does, doesn't it?"

"That's crazy."

"I agree. Your father, the pacifist, packing heat."

Evan can't take his eyes off the gun. *Nambu.* Is that what Griff called it? The name rings a bell.

"I took him once to the range when he was old enough. Couldn't hit a damn thing."

"I don't believe you."

"That your father was a lousy shot?"

"No, not that—him stealing the gun. It'd be crazy. How would he ever get it across the border?"

"Dumb luck, I guess."

"No way! He wouldn't have risked it. Anyway, he didn't believe in war. The last thing he would have wanted was to be caught with something like that."

"He was a naive boy," says Griff. "He'd never been anywhere near an international border. Wouldn't have known the first thing about customs officials. Anyway, back then security was lax. Canada wasn't yet considered a hotbed of terrorists. 'Canuckistan,' as someone once called this home of yours."

Griff seems to find this funny. "Anyway, faced with some scruffy-haired, pimply no count of a boy, the customs folks were probably looking for drugs, if anything."

Evan shakes his head. "Dad hated guns. I wasn't even allowed to play with toy guns."

Griff nods, then he fixes Evan with a look as sharp as a spear. "Pity," he says. "But you are right, he did hate guns. Lectured me on the subject a time or two. But you see, he hated me more."

That message of alarm in Evan's head is making its way to his limbs at last, carried by a mule train of neurotransmitters, a slow seeping of electrochemical charge. He inches to the side.

"You think I brought it with me, then?" says Griff. Evan stops. "You think that's how this got here? Like I was going to plant it, or something?" Evan doesn't say anything. "Have you traveled by airplane lately, son?"

Evan shakes his head.

"That much is obvious."

Evan slides another inch to his left. *Just fucking run,* the voice in his head says. But Griff is squinting at him now, as if he can hear the alarms going off. "He never showed you, did he?" Evan shakes his head. "Never bragged about it — getting one over on his old dad?"

Evan just keeps shaking his head, and Griff smiles a nasty, triumphant kind of smile. "A man could write volumes about the things you don't know, son."

Griff shoves the magazine home, clicks it into place. Weighs the heft of the gun in his hand. "And speaking of volumes," he says, "I gather there's one you've been dipping into lately."

Now, we're getting to it: the point of this whole little scene. The point of the locked doors and the single light on. The whole thing was staged.

The gun lazily shifts in Griff's hand.

"I don't know what you're talking about," says Evan.

Griff raises an eyebrow. "You're not much of a liar."

"If that's a compliment, thank you."

"It isn't a compliment. You *are* a liar—you're just not good at it."

"Okay. That's fair. And that gives you the right to enter my room and go through my stuff?"

Griff freezes for a millisecond—just enough for Evan to realize he's surprised to have been found out. Surprised that Evan had been home earlier. He shakes his head, and he sighs with a clear note of contempt. "My, my, my," he says. He looks down at the gun in his hand. He slips his finger onto the trigger. "I'd really appreciate it if you would just lighten the load on your conscience and tell me what the hell you're up to."

"I'm about up to here," says Evan. He's holding his palm at eye level.

Griff holds the gun up to the light, closes one eye, looks through the rear sight. Then he holds it out for Evan's benefit. "See this trigger guard here? See how big it is? That's because Japanese soldiers who'd been fighting up there in Manchuria complained about not being able to fire when they were wearing bulky gloves."

Then just like that, Griff points the gun at Evan.

"What the fuck!"

"When I ask a question, I'd appreciate an answer."

Evan backs up. "There's no bullets in it."

"Good eye, soldier. And you're *almost* right. There are no bullets in the magazine. But there is one in the chamber. And from this distance, it only takes one."

278

"Come on, Griff. This is fucked! Put it down."

"Are you going to talk to me?"

"Put that thing *down*!"

Griff lowers the gun, but he doesn't take his finger off the trigger. "I don't want you taking off on me, you hear?"

Evan just stares at the gun, and Griff chuckles.

"Do you really think I'd have aimed it at you if it was loaded?" he says.

Evan looks at him and nods.

"Shows how little you know me."

"This is what I know," says Evan. "You are totally insane."

Griff aims the gun at the lamp and pulls the trigger. *Click.* He looks back at Evan, one eyebrow raised, and cocks his head to one side. "Not quite totally," he says. "But it's just as well you think I am insane. Might help you to make up your mind about filling me in."

Evan backs up. There's a big old chair in the corner of the room — he feels it against the back of his legs and almost falls but resists, steadies himself with a hand on the chair's arm. "Okay," he says. He takes a deep breath. "Leo called asking if Dad had received the book. I didn't know who he was, so I didn't tell him Dad was dead. I started reading the book. And the next time Leo called, I told him the truth. That's when he told me about the letters from your lawyer and he wouldn't tell me anything more."

A grunt of scorn explodes out of Griff's mouth. "God, I hate a liar."

"It's not a lie."

"I'm beginning to think I might shoot you, after all. I'm sure there's some ammo around here somewhere. Twenty-two mil, is what I need." He smiles. "You might remember how I said I never forget a caliber."

Evan shrieks—surprises himself, but not Griff.

"They don't have capital punishment up here, from what I can tell. Hell, I'm so old, I'd be dead of natural causes before any court could condemn me."

"What do you *want*?"

Griff stares at him with loathing in his eyes. "I want to know what this Leonardo Kraft fellow and you are cooking up." He pauses. Evan says nothing. "So?" Griff lazily moves the gun around in the air, watching it the way you might watch the head of a cobra dancing for a snake charmer.

"I told you the truth. Leo refused to give me any info, once he found out about Dad. And I don't really care if you believe me."

"I'm willing to believe what you just said. But I can tell that you know more. I've done a fair bit of interrogation in my life, and I can always tell when someone is withholding something on me. Ya hear?"

Evan nods. His mouth is dry. He swallows. "I need water. I need you to put that . . . that thing back where you found it. I need for this not to be happening in my father's bedroom."

Griff seems to consider each item on this list of conditions. Nods. Then he reaches down to the floor where an old oil-stained rag sits in a shoe box. He bends over, wrapping up the Nambu carefully, and nestling it in the box as if it were a baby. *He acts more tenderly toward that gun than he does to his grandson,* thinks Evan. But then, guns don't talk back to you; they talk for you: quite a difference. And then, just as the last flap of cotton folds over the thing, it hits Evan where he's seen the gun before: in one of the drawings by Benny Yamada, the soldier parting the bamboo.

"That's Ōshiro's gun."

Griff looks up from where he has just placed the top on the box. "It is."

280

"You . . . you took it from him."

"I did."

"After you killed him," says Evan.

He doesn't care anymore—he has to say it. *You want some truth, old man? Well, there you go.* He feels this wave of euphoria overcome him, like when you finally throw up although you've been trying not to. He can feel a taste in his mouth as foul as vomit.

Griff looks him up and down, but when his gaze comes to rest, the contempt of moments earlier has lost some of its bitter edge. "Is that what happened?" he says, and it strikes Evan as odd that there is no challenge in the question. He wasn't asking if this was what Evan thought. It was as if he didn't know what happened himself.

CHAPTER TWENTY-THREE

Evan fills a tall glass with water at the kitchen sink. He joins Griff in the dining room. Griff has poured himself a scotch. They sit across from each other. Evan sits in the same seat where he sat across from his father in this very room, watched him slide a narrow ship into a bottle and pull the strings that raised the masts and sails. And as he went about this harmless pursuit, this hobby of a lifetime—making models with loving details, making small what was large, making a toy out of what had been an instrument of war—Clifford had told him that his own father was a murderer. And Evan had thought it was just his father blowing smoke. Just caught up in this huge hate-on that he couldn't seem to escape.

Eighteen days ago.

He looks at the man, tries to measure his state of mind, what he might do.

"So," says Griff.

He is resting his elbows on the table. He looks tired. Not so tired you'd want to try anything silly. Weary but wary. Evan searches for that questioning look he'd seen in Griff's eyes in the bedroom, but no. It's gone. He may be tired and old, but he's battle ready.

"So," says Evan. "What I think happened is this. While you were gone from Ōshiro's fort, when you went back down to your boat—after you'd delivered the picture with the treaty in it—this phantom storm came along, and Ōshiro, up in his tree, was struck by lightning."

Evan takes another long drink of water, one beady blue eye on his grandfather.

"You're really beginning to piss me off," says Griff.

Evan puts down the glass, wipes his face. "Only just beginning? I got the feeling I'd been pissing you off ever since you stepped inside this house."

"Just give me a straight answer, like a man, will ya?"

"No. You're the one who should be doing the answering," says Evan.

"You think?"

"Listen. What do you want me to say? This isn't anything to do with me. I'm not about to phone the newspaper or something. I'm not about to call the cops. Why do you even care what I think?"

Griff looks down at the table. Evan watches him, sees his left hand trembling, again, involuntarily—some kind of palsy. Watches how Griff covers it with his right hand, as if to hide it. It isn't just nerves.

"I do care what you think," says Griff, his voice low. "Why

do you suppose I was trying to hold up the publication of this damned book?"

"It's pretty obvious, isn't it?"

"So you *believe,* but you don't *know.* Those fellas out there in California: Kraft's son, Leonardo, and this Yamada crony of his." He looks up. "Oh, I forgot. You don't know anything about their plan."

It's no use faking it anymore. "I figured it out," says Evan. "Leo wouldn't talk, but he happened to mention he'd e-mailed my dad."

"'Happened to mention,'" says Griff derisively.

"Happened to mention," says Evan again. "I looked in Dad's e-mail, saw you'd erased whatever it was he sent. So I accessed the server and read about the idea for the graphic novel. That's the truth. Take it or leave it."

Griff glances at him, under hooded eyes. He nods. "Okay. So they offered me money to give them the rights to put out this comic book. I don't want their money. They think I'm some old fart who doesn't care any longer. That's what I hate. I do care." He looks up. The blue of his eyes is watery with that milky patina Evan hadn't noticed until they were up in his father's room. It's as if age has caught up with Griff at last—as if it is accelerating at a pace and the man is only one step ahead of it.

"They think they know what happened, but they're wrong. Just as you are."

"That isn't what you said upstairs."

"What did I say?"

"You asked me if you killed Ōshiro. Like you weren't sure."

And there it is again, the hesitant, almost vulnerable, look. Evan stares at his grandfather, feels as if he's seeing something of him—the real him—without all the bluster and spite. Just a sliver, like when a person opens an apartment door and they've got the chain lock on. All you see is this inquiring eye with a bit of fear in it.

Griff takes a sip of his drink and grimaces as if it wasn't what he'd expected. As if someone had filled his glass with some awful medicine.

"Are you trying to tell me you didn't kill Ōshiro?"

Griff hesitates. Shakes his head.

"What does that mean?"

"It means . . ." Griff shakes his head again. He swallows, straightens his back. "What if I said to you: trust me."

"Why? Why should I?"

Griff takes another drink. As soon as he lifts his right arm, his left hand slips off the table into his lap where a person couldn't see it tremble.

"In the marines, you learn to trust your buddy. There's this saying that the most important man in the world is the one standing beside you, and, goddammit, you have got to believe that. Believe it with your whole heart." Griff smacks himself in the chest with his fist. "Your life depends on that guy beside you thinking the same thing."

"The same thing," says Evan.

"Damn straight," says Griff, and all the macho bluff is back.

Evan frowns. "You know, that's the problem."

Griff rolls his eyes heavenward.

"No, listen to me," says Evan, poking the table with his finger. "You don't trust anyone who doesn't think exactly the same as you do. You don't trust Leo or me or anyone to listen to you with an open mind."

"Open? My, my, son. You think you're up to that?"

He sits back in his chair, waggling his head around as if trying to get Evan in focus. "You've been brainwashed from birth by your father to detest the likes of me. To hate the very ground

I walk upon. Don't say otherwise! From the moment I walked in your front door, it was as plain as the nose on your face."

Griff tips an ice cube into his mouth and crushes it with his teeth, with his eyes all the while on Evan. And Evan can't help wondering if this is to show off a full set of teeth — teeth that he could eat you alive with, if he wanted to. He wonders if Griff ever does or says anything that isn't meant to intimidate. And yet there was that glimpse . . .

"You've got a belly full of half-truths in you," says Griff, "and you seem to be satisfied with that — with half the story."

"Well, enlighten me, then. Trust me." Evan pounds himself in the chest, aping the old man. "What's stopping you?"

The air is filled for one long moment with no sound at all. Then Griff clears his throat, places his glass down on the coaster, and stares at it.

"Because what really happened isn't believable, Evan," he says without looking up. "I am not going to try to tell people something they won't believe — that I do not . . . that I . . . that I can't quite believe, myself."

Evan has this odd feeling that the whole conversation just got away from him. As if he fell asleep at some critical exchange and has no idea what Griff is saying anymore. "Yeah," he says. He scratches his head with both hands. "But . . . but the thing is, because you won't tell them, Leo and Benny Yamada — won't tell them *anything* — all they can think is that you're guilty."

"I know," says Griff. "I know what everything points toward. In the one communication I sent to them, I said as much. 'I know how it looks, but I would like you to believe otherwise. I would like you to take it on a soldier's honor. I do not wish to say anything more on the matter, and I do not consent to the publication of a comic book or a movie or any damn thing else that suggests otherwise.' That's what I told them. And

286

I reminded them that the property was mine. Those diaries. I found them. I only lent them to Derwood. Legally, they haven't got a leg to stand on."

He won't give up, thinks Evan. *He won't give an inch. You take the island and you hold the island, no matter what. You don't hand it over to the enemy.*

"Why not set the record straight?" says Evan, his voice mild, as close to friendly as he can manage.

Griff sniffs. Finds a handkerchief in his pocket and wipes his nose. Evan has heard of handkerchiefs but never seen one in the flesh. It's ironed. The man irons everything. Nothing that comes near the man with any creases in it gets away from him un-ironed.

Griff puts the handkerchief away. "Sometime in the not-too-distant future," he says slowly, "I will be deceased, and everyone can do whatever the hell he wants. For now, I'm going to stick to my guns. Make 'em wait."

"Are you sick?"

Griff looks taken aback. "Do you care?"

Evan frowns. "You said sometime in the —"

"I know what I said. I am not sick. I was referring to the law of averages, which suggests, at my age, I am not going to be around a whole heck of a lot longer."

Evan nods. He's as surprised as Griff that he cares. Maybe he just can't deal with anyone else dying right now.

His glass has left a watermark on the table. He rubs at it with his finger. "Won't you care about them making the movie? I mean even if you're dead and they're saying you did it?"

"How am I going to care?"

"What about your reputation and all that?"

"Nobody today gives two hoots about a veteran or his repu-tation. They laud you when you come home from some theater of war. They honor you at the football stadium come Super Bowl Sunday, but they don't care for soldiers, don't look after them. Nobody really wants to know about them or the dirty business they're honor-bound to carry out."

Evan stares at his grandfather. He cannot figure him out. The man is the most infuriating thing he has ever come across. He sighs and rests his head on the table. He is overtaken by tiredness. Exhausted. The incident with the gun has taken it right out of him. He realizes he must have been on some kind of adrenaline high, because he can feel the hangover coming on. He feels a little sick to his stomach. His head is spinning. He leans back from the table.

"You won't tell me what happened?"

Griff shakes his head. "I would like—" He stops. Looks down. Traces an imperfection in the grain of the wood. "I would like for someone to believe me. Have a little faith. Take an honest soldier at his word."

Evan shakes his head. "I've got to go lie down," he says. Then he glares at his grandfather. "And I'm *not* running away."

Griff acknowledges the statement. He looks beat, himself.

"We'll talk in the morning?" says Evan, as he stands. He has to grab the edge of the table, he's so wobbly on his feet. "Make that the afternoon."

Griff looks up at him, all the bluff gone out of him, the glint in his eye extinguished. He looks disillusioned. There is a pallor to his leathery skin that Evan hasn't seen before. "It's all there in the story, Evan," he says. "I was hoping maybe you could see it."

"See what?"

"The truth."

CHAPTER TWENTY-FOUR

Evan is standing in the enclosure, the broken-walled fort of the Emperor of Kokoro-Jima. He looks around him, at the cabana, the palm leaves of its roof lifting with a small breeze, the single hammock in the shadows, swaying slightly, almost as if someone had just risen from it. Something has been eating away at the palm leaves. Some kind of rot. There was nothing about that in the story. He is here. He is here because Griff is here. That's the way it works. He and the other ghostly familiars are tethered to the soldier by invisible strings, and he — Griff — is here in the compound waiting. Waiting for Ōshiro.

Evan feels the breeze take his hand, and when he looks, the girl is there, the blond ghost, more sun-spun air than anything else, and yet he can see her face and she is smiling at him. He smiles back at her. Yes. She is Griff's ghost as well. One of them. There are others, his extended family. One of these children is his own father. He looks around. They are everywhere, a dozen or more: Griff's lineage. The girl ghost pulls on Evan's hand, and when he looks at her, she points toward the entranceway, the fallen-open gates.

Ōshiro.

He has come. Beside him appear his ghosts. He stands at the threshold of his home, staring at Griff. Griff rises. He was crouching over in the northeast corner of the compound. Evan has no idea why, but now he is on his feet. And Evan sees that his face is angry. Why? Isn't this what Griff wanted? Isn't this why they are here? Why Griff brought the framed photograph of the treaty? Was it meant only to be a trap? No, that doesn't seem to make sense. Would Griff lure this man with a white flag tied to his rifle? Evan feels the girl ghost squeeze his hand. He glances quickly at her, sees the same consternation he is feeling, then they both turn toward the gateway just as Ōshiro steps over the threshold.

Which is when it happens.

The sand at Ōshiro's feet suddenly erupts as if he has stepped on a mine, and up through the ground reach hideous grasping claws—talons—wrapping themselves around Ōshiro's leg. Then there is another explosion of sand and a mighty head emerges from the grave, a hawklike head with fiery eyes. Its beak opens and emits a scream that makes Ōshiro cower—thrown backward by its force. His own scream of pain blends with the monster's scream of lust. Then wide shoulders of matted and dank fur rise farther from the sand, and a second limb is freed, slashing at the man who falls to the ground, grabbing at his throat.

Evan wakes up screaming.

He sits bolt upright in bed. Has no idea where he is. He is still on that island—his ghostly self—where even now the monster has Ōshiro in its clutches. The screaming in his blood subsides, but his heart is pumping like mad. He falls back against his pillow, his hands on his chest, half afraid he will die of shock. But he knows it will not be like that. His father's death was caused by the thickening in the walls of his heart, and as Evan's fear wanes and his pulse gradually flattens out, he knows with a certainty that the walls of his own heart are strong—if temporarily way too thin!

When he feels he might be able to stand, he does. He sways there, still feeling the distant reverberations of what happened. What he *knows* happened. The answer to the mystery.

His grandfather is in his pajamas, but he is not in bed nor is he asleep. He is sitting in the green wingback chair, sitting in the dark but for the light from the television screen. He's watching some old movie on TCM with the sound off. Silvery-gray people float across the screen. They seem miraculous to Evan. Beings from another planet. Fred and Ginger, dancing.

Griff turns his old head to look at Evan. He switches on the lamp beside his chair, blinks, fumbles with the remote but manages to click the television off.

"What is it, Evan?" he says, his voice soft. Evan swallows. Griff sits up, stares at him, his eyebrows pulled together with concern. He reaches out with his left hand, the one that trembles, and pats the footstool upon which his feet had been resting when Evan first entered the room.

Evan walks toward him, a bit like a zombie, and sits obediently.

"You had a dream?" says Griff. Evan nods. Griff nods. "I heard you scream," he says. He slowly leans back in his chair,

291

nodding as if he's had the same dream. He folds his hands in his lap, the right over the left. He waits, patiently, his eyes never leaving Evan's.

Evan collects his wits. Rubs his face vigorously with his hand.

"It was *Tengu*," he says, in little more than a whisper.

Griff stares at him, a vein on his forehead pulsing. Is it Evan's imagination, or does he see some of the darkness clearing in the old man's milky eyes? Slowly, he nods. Only once.

"*Tengu* killed Ōshiro," says Evan.

Griff swallows; his stringy neck muscles constrict. "Did he?"

That question again. The look in Griff's eyes is one of pleading. Evan nods. "I saw it," he says. "I saw the thing just erupt out of the ground."

Griff holds his eye, wanting to believe him.

"I've tried to tell myself," says Griff. "It was all so . . ."

"Fucked up?"

Griff frowns.

He wants everyone to believe him, but he doesn't even believe it himself.

"You . . . you were there," says Griff.

Evan nods. "You said it was all there in the story," says Evan. "You knew all along we were there: Dad and me and the other ghosts. Is that what you were after?"

Griff looks befuddled. "What are you saying?"

"When you found out Leo was talking to Dad. When you knew Dad was going to read the book. Did you hope that he would be able to see what happened—the truth of what happened—because he was there?" Evan waits, but Griff's expression is mute. He's fought enough. "You wanted Dad to be able to see through the words on the page and recall what happened—like I did, just now. You wanted him to believe in you. Just once. Is that it? Is that what this was all about?"

Griff looks back toward the TV screen. Evan holds him in his gaze, waiting for something, anything. Waiting for intel. And then there it is, but to Evan's surprise, Griff shakes his head.

"I thought I killed him," he says. "Ōshiro: I thought I killed him—*me*! And then I somehow made up this awful thing. Concocted a monster because . . . because . . ."

"But when you read the book," says Evan, "and it was there, *Tengu*—"

Griff shakes his head again. "I wanted to believe that I had not—that I *would* not ever . . ." His voice trails off. Then he finds it again. "I was twenty-one years old, Evan. I'd seen so much. Too much. But what happened on that island . . ." He rubs his face with his hand, takes a deep breath, grips the arms of the chair, and then lets go. Settles.

"Your father wrote me, just before he died," he says. "He wanted me to tell him what really happened. He didn't care about the project, what Leo thought or wanted. That's what he said. He just wanted to . . . to believe there was some other explanation."

"He was upset," says Evan.

"He wanted it not to be true—what they thought—hell, what I thought, myself, deep down inside."

And now, as Evan thinks back, it makes sense. His father had only seemed to be beating on the same old drum that last night. He didn't want to believe that his father was a murderer, despite all the things he said. "I know," says Evan.

Griff clears his throat. "This lad, Leo," he says. "He never experienced the island, the way you just did. He believes in his father, believes what he and Ōshiro had to say, but he never experienced it. I asked him outright."

"But even if he did experience the island, he wasn't there when Ōshiro died. Derwood was long gone."

"Right."

"So how'd you expect him to figure it out?"

Griff shakes his head, hunches his shoulders. "I wrote your daddy back. But . . ."

"But he died."

Griff nods.

"Before he got it?"

Griff nods again. Shakes his head sadly.

"What did you say?"

Griff's face sours. "Does it matter now?"

Evan nods. "I think so. It matters to me."

Griff stares at him, assesses him. Evan never lets go of his gaze.

"It'll be there in the . . . what'd you call it?"

"On the server. Webmail."

"Right. See for yourself."

"Just tell me," says Evan. "Trust me."

Griff acknowledges the challenge. "All right," he says. "I told Clifford that wanting it not to be true was generous of him. I told him that I wanted it not to be true as well, but I wasn't sure. I asked him to help me out if he could. If he believed what he read about the ghosts, then he was there, too, even then. I asked him for his help, if he could find it in his heart."

His voice has gone so quiet, Evan has to stop breathing to hear what he is saying. And when the old man stops talking and looks down, looks away, Evan's heart, already broken in two, breaks all over again. It would have been all his father needed to end the war with his own father. Just that.

Chapter Twenty-Five

Griff looks at him, looks away, comes to some kind of resolve. Checks on Evan again, frowning, as if this is all some elaborate trick. But there is no trickery in Evan's face. Griff's breathing is ragged. He's nervous but not afraid.

"How much did you see?" Griff asks.

"You came back," says Evan. "Back up to the fort. And you were angry about something." Evan shakes his head, picturing the anger again. "That's what started it." He looks at Griff for corroboration. Griff looks down at his hands, the one still, the other subdued.

"I came back," he says. He stares at the empty television screen as if he is seeing it there.

"It was getting gusty out on the water. I was worried about getting caught in a storm. I wanted to leave him as much time as he needed. Ōshiro. I didn't know his name. I just knew he was there. I'd always known. Kraft was anything but crafty." He smiles a wan smile. "I decided to keep the operative's existence and position to myself. There was a war to fight. And then, finally, it was over. He—Ōshiro—deserved to know that." He glances at Evan. "You see, there is this horrible paradox a soldier lives with: the only other person who really gets him is his enemy. Do you see that?"

Evan nods.

"By the time I made it up to the fort that second time, the trees were filled with wind. I remember stopping at the top of the hill and looking out across the lagoon. It was getting bad."

He looks at Evan with consternation.

"That is relevant information," says Griff.

"Yeah," says Evan. "I felt it. In my dream. The wind."

Griff's frown deepens.

"Anyway, I got to the fort, the broken palisade, the face of it all overgrown and coming undone. Teeth missing, where the doors had once hung. He wasn't there."

"You got there first," says Evan, to help him along.

Griff nods, seems to gain something from Evan's enthusiasm. Sits upright in his chair.

"I looked around the place, noticed all the stuff Kraft mentions in the book—how well organized it all was, and yet now overgrown, untended. I found my way to this one corner where there was a little altar of rocks. I'd noticed it when I first went up. Wondered about it. I just stared for a bit. Something told me it was a cache of some kind. Weapons, maybe. Something worth checking, just in case." He pauses. He looks at Evan as if he's expecting a rebuttal. Evan just nods. *Go on,* say his eyes.

"I moved the top stone, peered inside, and saw these books,

several of them. I squatted, flipped through one and then another. I remember suddenly looking up toward the broken gateway, feeling as if I had wandered into a trap. It's a second sight you develop as a soldier. There was no one there. And so I turned back to the cache. My attention was drawn to a flat tin box with black letters in a red bull's-eye on the cover. The image was dented, scratched, the words almost obliterated. The letters read: L _C_ _ S_R_K_. I remember that tin, all right. Between the letters, fragments of black were left, a bit of ragged curve, a cross bar. 'Lucky Strike,' a cigarette case. I opened it."

He stops and shakes his head.

"There was this snake's nest of thin chains and flat metal rectangles. Oh, my Lord, I was perturbed to see that. I reached in and selected one of them, pulled it out, separating it from the others. It was a soldier's ID necklace. This box held a load of dog tags." He shakes his head. "I read through a number of them. No one I knew, not by name or rank or number. But one or two from my division, all right."

He looks at Evan. "Can you imagine what I was thinking?"

"I think so."

"I could feel my blood beginning to boil. Those ghost children you read about. They were there with me. Infernal critters. Well, they pulled away from me, right then, I'll tell you. I think they were frightened of me—my own kin, if what Ōshiro says is true about what those things are." Griff shakes his head. He has spent a lifetime not believing any of this. Evan waits.

"I guess they could just feel the heat rising off me. I snapped the lid closed on the Lucky Strike tin, undid the button on my breast pocket, slid the tin into it, closed the button." Evan watches him mime the operation, patting the breast pocket of his pajamas. "And, as if on cue, he was there."

297

"Ōshiro," says Evan.

"Right. He was staring right at me. Had no idea he was there. Could have picked me off easy. Instead he just cried out.

"'No!' he shouted. In English.

"I didn't wait for him to make the first move. He'd had the drop on me, but the fact that he had not taken advantage of the situation in no way inhibited me. I had my rifle off my shoulder lightning quick, aimed right at his chest.

"He threw up his hands. He had no gun on him, as far as I could tell, but you never know. Christ, one of them, up in Okinawa, wounded—emaciated—wearing nothing but a G-string, pulled a grenade out of it, if you can believe it . . . almost killed—" He stops. Shakes his head. "Wrong set of memories. Let's just say I wasn't taking any chances.

"I indicated the framed newspaper leaning against the pole at the corner of his sleeping place. He knew what I was getting at.

"'Yes,' he said in English. Then he bowed slightly, not taking his eye off me or my rifle. He seemed to struggle for a moment to find a word. He'd gotten both his hands in the air, but one of them was pointing upward as if he were trying to grab at some thought. Finally, he figured out what it was he wanted to say. 'Over,' he said.

"'The end,' I said.

"'Yes. Over. The end,' he said back to me. I guess Derwood had taught him some English.

"I wasn't relieved. I still had that metal box in my breast pocket. I hadn't come here looking for trouble, but those dog tags . . ."

Evan watches Griff nod to himself. His eyes fixed on nothing in this room—focused entirely on something that happened

298

to him three-quarters of his life ago, and yet was still here, as clear as anything. Burned into his memory.

"A strange thing happened," he says. "The ghost children — his ghosts—all took up a protective position in front of him. They were acting out of some instinct to preserve him, I guess." Griff's face looks as if he is in pain. As if there were other things he could understand, but this—this was beyond knowing.

"When I read Ōshiro's idea about them. How they were the children yet to be born. Well, that's just plain insane, that is. And yet, it made sense, I guess. Not at the time. But when I thought about it later." He looks at Evan, and Evan nods. "Especially now." Evan doesn't nod again, but he knows some kind of a pact just got signed between them. Two people both accepting something on faith.

"They didn't even exist yet and yet their DNA *did,* if you want to call it that. Their future was in this man. And protecting him was as crucial to them as it would be for a mother protecting her baby child. Extraordinary."

Griff closes his eyes. Rubs them with his knuckles, opens them again. *The unbelief in his eyes, the terrible impossibility of it is something he's lived with all his life,* thinks Evan. *Do not hurry the man,* he tells himself.

Griff sighs. "I walked toward Isamu with my gun lowered, but with a pretty damn unsympathetic look on my face. By now, he was inside the gate a couple feet. Not making any attempt to run. I stopped. I guess I'd have been about fifteen yards away. With my free hand, I undid the button of my pocket and fished out the Lucky Strike tin. I held it up for Isamu to see. 'What the hell is this?' I asked him, or something like that. I rattled the tin at him, accusingly, so you could hear those dog tags rattle. So there'd be no doubt what I was talking about.

"And he nodded, looked kind of agitated. 'Yes,' he said. 'Bury.' And as he said it, he made this sudden movement." Griff pauses. "It was the suddenness I noticed, his one hand reaching down as if maybe he had something concealed in his pant leg. I dropped that tin so fast. I had the rifle to my shoulder, aimed at him, my finger on the trigger, before it registered on me what he was doing. He was shoveling—pretending to shovel. Not reaching for a concealed weapon. 'Bury,' he had said, and he was miming it for me. He had buried those soldiers." Griff rubs his steady right hand through the bristle of his hair.

And Evan says, "And is that when it happened?"

Griff nods, his eyes wide. "Out of nowhere."

"Out of the ground," says Evan. "He was standing right over the trap. *Tengu*'s grave." Griff nods again.

Evan waits. Then he says, "Go on, Griff."

Griff stares at him, rubs his face. Rests his hands on the arms of the chair.

"I started right in, firing on that thing. I fired again and again, my aim good—perfect—hitting it with every shot, peppering the shoulders and head of the thing. It was mauling Ōshiro, and I just strode right up to it, firing. By now, the upper half of its body was fully emerged. I emptied my rifle into its hide, and when I was out of ammo, threw it aside and drew my service revolver. I fired straight into the damn creature's screaming face, one eye, then the next, standing at close quarters until finally those talons let go of him. Let go of his bleeding body."

Griff pauses to breathe. He sounds dead weary when he speaks again. "Kept on firing, round after round, until with this awful gurgling, the creature slid back down onto the sand. Dead. Again."

Evan waits. Then he says, "And it was too late?"

Griff nods. "As careful as I could, I dragged the fallen

soldier away from the churned-up sand—out of the reach of the thing, in case it somehow came back to life."

"Ōshiro was dead?"

"Not quite. Chewed up something awful, but not quite dead. The worst of it was this cruel slash across his throat, leaking blood at an alarming rate."

He looks suddenly at Evan, frightened, distrustful. Even now he can't believe it. Evan nods for him to go on. "I wrapped my hands around his neck," he says, "and the blood, it just bubbled up through my fingers. I could just barely feel his pulse." He shakes his head, angrily. "Damn heart," he says. "Pumping blood *out* of the body, and I had nothing to stop the wound. Nothing I could do. Then I saw my rifle with the white truce flag tied to it. Letting go for a moment, I tore the flag off and wrapped it around Ōshiro's neck. But there is this terrible truth about a neck wound: you cannot make a tourniquet. To stop the blood is to close the windpipe. The white flag was drenched red in no time. Even as I tried to stanch the wound, I could see the life slipping away from him. I had seen it enough times to know. I stopped and just sat there on my backside to cradle his head in my arms."

Evan waits, watches. Listens.

"I'll never forget his dying gaze. There was no anger there. He tried to speak but had no voice. I nodded and nodded. The shock of what had happened finally made way for what had gone before, the moment when he had made the gesture of someone digging. 'Bury,' he had said.

"'You buried the soldiers,' I said to him. He couldn't nod, but I know now that's what he had been up to. It was all in the book. All those dog tags had been saved, but they were not a murderer's trinkets. I truly believe that."

Griff goes silent. Evan watches him. Waits. Knows there is

301

more. Can feel it, the story, throbbing inside his own blood. It is nothing he can explain. He can only attend this old man.

Griff makes a strangled kind of sound of anger and anguish, as if he's seeing the next part.

"What happened?" Evan asks.

Griff looks up. "Maybe the strangest thing of all. I was plumb exhausted. Still sitting there, holding him, I closed my eyes. Just closed my eyes. Then I must have heard something, because I snapped 'em open and there were the others. Not the children, those confounded . . ."

"Jikininki?"

"Yeah, the flesh-eaters. I'd never laid eyes on them—sure as hell never seen them at work! They'd made themselves scarce when I'd been there with the troops. But now they were converging on him—on the two of us—and I knew well enough what was up. They were approaching from the clearing in front of the broken gate, sniffing the air, drawn to the smell of blood, I guess. I could hear them moan. I lay down the dead man and grabbed up my automatic. I loaded up quick. I fired at them and watched holes appear in their flesh, holes that did not stop them moving in. I kept on firing, again and again, to no avail.

"Which is when the ghost children closed in. They were there all along, but now they closed in on Ōshiro. One of them stared at me with this knowing smile. It was as if he was relieving me of my duty. As if they were going to take over now. There was nothing I could do, anyway. I backed off. And I watched the ghost children wrap themselves around the dead man, guarding him."

Griff blinked tears away, sucked it in. Went on.

"Those zombies . . . My, but they squealed with rage. God, what a sound! There was nothing of the man exposed to them—not a square inch. They circled the body, gnashing their yellow teeth. Their red eyes filled with this wretched look of sorrow and helplessness and indignation, while these insubstantial children, so much less sturdy than the ghouls in every conceivable way, made a shield of their bodies over him. They had this one power, you see. The zombies would get none of their man." Griff shakes his head in awe. "Ōshiro and his memories belonged to his own people."

Chapter Twenty-Six

Tuesday, July twenty-second. Griff arrived late on Saturday night; he hasn't even been here three whole days. Evan tries to remember how many days it took the Americans to take Tinian. There was a footnote in the book somewhere: something like a week, he thinks. Anyway, not long. It feels as if there has been a war here. He's not sure who won. He would like the book back, and he has no idea where Griff's head is about Yamada's graphic novel. So there is unfinished business—it's just a question of whether it's any of *his* business.

And then Evan is suddenly crying, weeping. It comes over him like a cyclone, a tsunami of grief. "I hate him," he sobs. "I fucking hate him!" But his anger only morphs into another wave of grief, as though he will drown Any Place with an ocean's worth of tears.

And it subsides. Not gone but in remission. The grief.

A little war and now a little peace: a lifting of something—some weight. He looks at his cell phone. Just after eight. The earliest he's woken in a month. He's not sure what time it was when they called it a day, but he feels rested, despite everything. He climbs out of bed. He needs a shower. A long, scalding-hot shower. There is shampoo. Griff must have bought it. He stands there feeling the streaming water massage his neck and shoulders. He showers until the water starts to cool. Back in his room, he puts on shorts and a plain white T-shirt. A peace offering.

Griff isn't in the kitchen. The door to the rec room is closed. Evan goes back into the kitchen. Griff's outdoor shoes are there, shining. Evan stands in the middle of the room, listening to the almost-quiet. The windows are open, and the distant hum of the Don Valley Expressway seems to have modulated to D major. A good sign.

He allows the idea of Griff being dead to take him over. It's not something he wants; it's something he fears. The old man had looked pretty gone last night. He might have stormed a lot of beaches in his day, but he wasn't heavily equipped with weapons to confront big emotion. If he is dead, lying down there in the rec room, Evan doesn't want to find him just yet or phone the authorities. He'll try bacon therapy first.

It works.

Not fifteen minutes later, the man appears at the kitchen door.

"Ah," says Evan. "So you decided to get up at last."

Griff shakes his head. "You might try using the splatter guard," he says. He points at a mesh utensil hanging beside the stove.

"Hey," says Evan. "I always wondered what that was."

He makes a big bowl of cheesy scrambled eggs and a log pile

305

of bacon. There's toast and raspberry jam, courtesy of Rachel Cope, a gallon of orange juice and a gallon of coffee. Saturday-morning breakfast on a Tuesday.

When Evan thinks it's time, he says, "Can I tell Leo the news?"

Griff looks bemused. "What news would that be?"

"What went down out there on Kokoro-Jima."

Griff shakes his head. "I'm not giving them permission, Evan, if that's what you're getting at."

"Why not? You didn't do it."

Griff sits up straight. He quietly lays his knife down on his plate, then pats his lips with his napkin.

Oops.

"Let's just say that I'm not keen on the idea of reducing war to a comic book."

"Have you seen Yamada's work?" says Evan. "He's, like, really amazing."

"Words in bubbles? It's a desecration, as far as I'm concerned, however talented he may be. Cheap and tawdry."

Tawdry, thinks Evan, and wishes he could draw out a word that well, so that it fills up with meaning. He makes himself nod, not in agreement but so as to show acceptance of the idea put forward, however insanely stupid and narrow-minded it is. He pats his own lips dry of grease. He made a deal with himself before launching into this conversation. He would not

1. swear;
2. be cheeky; or
3. leave the room.

Griff is watching him closely. When Evan doesn't speak, he picks up his knife and recommences buttering his toast.

He's under the impression that I'm done, thinks Evan. He clears his throat. "Okay, but even if you're not going to allow the project to go forward, it'd be cool to let Leo know, wouldn't it? I mean that you're innocent. I can even corroborate it. I'm an eyewitness. Sort of." Griff is frowning, which is not like glaring. "You didn't tell me what happened. I saw it myself and then you filled in the details. That's got to count for something." He manages to keep his voice light, as if it's no big deal. He peers at Griff. He's helping himself to another cup of coffee, doesn't look too close to blowing up. There's a little container of pills he has to take. Evan has never seen it before because they've never had breakfast together — never had any meal together. He waits, but he has never been big on knowing when enough was enough. "You'll end up coming off like a hero, Griff."

"I don't need a cartoonist to glorify the incident."

"But he can tell your story. Get it right."

"What if I don't want my story told?"

Evan considers that, shrugs, and takes the last of the eggs. "Okay," he says. "Your call."

Griff nods. "Damn straight it is, son."

Then he sits with a piece of toast dangling from his hand, looking out the window. It's that kind of thousand-yard stare you see on a person when they have pretty well left the room, so Evan feels free to observe the old man. And that's when he sees the mask for the first time. It's so thin and perfectly made that it's almost lifelike, except that there is a tiny part of it that has flaked off, just under Griff's right eye. Maybe the tears Evan saw there last night, ever so briefly, dissolved some of the mask.

Griff doesn't raise his voice or look up when he speaks. "You have no idea," he says. "No idea whatsoever." Evan watches as another flake falls away from the man's face. "You think a few pictures say anything about what we went through out there?"

His hand with the toast gestures toward the window as if Any Place were a war zone. "You think?"

"No, sir."

Griff snaps his head around to look at Evan, expecting insolence even now, but seeing none. He's spent a lifetime with boys not much older than Evan saying "Yes, sir" and "No, sir," with respect and an edge of fear. *He doesn't think I respect or fear him,* Evan thinks, *because he hasn't spent a lifetime knowing this boy. Too bad.* There is no sneer on Evan's face, no snide remark lurking at the corner of his lips.

"No, sir," Evan says again.

Another tiny flake of the mask falls away. Griff scratches his cheek, and now Evan catches a glimpse of what the mask has been hiding. He waits. The mask — the armor — is crumbling as if it were a thin slip of clay, falling away, but Evan isn't going to draw attention to it. Let the old man gather up the crumbs of it, sweep them from the table into his fist to dispense with later when he is alone. He isn't a man who reveals himself too often. *This must be hard for him,* thinks Evan.

He goes back to his cold eggs. He looks up to see Griff looking out the window again at the nothing of consequence that happens on a daily basis out there in Any Place.

"What?" he says.

"Excuse me?" says Evan.

"You're itching to tell me something. Fill me in."

Evan smiles.

"Don't patronize me, boy."

"I'm not, sir. And I know you're right. I don't think anything can capture what you went through out there." He nods toward the outside, the everywhere that stretches from this small place where Evan has spent his entire life. "But maybe there is something that can come of it. Telling the story."

"It's not a story, Evan. That's my point. A story has some shape to it, a point. War doesn't have a point. And it doesn't have a convenient end to it, either."

"It doesn't end?"

"It ends and then it starts again, and the end of one war inevitably grows out of the war that came before it. There's no . . . what do you call it . . ."

"Resolution?"

"I don't know. Yeah. That."

Evan nods. "So, how about if Yamada could get across this one single truth — just one."

"What would that look like?"

"I don't know. Just the idea that something looks like it happened one way, but it didn't really happen that way." He waits for Griff to counter but sees that he's not going to. "That it was something bigger than you that killed Ōshiro. Something that can't die, no matter how many times you kill it."

Griff favors Evan with a wry grin. "And y'all think there's a living soul out there who'll believe it?"

Evan nods. "I do. That's a start."

Griff shakes his head, but there is no look of disparagement on his face, just a lifetime of people who didn't get him — didn't understand.

"Listen," says Evan, leaning forward, his fists on the table, but his voice even and filled with clean clear possibility. "You were talking just the other night about how the truth isn't what people tell you happened — how it's something else. Isn't that what you were saying?"

Griff nods, but his right eyebrow arches. "You mean you were listening to me?"

"Oh, yeah. I heard you loud and clear. It's just that I'm not in the habit of saying 'yes, sir' every time I'm told something."

Griff laughs. "What I said was, the truth is bigger than the stories people tell themselves and bigger than the lies they live with."

"Right, so . . ."

Griff holds up his hand, a stop sign, a shaky one. "Hold your horses, Evan," he says.

Evan nods, and now he knows to stop. For the time being.

Chapter Twenty-Seven

Evan knocks at the Reidingers' blue door. He hears the muffled shout of Lexie Jane announcing that she'll get it. The door flies open.

"Oh, hey."

"Hey," he says.

She looks past him. "Is it time to do the lawn again?"

"No," he says. "Well, yeah, actually it is. But I'm going to do it. That's not why I'm here."

Which is when she notices that his hands are behind his back. Which is his cue to show her what he brought.

"Oh, wow! The *Constitution,*" she says.

"Yeah. Sorry it took so long to get it."

She makes a quizzical expression, and he realizes that she might not have even known what happened the other day when he balked and left her standing in the garden waiting. "Anyway," he says. "It's yours."

"Are you kidding?"

"Do I look like I'm kidding?"

She smiles and, with his prompting, takes the bottle from him, carefully, in two hands. That's when he sees just the tiniest glimmer of something like disappointment in her eyes. Really? "Don't you want it?" he asks.

She looks surprised—caught out. "Oh, yeah, it's great," she says.

"Whoa, that wasn't very convincing." Now she looks embarrassed. "Come on, level with me," he says.

"There was this other ship," she says. "The *Bounty*?" He nods. "Well, it was my favorite because it's a way better story, and your dad let me paint it—the hull, anyway."

"You're kidding me." She shakes her head. "Then, give me back the USS *Constitution* and let's go get the *Bounty*."

"Honest?"

"Honest."

Then Lexie Jane hands him the boat and yells back into the house. "I'm going over to Clifford's," she shouts. Then she looks at Evan and her face darkens.

"It's okay," he says. "Go on. You know where it is."

Evan and Griff build a fishpond for Clifford on Saturday.

Rollo comes over to help with the heavy lifting. Griff actually just sits in a deck chair on the newly mown lawn, in charge of the lemonade and dispensing advice. Helpful stuff like: "That rock won't move itself." Or: "Do not—either one of you—even think about a career in garden maintenance. I mean it."

Rollo loves it.

312

"You two've got to be the most hapless pair of shit-for-brains ever!"

"That's what we'll call the band," says Evan.

"Shit-for-Brains," says Rollo. "Got a good ring to it."

"What is this? Break time again?"

Evan's father kept a book about his garden, what he'd planted where, when things came up, what to do with different pests. He'd drawn a good plan of how the fishpond was supposed to look, and all the supplies were there. They spread his ashes in the hole before they lay down the rubber liner.

The three of them stand there, and Evan wonders if he should say something. Then he looks sideways at Griff, expectantly. But no, it's too late for him. Any words he might have said died long ago.

The pause is a long, respectful one, and into it floods another wave of anger. Evan isn't done with it yet, he realizes. The anger. But now is not the time for it. Now is the time to do what his father never got the chance to do.

"Rest easy, Dad," Evan says.

Then something hits him. An idea. Rollo is already reaching for the shovel. "Wait a sec," says Evan, and takes off toward the house. In the Dockyard he scours the shelves until he finds it. The USS *Chesapeake*. He carries it out to where Rollo and Griff are waiting at graveside. He shows it to Griff. "Was this the one?" he says. Griff takes it, looks it over. Nods. The ship his father sent Griff: the one with the sketchy history. The boat Griff sent back. On his knees, Evan places the boat in the grave. Then he stands up and rubs the dirt off his knees. He can't look at his grandfather, but he feels him looking at him. Then they fill in the hole.

* * *

313

Rollo can't stay for supper. "I'd love to get some more abuse," he says to Griff, "but I've got a date." He turns to Evan. "Oh, yeah. It's with Bree. Is that her name?"

Evan punches him in the arm.

"I'm out of here," says Rollo.

"Shiftless bastard," says Griff, and Rollo howls with laughter. He walks to his car with his fist in the air.

"Yes!" he says triumphantly. "Shiftless bastards rule the world!"

So Griff and Evan grill hamburgers on the barbeque, and Griff makes a potato salad, southern style. "Got to have the sweet relish," he says. "Any fool knows that."

They move indoors for dessert, a store-bought pecan pie. And when they're sitting down to it, ice cream on the side for Evan, none for Griff ("A desecration, if you ask me"), he says, "I contacted Leonardo Kraft."

Evan looks up. Waits. They haven't talked about the book since Tuesday night. Evan found it on his desk the next day, but with no note of explanation.

"I told him I was making you my legal executor."

Evan lowers his fork. "Are you kidding?"

"Yes, of course I am. You think I'd want you as my executor? Anyway, it'll be years before I need anyone signing things for me. Brain like a steel trap," he says, tapping on his noggin with his finger.

"Okay," says Evan. "Got it." He's not sure what he's got, but he's had enough of arguing with this coot.

"As far as this comic book business goes, I'll sign some kind of affidavit or whatever saying you can speak for me."

Evan eats a mouthful of pie with too much ice cream and immediately suffers glacier-grade brain-freeze. He grabs the edge of the table and concentrates on melting the iceberg in his mouth.

"You going to die on me?" says Griff dispassionately.

Evan gives him the finger, and Griff actually laughs. "You are brash, son," he says, and Evan nods.

Finally he can talk again. "When you say 'speak for you,' does that mean I'm doing what you direct me to do or what I think you should do?"

Griff puts down his fork with a clatter. "For God's sake, son, if I wanted you to do what *I* want, I'd just do it myself."

"Right," says Evan. Griff rolls his eyes, then attends to his pie. Evan gives it a minute. "Okay," he says, "so I can give them the green light?"

Griff finishes his mouthful. "You really think this Yamada character is any good?"

Evan nods. "Really good! Didn't you look at the drawings on his website?"

"I did not. They weren't supposed to be there at all. But I'll overlook that."

"So did you tell Leo the real ending?"

Griff looks as if Evan just drizzled dog urine on his pie. He puts his fork down again and curls his hands into fists on either side of his plate. "I guess I did not make myself clear," he says. "I don't want to have anything to do with this project. You will be my representative and have contact with Leo and the artist and the publishers. Got that? Is it totally comprehensible?"

"Yes, sir. Loud and comprehensible." Evan is about to salute, but doesn't want to stretch his luck.

Griff goes back to eating, mumbling something about the pie not being a real pecan pie, but Evan's mind is elsewhere.

315

"I know you don't want to talk about this, but I may want to bug you for more details," he says.

"So be it," says Griff. "But when I'm back at Hopeless Manor, I want to hear as little about any of it as possible."

"Hopeless Manor?"

"It is called 'Hope Manor,' which seems to me to be about as bad a name for a senior residence as is possible."

"So why'd you move there?"

"Because I had to go somewhere and, well, I'll grant the place this: it's a good location. A bluff overlooking the Cape Fear River."

"Cape Fear? Like in the movie with Robert De Niro?"

Griff makes another of his sour faces. "No, like in the movie with Robert *Mitchum*. But yes, that's the place."

Evan gets this grin on his face. "I am so going to visit you."

"Like hell you are."

"I'm doing it."

"As soon as I get back on that plane, you're going to come to your senses and realize you've seen about as much of this old soldier as you can stand. Mark my words."

Evan stares at him as the old man breaks off a little corner of pie and brings it to his mouth. There was so much bundled-up loneliness in what he said. It was as if he was going out of his way to keep people at bay. But why? Evan sits back in his chair and something comes to him. Something he'd meant to ask but had forgotten about in all the excitement. Something else he doesn't understand.

"Griff?" he says. Griff looks up. "In my dream of being on the island, there was this girl ghost." He waits.

Griff just looks at him matter-of-factly. "It was a dream, Evan."

"I know."

"Maybe you're just lonely. Did you think of that?"

Evan nods. "I sure haven't had any good company around here."

Griff smirks, looks down at his plate. But as if he can feel Evan's gaze on him, he looks up again. He puts down his fork, gently this time, and stares out the window—*always staring out the window,* thinks Evan, *as if houses are something he's never figured out.* It's dusk. All the neighbots of Any Place are turning off their water sprinklers and heading indoors to a night of unbridled television watching.

"I suppose you should know this," he mutters. Evan hears him but doesn't bother to respond. He can hear Mr. Gupta, next door, calling his dog, Rudolph. Rudolph barks. Then the Guptas' door closes. Griff seems to be waiting for the quiet to close in on them. In a bit, it does. He gets up, wipes his lips on his paper napkin, and leaves the room. Just like that. Evan smiles to himself, shakes his head, and returns to his dessert, although there's only a pool of melted ice cream left. Then Griff reenters the room with the remainder of the bottle of scotch and a tumbler. He sits, rests his hands on the tabletop.

"I might need this," he says. He stares at the bottle but doesn't pour a glass. Then he begins.

"I was only . . ." He stops, looks down at the few crumbs on his plate. Evan watches the old man gather his strength together as if there were some wall he had to climb and he'd forgotten how. "I was only ever once in love," he says. "In my whole life, only once. Sadly, it was not with your grandmother." He looks up. And Evan wonders what it might have been like for a kid to hear this confession if the kid had known his grandmother. Awful. But it's not awful to him. Grandmother is just a tiny black-and-white picture of a young woman with a big twist of hair in a locket.

"My first deployment in the war was to Iceland."

"World War II?"

"World War II. But America wasn't in it when we got shipped up there. It was July of '41. The Brits and the Canadians were guarding Iceland. Churchill . . ." He stops and levels his gaze at Evan. "Tell me you've heard of Churchill?"

"I've heard of him," Evan lies, knowing he can Google it later.

"Churchill was afraid the Germans might take Iceland, which would give them control over the North Atlantic and would make a good place to prepare for an invasion of North America, if that's what they had up their sleeve. So, as I was saying, the Brits and—"

"Wait! Should I be taking notes? Is this going to be a history lesson?" Griff's eyes flash. He is not used to being crossed. "It's just that if it is," says Evan, "then maybe I'll need some of that scotch, too."

The surliness on his grandfather's face withers. "Are you telling me to cut to the chase?"

"Not exactly telling."

"Oh, good. I'm not partial to being told what to do." He lets that sink in, and Evan suppresses a smile.

"Her name was Snaedis Hillgrimsson." Griff's eyes light up. "You know, I don't think I've said her name out loud for over seventy years. Strange, how someone can be on your mind your whole life, and yet you don't ever utter her name." He clears his throat. His eyes look anywhere but at Evan. "At the risk of annoying you with further historical detail, let me bring up one more significant date: December 7, 1941. Does that mean anything to you?"

Evan shakes his head and knows somehow he's in trouble.

"What exactly do they teach you in school?" Griff asks, but

318

does not wait for an answer. "The attack on Pearl Harbor," he says, grumpy as all get-out.

"Oh," says Evan. "When America finally decided to join the war, right?"

Griff rubs his jaw. "I forgot you were a Canadian," he says.

"Griff. I'm dying here. Get on with it, okay?"

It's then that Griff's pretense of being upset evaporates. "It's not easy to talk about," he says. "By January of '42, I was on a troop carrier heading back stateside. I wrote her — Snaedis — every single day of that journey home. I've never been much for writing, so I just told her everything that was happening, every little thing that came into my head. What I saw, what anyone said as long as it was amusing and as long as it was halfway clean and respectable. Every day. Fourteen thick letters I was going to send the minute I was free to do so."

"You mean when you landed?" says Evan. And then sees something in Griff's eye and says, "Not when you landed."

Griff shakes his head. "The way I saw it, I would not be free to send those love letters to Snaedis until I had formally broken off with Mary."

"You were married?"

Griff looks exasperated. "No, son, I was not married. Nor was I engaged. Mary and I . . . well, I guess there were expectations on her part, and until I'd severed those ties, I could not bring myself to pursue any other option."

Evan thinks of the locket in his bedside table. Those two people locked in the darkness of that narrow little silver heart.

"So, what happened? Wait, let me guess." Evan smacks the table with both palms. "She was pregnant." Griff closes his eyes. "Sorry," says Evan. "I will now totally shut up."

The eyes open again, filled with warning. Evan zippers up his mouth.

319

"She was not pregnant. Had she been, it would not have been my child, and so that would have been . . . how do I put this . . . very convenient. But Mary was not one for making things convenient. Unbeknownst to me, she'd moved in with my parents."

"Whoa!"

"My father had become quite ill and Mother Griffin was always fragile, so Mary took the opportunity to get her foot in the door under the guise of being helpful. That will no doubt sound cold to you, but you never knew your grandmother."

"So the letters?"

"Burned them."

"But you wrote her—the Icelandic woman—you told her?"

Griff shook his head. "I was home for a one-week furlough before heading off to San Diego and then New Zealand for training, and then the Pacific Theater. I didn't know what to do. I thought maybe when I finally did make it home, things would have changed. Hell, there was every chance in the world I'd be dead. So, I did nothing."

Griff looks at his watch. "The long and short of it, Evan, is that I never again communicated with Snaedis Hillgrimsson."

"Oh."

"Yes, that about sums it up."

"But wait. The girl in my dream. The ghost girl," says Evan. And then he says, "Oh," again. "Snaedis got—"

"Yes," says Griff. "That would be correct."

He looks beat. It is, to Evan, as if Griff had locked up the past in a steel vault for so long that the door rusted shut and this attempt to enter it required an inhuman effort.

"But if you never communicated with her again—"

"Her daughter. My daughter. Our daughter . . ."

"She got in touch with you?"

"She did. She did more than that. She came to the States to go to school. By then — this is about 1960 — America had strong ties with Iceland. There was the big air force base there for one thing. There were also scholarships. Eyja was a smart girl. She enrolled at Georgia Tech on a full scholarship. And then went about tracking me down."

"Eyja," says Evan, savoring the name. "Was that as bad as you're making it sound?"

Griff looks surprised. "No. No. I wondered, when I first heard from her, what she had in mind, but all she wanted to do was meet me. We met a few times. Beautiful girl. Beautiful." He pauses, scrunches up his mouth. "But I . . . I guess I found it too painful. Just couldn't do it. So I asked her to stop."

Evan is thinking hard. "So my father had this half sister," he says. "Eyja?" Griff nods. "Did Dad know?" Griff looks at Evan solemnly and shakes his head. Evan is filled with rage. Oh, it is there. So much of it. But he punches it back down. He looks away. "So I have an aunt and maybe cousins."

Griff nods. "I thought about that, after what you said. Your dream. That girl . . . the ghost you saw; she couldn't have been Eyja. I mean if this crazy business of a child being born out of the island and into the real world . . ." He stops, unable to say it; unable to believe he is talking in such terms. But Evan knows where he was going.

"Eyja wouldn't have been on Kokoro-Jima in September of 1945. Is that what you mean?" Griff nods. "She'd have been born, like, in —"

"Nineteen forty-two. August."

"So the girl I met" — he laughs at the lunacy of that verb — "She would have had to be a daughter of Eyja."

"Something like that," mutters Griff. And Evan thinks how

nothing in Griff's handbook on being a marine would have prepared him for any of this.

The room floods with silence—a deluge of it. A tsunami of silence.

Then Griff speaks. "I couldn't do it, Evan. I don't expect you to understand. I'm not sure at this late date that I understand it myself."

"And so you shut out everybody. You never loved Mary. You said so yourself. So it sort of makes sense why you never loved my father, either." He doesn't mean to sound so bitter, but he can't help it.

"That would be a fair summary," says Griff. He stares at the bottle of scotch, seems about to reach for it, but changes his mind. He leans back in his chair; his hands fall to his lap. His shoulders are hunched, and then he recalls himself and sits up straighter. "You have every right to your judgments," he says.

"Forget it," says Evan. He's not about to forgive the man. Right now, he can't even make eye contact with him. Won't. He gets up from the table and gathers their plates and forks and heads out to the kitchen.

The other dishes are on the counter. He starts running water in the sink. The dishwasher broke almost six months ago, and Clifford said one evening, much to Evan's surprise, that he liked washing dishes. Not as much as making ships in bottles, but enough to not bother replacing the dishwasher. Suddenly Evan misses his father so badly he can hardly bear it. He doubles over in pain, holding on to the counter so as not to fall in a heap on the floor. All that anger that was holding back the grief—pressing in on it—has lifted a fair bit now, enough to allow it to surface. A mixed blessing.

He recovers. He stands up and looks out the window at

the pool. The only thing missing is fish. He'll get fish. Those big gold Japanese fish. He looks down, sticks his hands in the hot water, feels the relief it offers, leaves them there, leaning heavily on the bottom of the sink as the soapy water climbs his forearms.

"We could find them."

He looks up. His grandfather is standing at the door to the kitchen. Evan turns back to the sink, turns off the water. Pauses. Starts putting dishes into the sink, quietly, not wanting to break the spell.

"We could find them," says Griff again. "Your relatives."

Evan almost laughs. *It's so crazily unbelievable. Is it worth trying to teach this old man anything? Yes,* he thinks. *But start easy.* "*Our* relatives," he says, quietly.

Evan turns to look at Griff. He is standing "at ease," his legs apart, his arms loose, his hands gripped loosely together in front of him. At ease isn't easy for him.

"What did you say?"

"Our relatives, Griff. They're your relatives, too."

Griff doesn't nod right off. *It's hard for him,* thinks Evan. That much steel in your backbone makes nodding a difficult task. And it is, after all, hard to grasp. This family Griff has mostly only ever met as ghosts on a faraway island. *Don't make this hard on him,* Evan tells himself.

"I'd like that," he says.

Griff just stands there. Evan isn't sure the old man heard him. He didn't say it very loudly. It is hard for Evan, too. There had only been his father and him. And his father had been an always kind of father. No fight ever lasted past bedtime. And here was a man who had managed somehow to stay in a fight that lasted a lifetime. So what he had just said—what

Griff had just said — why, you'd have to classify it as a minor miracle?

We could find them.

Evan turns to face his grandfather.

"I'd like that," he says again. And watches a smile crease the old soldier's leathery face.

Acknowledgments

This is a work of fiction. Alas, World War II was not. Wherever I have mentioned real battles, I have endeavored to get my facts straight. And where military matters are involved, I also hope that my research has been thorough. I am especially indebted to William T. Paull, who served in the U.S. Marines in the Pacific. His memoir, *From Butte to Iwo Jima,* can be found at: www.sihope .com/~tipi/marine.html. I borrowed two or three excellent details from the chapter called "Boot Camp, Camp Elliot & Brawley, CA." The memoir is well worth reading as a personal narrative of the war. Paull died in 2007.

This book has gone through many incarnations, helped along by the encouragement and excellent advice of loved ones and writer friends who have generously provided information, read one or more versions, or put into my hand just the right book to read. I would like to thank, especially, Steve Bramucci, Sheryl De Paolo, Ikue Endo, Amanda Lewis, Dana Walraith, Pam Watts, and Lewis Wynne-Jones.

Mal Peet was also a big influence. His book *Tamar* finally helped me to understand where it was I wanted to go with this story. I was so looking forward to sending him a copy, but sadly he died early this year. He was a great author, a grand, good man, and a new friend. He will be missed for all of those reasons.

Thanks as always to my brilliant editor at Candlewick, Liz Bicknell, as well as to Kaylan Adair, who braved the Very Long Draft; Sawako Shirota, who reviewed and corrected my Japanese; Carter Hasegawa, who helped to steer me through the sticky bits; and Erin DeWitt, who did an inspired copyedit.

Ōshiro is a very common name in Okinawa, but the Okinawan reading of the *kanji* characters would render it as Ogusuku. I have gone with the Japanese rendition, because I think Isamu would have adopted the name Ōshiro so as to avoid discrimination when he joined the army. The name in either form means "big castle." I'm sure the Emperor of Kokoro-Jima would have loved to have such a grand surname.

Rachel Cope, Sandra Nickel, and Nicole Valentine each contributed substantially to the Vermont College of Fine Arts scholarship fund for the chance to have a character named after themselves or someone of their choice in this novel. Thank you. And thanks as always to my colleagues and the endlessly inspiring students at VCFA, who have listened to me read excerpts from the novel-in-progress on at least four occasions.